CHILDREN OF THE BURNT EARTH

Beverly Johnson

♚   ♟   ♞

"When the game is over, the king and the pawn go into the same box."
-Italian proverb

TABLE OF CONTENTS

PROLOGUE:
A SHORT HISTORY OF
EVERYTHING I'D RATHER FORGET

IT WAS THEIR last hope, he said to me.

The sun danced. The moon sank and rose, and the earth smoldered. The men gathered their goods, planted themselves on new ground, dug their shovels into the soil, and the land sunk under their weight.

Our land of Belvidere was built a hundred years ago, a slab of an island off the coast of nowhere. It's all I've ever known.

My father told me bedtime stories of how the first men came, from burning earth and sea-swallowed villages. They pitched their ships onto the shore, saw the trees sprouting new and green from the earth, and wept. He told me they wept, because it was so beautiful and new, and they thought they'd never see good land again in their lives. Half the word is burnt black, he said. Half the world is ruined for good.

The story never had an ending. He always stopped it short – he didn't know what happened after that. The old world is all a blur, a wreck, a ruin. No one likes to talk about it. "How'd it all come to this, then?" I'd ask, but he just shook his crown.

The first kingdom was named Wickwolf, settled on the curving coast of Belvidere. The second was Kosta, the diamond country of grass and forest, with trees like pillars shooting into the sky. Then came Uppica, with its mineral-rich edge of earth, and dark, churning water. Last was Lusk, where gold was struck, gold stockpiled deep into the ground, as if hidden and hoarded by some ancient race.

It's all we've ever known.

We knew even less back then. I couldn't see beyond the interior of the castle walls. Every morning, my face was powdered beyond recognition. My hair was slicked back and secured. The royal ceremonies rolled on and on and I understood none of it.

My birthday was celebrated with red fireworks. All around me, the shape of the Wickwolf horn – in the sky, in the air, in the eyes of my wonderstruck, neighboring-kingdom friends. People were starving and suffering beyond our balconies, and we were burning things for good luck. We didn't know any better. We were children.

I wondered why the doors always closed when I entered a room. I wondered what made me so special. I wondered what was really in the forest, if not magic.

I wondered, where does the world go when I close my eyes?

Hazy summers were spent underneath the neighboring palace trees, gulping down water to try and stay cool. But the winters were different – a second in the outside air would chill your bones. Or so was the story. We stayed solely indoors and the snow froze everyone near death, all those tiny, imaginary people with no good fortune. The view from the window was pure, piling sleet. We were shielded by solid gold walls, never subject to the icy outside.

The time in between, that morphing time of mild warmth and cold – that was always my favorite. When the clouds rolled in the sky, and the rain washed everything clean. I used to be able to love it. I was happy, wasn't I? Wasn't I happy? I don't know. I had never seen sadness. I had never felt anything more than simple contentment and clueless, golden-wall bliss.

Until the Regicides. Until the cracking of the sky.

DECEMBER 1

MELCHOR CITY

The tiny details I remember clearly; they are unmelting ice in my mind.

Our city held a white mist that day, and a musical air danced over the fresh snow. The cold air gasped and wheezed on my young face. I could see our palace from a distance, towering red and gold into the clouds.

The red chariot rolled out into the borders of Melchor City, shielded by thick glass. White coursers and spinning wheels, rolling like clocks.

Mouths moved, but no voices escaped them.

Everything was quiet — no shouting, no singing, no screaming; no rabble-rousing in the streets, not even a trace of trouble — just gazing in awe at the Wickwolf royal family. I remember a stunned face staring at mine, smiling a nervous smile — waving faintly. One eye was green, the other brown.

Then, a gunshot.

Thin shards of glass whipped down at me and stung my arms, debris scattering like feathers from the chariot's lid. Everything moves so slow in memory.

I caught a glimpse, just a frozen frame, of the single bullet through my father's throat.

My mother's shaking scream seemed to shatter the glass, though it was really the storm of voices, pounding their way in — and the bullet. Some nights, that same scream still echoes when I try to fall asleep. She sent tremors through the glass and her scream filled my world, now fractured beyond repair. And then her long black hair, as it swung down on my face and guarded my huddled body.

The sound of a second shot.

All was dark.

CHAPTER I:
A BRAVE COWARD

ALL IS DARK.

My last night in the velvet bed I know is spent staring daggers at the sky. Only a scattering of stars in sight, the moon a shred of silver. I'd like to rip it out and shut out its light forever. I'd like to pluck each star from the sky and stomp them under my bare feet. Yes.

September the third. The exact date, I can remember for one reason only: three royals were murdered, six years ago, today. Under these same wicked stars and trees and cold, cycling planets.

You'll be safe here. They've had their way with us.

I lay in bed, gripping the rusty golden handles of its headboard until my knuckles ache, looking out the picture window nearly covered by a long sheet of silk. The night is too dark to see much color, but I can make out the faint glow of red.

They are no real threat, my prince.

Outside, the city is inky and shrouded by the forest trees that used to protect the palace. The woods, where I've never dared to go – even when it was wild and beautiful and free.

They only wanted to strike fear.

My chest aches for everything, a long list of sadness that rolls through my head. My still, silent mother. The dry-cracking cold that envelopes Melchor City. The war-wrecked ruins of our castle in which I lay tonight. Years of mourning that will never be done with. My father's murder.

My father, the King, stood at the peak of the Royal Hall and spoke in a grave voice that seemed to send itself off into every corner of the burnt-earth world. I remember every word of it.

"September the third. Today we remember our fellow Belvidereans whose lives were stolen by this hidden, vicious horde... of Kosta, their Queen Merris and King Karan... of Lusk, their Princesses Krysanthe and Oriana, and their Prince Jorson..." His voice echoed off the walls, carrying the weight of each name. "And of Uppica, their King Victor, Queen Ayana, Prince Clayr, and their Princesses Fey, Eris, and Stelle. May we all celebrate their lives and mourn their tragic ends... I promise you, citizens of Belvidere, children of the burnt earth, we will find the Regicides."

Then my father was shot through the neck.

Sleep.

King Loupe Wickwolf joined the roll, his royal promise dead and gone.

Don't torment yourself like this, Prince Wickwolf.

The assassinated royals, killed by the Regicides, hang like a curse over Belvidere. They are masters of disguise; they are shadows in the night. No one knows who they are. They travel in packs. They are looming, they are elusive, and they are quick. Invincible, it seems. They are not a gang but a force of nature.

They are long gone, and you are safe.

I can't forgive them, yet I don't know who they are. Dozens of figures with gray masks. From everywhere, from nowhere. They are my mother's misery, my father's grave, my terror and trembling and pain.

Stay.

I am paralyzed with fear — yet I want to run until my legs collapse. There's a kind of dark glory to the word *fugitive,* but it tastes like a curse on my tongue.

We need you.

I've chosen to abandon my mother, my never-moving mother, the only person in this world who loves me. Frozen with fear after what happened to the King, confused and incompetent — simply and deeply inept at everything my title entailed — I guess I was an awful prince anyway.

Your kingdom needs you.

Yes, was. I've decided: I can be a prince no longer.

The dread of my murder is hanging in the air and eating me alive. My given name, Ezra, I'll get rid of it. Then all the decorative ones in the middle that mean nothing to me. Then wolf, the symbol of honor.

They will not hurt you again.

I'll keep Wick, though, or there'll be nothing left of me. I'll become Wick and escape this place. I can't keep living under the delusion that I am indestructible.

I have to escape. I don't want to become a part of that speech. I don't want to be killed like my father, at the hands of masked people who hate that I was born. I don't want to sleep on a grave anymore, a grave that shakes under the weight of my nightmares.

The darkness is holding my hand, and it begs me not to go.

No. It has to end. My voice trembles now whenever I speak, mostly to myself. I lock my bedroom door, bolt the exits, close the curtains all nights but tonight, disappear into the corners, eat quickly and sparsely and quietly, avoid all eyes, and sleep sleeplessly. I've broken dozens of locks from twisting them so hard. My hands seem like claws these days; they cannot hold anything without destroying it.

Anyone, at any time, could be next, and that could be me. Will be me, if I don't leave. I don't want to be a part of our feeble, crumbling kingdom any longer. I have to, want to, need to escape where I could never be suspected.

They cannot hurt you again.

A quick knocking at my door makes my heart fly.

"Prince Wickwolf?" The voice belongs to Emelin, the chambermaid. My mother loved her and wished to keep her close, so she clung to the shelter ground with us and heard the scream of bombs as they hit our kingdom. The only other survivor.

I open the door, my hands trembling in the dark.

"O-oh. My. You don't look very good." She holds a bowl of soup up to me. "Her Highness was saying you haven't been well lately... are you having those nightmares again?"

"My... my mother is speaking again?" I take the bowl, but it shakes in my grip as I tilt it up to my mouth.

"She —" Emelin furrows her face with some terrible and mysterious grief. She knows every word will hurt me. "Her Majesty speaks, but her words are barely discernible, I'm afraid. She is still..." She gulps. "...just above comatose... Immediately, immediately as she woke she mumbled about your welfare... her Majesty said, *'Ask if he is well...'"* A lie. She hasn't said a word in years. "Would you like me to stay here and keep you company?"

"I'm — I'm fine." I'm a good liar, too. "The nightmares aren't so bad, of late, honestly." Brilliant, even. "Thank you."

"Sleep." Her small voice shakes, and she raises her head from its usual bow, meeting my gaze. I didn't know her eyes were brown. "Sleep, Prince Wickwolf, *sleep*, I beg of you. You don't look well."

She's right. I look absolutely awful. I look like I just crawled out of hell.

"It's sweet of you to think of your father... still, after all this time – but to mourn for so long... I beg of you... please, think of yourself. You are most cherished by your kingdom, and your law tutor awaits you downstairs."

I nearly laugh, but it's just a slight, sick twist of the mouth. I couldn't squeeze an ounce of care from me about the *law* right now. And the tutor is the last person I want to see.

My tutor is a crooked-toothed old man from Uppica, God knows how he came here. His name is Gresky, or Gresty, or something like that. Took his old blue backwards trolley all the way to our lovely wasteland, probably had to wriggle his way through the law to do it. He's got about four teeth total, and speaks with a lisp that makes him sound even older than he is. There's really only two things the he'll bother teaching me nowadays: law and human psychology. The operation of a government – a king's duties, a king's burden, why such things came to be. But there's no one left to govern, so there's nothing left to learn. And psychology – I don't think I'm qualified to psychoanalyze anyone when I can't stand straight without trembling. So the old man just hands me three-foot-wide textbooks and leaves me be.

"Thank you for your concern, Emelin." I put a trembling hand on her shoulder. She nods and walks away with her brow knotted, and with a jolt, my soup bowl clatters to the floor, breaking into shards, spilling broth over the velvet floor. She's put two lithium pills in it.

"God" is all I can choke out, not bothering to pick up the pieces. Instead I bolt back into the room, and the flying chips of chariot are stinging at my skin once again.

But this time my mother can't cover me. I have to do this on my own.

I leave at midnight with my small pack full to the brim — matches, compass, berries, canteen, a warm coat, extra clothes, a decent knife, and my Wickwolf pendant, my father's precious map. Packed light.

Six hours. I need six hours.

The library still stands – just barely.

The shelves are singed in half, the floors are smeared with ash. We're lucky the bombs were old and weak, or the damage would be much worse. And we wouldn't be around to see it. With the bombs of the old world, we'd be blasted out of the water – that is the new world's only mercy. We have not yet found a way to completely destroy ourselves.

Pages are scattered across the floor, burnt at the edges. The same searing black type. A clutter of ash. Words, strewn everywhere.

his vengeance need not be feared
a true friend and a true enemy
. علي المرء أن يكون ثعلباً ليعرف الفخاخ
and a lion to terrify the wolves.

It's enough, though. It's enough for me to hope a little. In the wreck of demolished books, the splintered ruins of walls, there are survivors – blackened and brittle, but intact. They don't crumble when you hold them. Their pages don't slip like black sand through your fingers.

I can feel now how they must've felt after the ruin, those that did survive. When the sea ate up towns and houses, and the blinding fire got the rest. They rose from their own ashes and struggled just the same. The words echo in my head: *nothing can ever be broken beyond repair. Nothing is ever destroyed completely.*

I want so badly to believe them.

One more time. I won't look into her face and see the woman who raised me. I won't round this velvet-decked corner and look into open, seeing eyes. I can't say goodbye because she won't be there to hear me.

In the last ravaged passage of the castle is that wretched twelve-foot-tall painting, hanging by a thread. A young, healthy-looking kid with a casual smile and silk stockings, jauntily leaning forward into a pleasant future, bits of very real rubble dotting the painted velvet he stands in. It takes me a minute to realize it's me. It was once me - the smooth-faced child who ran in between trees and jumped into forbidden lakes and ate twelve-course meals at galas.

Before.

My neatly-folded life unfurled into the wind, and was tossed about at sea.

The realization hits me, cold and coarse and unforgiving: none of us are how we were before, and never will be again. These are things that cannot be rebuilt, cannot come back to me. Everything is gone forever.

I inch toward the Queen's Keep, my boots quiet on the velvet ground. The door groans, golden and ancient. The room is overwhelmingly dark, as if caught in perpetual night. The ceilings are cloaked in red and black, and she lies her long, wide throne, sprawled out. Black hair. Half-open eyes. Awake.

"Mother." I press a hand to her face. Turn my heart into stone. Will the water back into my eyes. "See me."

No. She doesn't see me, but the blur of me formed by tens of thousands of distant, foggy memories, one that isn't me at all.

Her lips part, and she whispers, "Loupe."

I run and don't look back.

The castle no longer stands. It slumps, like a ruined cathedral. Holiness, demolished.

There are no dynasties. There are no other kings. There is only Wickwolf.

The air is cold outside the castle as I hear the boom of the closing gates. I no longer care if anyone hears me. I no longer care if the bitter cold burns my skin, if I collapse onto stone and no one can see me fall.

Melchor city is dusty, dark, painfully quiet, so much that its silence squeezes me. The bombs, the bombs, of course. How many people are left? How many humans walk these grounds? Had anyone else taken shelter?

There used to be people here, I shudder to think. Laughing people. Walking people. The sun used to shine on us. Everyone can't be gone – impossible. There must be a human soul, there *must* be.

But as I leave Melchor and come to Endlos, the darkness only follows me. There's not a single trace of life.

Asphodel is marked by a trail of rubble. Stars begin to shiver in the sky. The darkness begins to clear, only a little – the sky a natural dark blue, instread of smoke-choked black. The destruction isn't quite so evident: not desolate, just abandoned.

Asphodel, a haven, I almost laugh to myself. The dready slums are safe. The air is breathable, the water is not deadly to drink. And yet, no one.

Had no one seen the bombs come? Had no one else had the luxury of living?

My answer takes shape in an run-down old beggar in the outlying city, smoking into the dead night sky, and probably blind drunk. I've stopped in my tracks, and he seems to notice.

"Boy," he chokes, relighting his cigarette. "Cm'ere."

I cautiously tiptoe over, as if each step will send the ground shaking. I can't waste much time with this urchin. "Good... day, sir."

He suffocates himself laughing. "Ah! Aha! Ha! Oh, God, good day to *you*, too, good *sir!*"

"Sorry – I'm in quite a hurry–"

"Oh, is that what y' call it?" He laughs through the smoke, but it sounds like more of an airless growl. "Are you who they say y' are?"

"Who–"

"Don't play dumb, the *prince*, boy. The *prince* survived, everyone else was blown to bits, yeah? Except for – ha, of course – us few lucky rats who ran fast to the sewers. Oh!"

"You said... they. There are more?"

"Ha!" I don't know if he's amused or choking on his own breath. Either way, he stares at me with tired, overlarge eyes – the color of a stormcloud – eyes that seem to stamp me into the ground. "More of *us*? More of us dirty beasts that you can tromp on? More poor, sad people to force your war on? Ah! Ha!" His voice loses its laughter completely. "My daughters and my sons? We live. We live in your gutters. We live in your wastebaskets, boy. You're despicable."

His words sting, probably because they're true. I am despicable. That's why I'm becoming someone else. "I'm sorry, I've really got to be–"

Then he grips my wrist, all yellow, rotting fingernails and bloodshot eyes, and breathes his vile breath on my face. "Run for your life."

Run for your life. It's the only option.

Keep moving, or it will kill you.

Now the prince is gone, and good riddance.

I race through the trees on this cold early-autumn night. Pain and paranoia: these two feelings are obvious in me, coursing, intense and red-hot, through my legs, filling me like little crawling bugs.

Then worry, lodged in my stomach. Regret in the shadows of the trees, relief in the breath pouring out of me, that god-awful homesickness in my chest. I'll have time for those later. I'll save them, keep them tucked into my head, and worry about them later. There's no time for regret. My body is running on instinct and memory alone. His words run through me.

Us few lucky rats who ran fast to the sewers.

We live in your gutters....

You're despicable.

Grimy, blurry tree trunks, brown grass, and rusty-looking skies.

The outside world I've waited so long to see... this is it. This is what they've done to us; the bombs aimed at our kingdom have done their job. It's a ghost world, dead, dust, desolate. The trees lay defeated, like fallen soldiers, and this war has been won.

I run through the dead forest, my too-long legs catching on branches. It isn't a forest so much as a trench of ugly, dying trees. I struggle to keep the lower half of my body from buckling; I've been running for miles now, and dry air fills my mouth. My breath cracks in my useless throat.

All the joints, all the muscles in my legs are shot and heavy. There's an unbearable feeling of intense cold and heat all at once.

And why am I running? As far as I know, no one is trailing me. Even so, running feels like the best option. At least, my gut believes it. Lurking shadows scare the living hell out of me — moving, unmoving — small, large — the shape of a squirrel in the leaves knocks me off my feet with fear.

Paranoia. That's what they call it. I'd seen glimpses of it in the darkness of my bedroom, but I'd never truly experienced it, real and raw, until now. The prince was always rational, wasn't he? He always thought things through. That's why he never did much of anything. He hid in his enormous castle and kept to himself, mostly. Then he became the good-for-nothing coward I call Wick.

My pace slows, and I give into the prickling fatigue, crumple into the ground. I taste blood. At this rate, I'll knock myself out before I reach my destination, whatever that may be. Killing some time could do me good.

The river that runs through the forest sits glittering in the moonlight, reflecting the gaps of stars between trees. I barely have time to think before I dive straight into it, feel my clothes grow heavy with the water, feel myself sinking into the stars.

Shivering in the cold, I gather the tools to make a fire and grate two sticks against each other. Finally, heat. I rub my hands together frantically, begging for warmth, and take a long chug of the canteen. The pristine water Emelin handed me has warmed inside the pack.

I swap the knife out of my pack and chop a lock off my hair. It's good luck to toss it in the fire – now I'll survive. Now I'll survive, I tell myself, as I watch its useless crackle.

"Flames for fortune," I say, and there's no one to prove me wrong.

I paw along in my pack and find the Wickwolf pendant I treasure and loathe. It's the shape of a crouching wolf, poised to attack. It shines by the fire with a sharp crimson gleam – the symbol of honor, of courage, of bravery, of which I have none.

I'm exhausted, purely and plainly exhausted. Alone with all my thoughts, I may eat myself alive.

Draw your mind away. Catch your breath and throw it back. Focus on the dusted grass, the bomb-struck sky, the stars that glow with a lofty arrogance. Focus on the darkness, the smell of destruction. See nothing but the manmade moon. Do

not

feel
anything.

At last the time has come for regret.

My mother, left alone. Everyone and everything she has ever loved has
been taken from her. By time, by war, by the Regicides. And I've been taken
away by my own fault, my own cowardice. That massive, cold, gray castle, and
her alone, just emerging from a long sleep. She will wake up in a matter of days,
weeks, months. She has to wake up sometime. Muster the strength to wash her
face. Eat her first breakfast in ages, lock her eyes on my bare throne and my
golden crown. The crown I tore right out of my hair. Ask Emelin where could I
be? Where could I be? *Where?* Look for me, tear my massive bedroom apart,
and find no one.

No one.

Where is Ezra? *Where is my son?* She'll shake Emelin by the shoulders,
with all the feeble strength she has. *I don't know, Your Majesty! I don't know
where he went!* Her face will wrinkle and redden and fall. It's doubtful I'll see
that face in front of me again. Awake. Alive.

It's doubtful I will see anyone's, because I'm good as dead. So I try to
grasp at every memory of her. I think of her black hair and the blue lines in her
eyelids and her long brown lashes and that red silk robe, and for a good while,
my mind is all colors and regret.

I don't want to feel anymore. I don't.

The stars start to spin in the blackness like tiny silver pinwheels, and soon
they blur together. I'm crying, choking back sudden, vicious howls that may
have been climbing their way up all along.

"I'm a coward," I think aloud, but it's only a garbled sob.

You're despicable.

This is the first time I've cried in so many years. Letting the tears spill, it
feels almost lovely. Like I'm a child again, and feelings are not a weakness, but a

strength. Like I'm born again, shocked by the frighteningly cold grip of this new world.

What I need is time, but what I lack, most horribly lack, is time.

Time heals all wounds, someone said, but they didn't see the bullet through my father's throat. More tears slither down, and everything is blurred in rough paint strokes of colors. I'm half-starved, drained, exhausted, and the world has decided to play lovely tricks with me. The trees go blue. The sky washes red. Every blade of grass, every speck of dirt fades to gray, and I can't trust the very ground I walk upon.

Those flying shards of chariot. The tallest tree in Kosta. My father's neck reeling back. My best friends I never said goodbye to, the sun on their skin. My mother's scream. The bomb shelters that did not hide the wail of the bombs. Emelin's bowl of soup, clattering on cold castle floor.

It all hurts.

I lie down on a rotting log, dumping my pack on the ground. Curled into a ball, I wrap my extra shirt, a limp brown rag, around my shoulders. The trees of the forest seem to close around me, guarding me. Or perhaps trapping me. Damn my restless legs, and damn my restless heart. Damn *me*, I wish I had taken those pills. They'd drown the loneliness in me and fill its place with warm, unbroken sleep. Finally, I force my eyes closed, force fake thoughts into my head: *I am home. I am home. Home, and safe, and not alone.*

As I drift slowly to sleep, I long to see life again. I long for the sky.

The stars are beautiful.

CHAPTER II:
THE SKELETON GUIDE

MY DREAMS ARE always, without fail, nightmares of my death. This time is no different; the same bullet cuts me through the throat, and my soul watches my body die.

I've been murdered more times in dreams than I care to remember. This time I wake up and I don't immediately vomit.

We're off to a great start.

When I awake I feel as if I had just finished crying — the smothered feeling in my throat, that enormous knot, the hot-stinging eyes, all stay. I can't stop the shaking. But I also feel new; almost empty. Everything has been washed out, and now I'm limp and hollow. This nightmare doesn't bleed into my life.

The end of the forest gives way to a clearing of vines and some type of dark yellow blossom, all waving in unison to the kingdom of Kosta... a parade of royal subjects, bowing gracefully.

The neighboring kingdom lays out before me, a marvelous painting. Our triumphant enemy kingdom. I'd forgotten what real warmth and life felt like, and the butterflies' colors are so vivid I almost feel like crying again. Brand new colors fill my vision, colors I haven't seen in ages. Everything feels green, so blindingly green, the color of Kosta. The kingdom of light, of green sparkling sea, of miraculous forests and soaring birds.

I haven't felt this kind of color for years.

Of course it all looks fresher, more alive, than in royal Melchor City. Most everything is dead and dark in the kingdom of Wickwolf, the leaves lying brown on the forest floor, the dust collecting in the bomb-struck streets. Yet the victors of Kosta seem to live in a land of perpetual, blooming spring.

We lost in this war, and Kosta has long since cut all ties with us. But I do remember some things, from peaceful times so long ago — maybe enough to survive here. Enough to infiltrate their palace.

Maybe, I could belong here.

In my memory, Kosta Castle is buried deep within the center of the capital city, Ordim, surrounded by thickets and invisible to those in the slums. A rumor, a magic-land — there'd be no knowing it existed. If my luck stays with me, I'll find my way. I know it.

Kosta's guarding wall soars above me, huge and rusted green. The Wall of Spikes, it's called — quite appropriately. Its circular edges are set off by needle-like golden prongs that stab at the nervous sky. Tall, terrifying Green Knights man the other side, with their cold, trained stares and pitchforks. An imaginary stone plummets through my stomach, and I know deep within me, I was an idiot. I could never surpass this.

So I clasp my hands in prayer and feel their desperate warmth. The hope is all but sapped out of me, but for the nearly-microscopic crack in the wall. Maybe I can take my knife and dig my way through before they can catch me? — No, I'll be killed. Go underground? — No, I would only bury myself.

Too powerful to die, too bright to be blackened. Will too strong to bend. Walls too thick for any enemy.

But I'm not an enemy to your kingdom. I held your prince's hand as we jumped into ice-cold lakes.

My heart's racing with that familiar mantra, *I'll die. I'll die, I'll die, I'll die* —

Suddenly, a door swings in and two skeleton hands are tugging me past the wall, into Kosta.

Death himself! I swallow a scream.

But no, no, it's not a skeleton, or Death himself, just two long, bony, white-as-death hands. Dirty fingernails. Translucent knuckles. A low hiss of a voice.

"No," he curls his lips and pauses, "questions." The man encloses his knock-bone hand around my shoulder. "No words. Come with me." He opens his mouth so slightly that I can just barely see the line of his frighteningly white teeth.

He's a Kostan guard, I suppose – the white skin, the haughty accent. Then why is we wearing a long black cape? — some kind of disguise? And why hasn't he killed me yet?

"*The King's blessing,*" says the man, pressing his bone-white hand to the wall, his voice barely audible from his slit of a mouth. In the course of two seconds, a ten-foot-tall, diamond-shaped hole has opened in the wall. He pulls he through, and with an astounding, sickening jolt in my stomach, I realize we are plunging down a tunnel, the metallic whooshing sound filling my ears like a real and tangible thing.

An onslaught of darkness.

We tumble down to the ground, our legs smacking the dirt floor of — what *is* this place?

"Onward," says the black-cloaked man, and what choice do I have but to follow him?

After we wind through a series of glassy passages, he examines a creaking underground trapdoor. It is coated with dirt, pierced with ancient blademarks, and covered in locks, which the man twists open with dingy silver keys. Over to the corner, I see a small glimpse of text — carved in with a pin or dagger. It reads, in urgent, fatal, impeccable print:

OUBLIETTE.

I'm going to die. Lost inside the earth. Shackles. Chains. Slabs of metal. I'm going to starve to death in a dungeon. I've escaped one prison just to be thrown into another.

Suddenly, the skeleton man jumps through the trapdoor, lands with a soft thump, and beckons for me to follow with that same bone-white hand. My feet won't go, so he yanks me down the chute, his sharp hands digging into my leg. Violence or urgency? I still can't tell. Everything about him is ambiguous. An assassin. A savior. He could pull out a knife or a tonic on me and I wouldn't know the difference 'till I was dead.

Inside, the Oubliette is black. Hints of light come from what I gather is the staircase, a mist of yellow glare.

With grave recognition, I look up at the man's white face. Instead of malice, or indifference to my coming death, he gives me a sincere nod and grips my shoulders with his bone-fingers. I haven't felt a human touch in so long, even a hostile one, that I become immediately tense.

"You're in league with the Regicides."

"No. Relax. I know who you are."

I realize my hands are balled into fists, my nails biting into the palms — but I refuse to uncoil them. I trust no one.

"H-huh? Ah... who do you assume—?"

My voice feels odd when it escapes my mouth. It's been lost to me for so long.

The man nears his face to mine, trapping my eyes in his, and speaks under his breath. My name, that dreaded name.

"Prince Ezra Wickwolf."

"Correct," I force false confidence into my voice, but it still comes out a thick, choked whisper.

"I will protect you." He lets go of my shoulders, then leads me by the wrist, and we walk into the light shining atop the dungeon staircase. We both duck for the doorway. Then his voice goes cold. "For a price."

I swallow my worry. "I'll be a slave here, sir. I'll do anything."

The greenish light illuminates the man's face. Black hair, long and eerily silk-straight. Pale transparent skin just a few shades lighter than the rimy blue eyes, with strange gray eyelashes. Razor-edge cheekbones that curve into a sharp jaw; a snarl on his lip.

And a voice like glass.

"There are no slaves here, Your *Majesty*. You are a pawn, *our* pawn —
delighted, obliged to do your work. Which will be..." He chews on each word,
bearing into me with his unearthly eyes — "absolutely any duty you are given.
Understand?"

"I — I'm sure I can handle that. Thank you, so much, sir." An ocean of
relief spills through me. Death dodged a second time. But I don't deserve it.

"You don't..." He examines my face for a long moment. "You don't look
like a prince."

I don't question this much. He sees me as I was: a long, weak, gangly
teenager with no princely grace and no princely manners. Dark, disheveled,
rumpled-up hair. Thick, angry eyebrows that would never match with my large
droopy coffee eyes. Freckles scattered across my cheeks, just remnants of the
sun of my childhood. Guess I look more like a spindly peasant than a member
of any royal family.

The sharp, dark, elegant Wickwolves. Graceful as ghosts. I'd never match
my father's strength, or my mother's politesse.

"And yet you recognized me, sir," I mutter, trying to smile and looking
back at a pale and unamused face. In the harsh, soupy light, his teeth jut out and
the hollows of his eye sockets are filled with shadow, giving him the appearance
of a talking skull. A single jade glitters at his throat, where his cape connects.

"It's not Sir. It's Pawnmaster Klosswarden. Address me like so, and get to
work." He picks up a long broom from the ground, along with a sack full of
clothes and a dust-brown kit bag, and tosses them in my direction. I fumble
with them until I get them in a comfortable carrying position.

"You are in Ward One, Room Eight. That's to your right. From there,
keep going straight, and if you see anyone, keep quiet, keep quiet, keep *quiet*. Or
I'll be the one to cut your neck, not a Regicide. Now begone with you, boy.
Thank me for your life." He flashes an almost-smile — maybe a grimace — with
his large, sharp white teeth.

"My deepest gratitude," I croak, and I'm running once again.

CHAPTER III:
WARD ONE, ROOM EIGHT

THE HALLWAYS IN the Kosta palace are long, wide, and brick-cold. Up ahead are the pawns' chambers, just one floor above the lonely dungeons. A barren place. The halls are slightly brighter, but the darkness glows a dull green-yellow. Looking down, I see my long, grim shadow.

"Hello?" I call out. I'm answered by echoes.

I try again. "Hello? I'm a new... arrival, looking for my room?"

My footsteps create a soft, thumping sound. I hear nothing else — but suddenly, my eyes trail over to a soft-edged, wavering shadow casting out from a gap in the walls. It moves, but only slightly.

This must be a person... at least a living creature.

"I can see you," I say tentatively, making slow steps towards the silhouette.

It's then that I notice the sound of hushed breathing — human breathing. Non-threatening, quiet... harmless, as far as I can tell.

"It's safe," I try.

The shadow moves out from under the low-cut crevice. A small cloaked figure, it stands a good distance away from me, its face shaded by the hood.

Maybe the shadow speaks a different language... maybe it can't understand me. I try simple words. "Hello — I'm... Wick. I... won't... hurt you." I judge that it's alright to come closer. My feet create a dull echo. One step. Two, three, four.

I clear my throat. "Can you understand me?"

"Of course I understand you."

Finally, a voice. *Her* voice, I guess — it sounds like a girl's. A slow, curious sound. "I can't see you, though."

The girl slips off the hood of her cloak. She flicks a switch on her lantern, releasing a sharp white glow that comes from a shining glob of kersone. "Oh, that's better."

The flash burns my eyes for a moment. A yellow-glowing hand tightening its grip on the stones, a dark unblinking eye flickering with lantern light.

Until now, I didn't realize how small she is, next to me. She's standing, but the top of her head only lines up with my chest. The cloak hangs limp over her body, dragging out on the ground beneath her.

I take in all the details of her face as if I'll never see her again. Her skin is pale, almost white in the glaring light, her face framed by long, wispy hair – honey-red, the color of a dying fire. Strands fall loose from her forehead into her eyes. Obviously a Kostan slumdweller, not from the colonies. All features point to it, all except for those large, dark eyes, like saucers, caught in a perpetual look of wonder. A long nose and a small mouth, curled at the edges, beginning to speak.

"You're scary." She stares up at me, looks down again, then stares up again, as if she has to go down for air every so often.

"Ah. I try."

"But also charming, in a way?" She tilts her head to the side, but her eyes flicker down again.

I don't know what to say to this.

"And your voice is weird."

"Oh?"

"You from the colonies or something?"

"Huh? Yeah. Kallichore."

"That's strange. You look sorta familiar."

"I — this is the first time we've met." Honestly, it is. I don't recognize this girl. I don't even know her name.

Maybe she recognizes Prince Ezra Wickwolf.

"You haven't met until you know each others' *names*," she recites, as if this is obvious fact. My confusion amuses her, I see. "I'm June Kinsel, junior palace handler. You a one-named wonder?"

"Just Wick."

June sighs. "I don't like nicknames. 'Round here they call me..." She lets out a nervous cough. "They call me 'the little ghost'."

"Why's tha..." I stop myself quickly. Yes, she really does remind me of a little ghost — her appearance is actually eerie, though perhaps it's just the lowlight. The way her long cape trails behind her. Her hair falling, almost floating, over her face — like a phantom. Her eyes... round and unnaturally dark blue, and now glaring up at me.

But when she grips my wrist, her hand is warm.

She leads me like a tall, ungainly dog into the pawn's quarters.

"Welcome to the gutters," she says.

"Ward One, Room Eight," I repeat, partly to myself and partly for her instruction.

"What?" she asks, widening her already-huge eyes at me.

"One, Eight, I said."

June mutters something to herself, a little vulgar chant: what I can make out is "Curse... Klosswarden... fool." I raise my eyebrows in inquiry.

"You have the ability to curse people?"

"Aye." She jabs me in the rib, and I flinch involuntarily. "You're cursed. A thousand more years of looking like a giraffe-turned-person."

She opens a door marked 8, and shoves me into the boxy closet-like cubby. There's a shelf, a cot lying rumpled on the floor, one patchwork pillow, June's kit bags, and a round miniature lamp.

"Always sleep in the corner, over there." She gestures to the right. "Store your stuff in the nook. Change in the washrooms. And always knock with eight soft taps to the door." She makes a drumming gesture with her hand. "Okay?" I nod quickly.

"Everyone's paired up but me," she fidgets with her hands and stares at the stones on the ceiling, "so it shouldn't be a big trouble. But I liked being alone..." Her eyes drift down to the ground again.

"You did?" I ask. "I've never met anyone who liked being alone before."

"I don't so much *like* it as..." She hesitates. "I'm used to it, I s'pose." Her eyes look gloomier than before, but they turn right back up to me.

With a deep yawn, June shifts out of her cloak. She wears what I assume is a pawns' outfit, baggy and black and lined with gray thread. She's a little bow-legged, and a little pigeon-toed. There are three bruises on her leg, and four on her arm. Finally, she smiles faintly.

"Everyone's a bit scared of me, or something."

I am so taken aback by her sudden smile I can barely move.

"Or something," I mumble. "Who did this to you?"

She looks down, tracing the sick yellow and purple of the bruise on her arm, wincing.

"I bruise easy."

CHAPTER IV:
THE MISSING PRINCE

THE PAWN HALL is barely a room. It's small and stuffy — an oak table in the middle, sparsely decked with wooden plates. Off to the side, there are boys and girls scooping oatmeal and crackers onto their dishes. To the farther right are what look like chutes or slots cut in the wall. Above are the words "TO THE FEED." On the ceiling, the Kosta regalia of the green diamond is painted, large and fading and cracked in places, but still penetrating in the gloom of the room.

I peer down at the pile of mush and bits on my plate. Well, it isn't repulsive, so I'll eat it. Food is food.

"What's with your scowl?" June whispers, sipping water from a paper cup.

"My scowl?" I hadn't noticed it. "What face am I supposed to make?"

"Smile. You're a happy pawn."

"And you're the shining example." I stare back at a pale, gloomy face.

"These days, I'm not a happy pawn," she says, scooping oatmeal onto a cracker, glaring at the grimy floor.

"Sorry."

"Not your fault," June mutters in what seemed to be her ordinary voice; it is airy, almost gentle, but it barely convinces me.

"New recruit!"

A small black-haired kid suddenly sits himself down next to me, bringing the mob of pawns along with him. They all file in, in plain black garments. The group scatters themselves around the table, the floor creaking below them.

Why are they all so *young*?

They all seem to be no more than eighteen, some as young as twelve, but their youth is betrayed by circles of sleeplessness under their eyes, the hollow look in their faces; though most have dark complexions, they look like the sun has never touched their skin. Many of their shoulders have curled, a permanent bow to the long-dead King. They are all wearing some variant of a dull black pawn outfit — loose, laced, some tied in the middle with a rope-like belt.

The black-haired kid speaks up again. He has a long, starving smile, and a dark bruise on his cheekbone.

"I'm Noor."

"Wick."

I extend my hand to shake his, but he grabs me around the neck and hugs me. I can feel the bones in his arms.

June crunches down a handful of crackers and shoots the boy a look that seems to terrify him. She turns to me. "He's excited 'cause today he has some sort of upper palace duties."

"Kitchen duty," Noor hums to himself, fidgeting nervously in June's apparently-frightening presence. He smiles, yet he has bruiselike rings under his eyes. "I got kicked upstairs, Wick."

"Congratulations... Noor."

We're talking, nervous and bustling, like friends. My first friend — as Wick, not Ezra — is a strange pawn boy.

"B... but what's so exciting about kitchen duty?" I ask him.

"High-ups," June interjects with a grave look. "The royals and aristocrats. And since Kosta is the *best* and *safest* kingdom... a large lot of the Lusks are mooching themselves off here."

"Shh!"

The Lusks. I remember them — Princess Krysanthe and Oriana. Prince Jorson and Leo. Most of them were killed by Regicide bullets.

"You're lucky, little ghost," Noor pouts. "You get to rub elbows with them all the time. How'd you manage that?" He gives her a joking grin that I don't understand.

I tilt my head at her in questioning.

"Klosswarden's my father," June explains, pivoting to face me and lifting herself from her seat. "Not a very good one, though." And with that, she slides her dish into the washing slot and leaves, her mouth still drawn in a straight, small, unwavering line.

I can already tell June is the kind of person I'll need to ask a lot of questions if I want to know anything. The things she says are so vague and unexplained. Not that she's an enigma — she seems almost the opposite. An open book, but every other word erased.

"She's a spooky one," Noor observes, feigning a shudder. "I can't believe she actually talks to you."

"Why does everyone call her that?" I ask. "'Little ghost?'"

A bony girl to the left of Noor shoots up in her seat in excitement. "I know, I know this one!" she exclaims, looking me in the eye. "My name is Ibby, by th'way. Nice to meet ya. Anyway, the girl—"

"June," I interrupt.

"— yes, June — was roaming through the castle the night she first came here. She was about twelve, I'd guess? — yes, that sounds about right — so anyway, she wasn't given her pawns' togs yet, and she was wearing an old nightgown. Which was white, and much too long, so long it dragged along the ground as she walked. She didn't know the way around the castle at all, an' so she wandered, like a stray cat — all up t'the Royal Hall, for God's sake!" Her voice pinches with muted enthusiasm. "The *Royal Hall*. The *thought* of it!" She takes a chug from her cup.

"Go on." Noor smiles eagerly. The other pawns grimace and goggle at their excitement.

"So she's in the Royal Hall, *very* lost and confused, so guess who she finds, also wandering? Guess." After a moment, she whispers, "Prince *Russel Kosta* himself!"

The name lights a match in me.

Russel Kosta!

"And what did she do?" asks Noor, his eyes aglitter.

"Asked him how he was, I 'sume. Whatever she said, he was just frozen with a spooked look on his face and then he screamed and screamed his head off and ran away like that." Ibby lets out a hearty little laugh. "And then, in the morning, the prince told someone about the little ghost haunting his castle, and then word spread, and us down here, we learned it was the new little pawn girl! Oh, she got a hiding for that."

Noor smiles guiltily, and I just stare at the table. So June has met Prince Russel — perhaps she gets to interact with the royals daily. Maybe once, twice, three times, she has seen the Wickwolf prince while he was on a visit. My old self. Dressed in dark red velvet and gold. My hair perfectly arranged, my face slapped with powder. Unrecognizable. Right?

Luckily, the little ghost girl is not high on the list of people who would kill me if they found out.

"That girl gets to see the royals every *day*," Ibby sighs, "plus the aristocrats, for God's sake. They're all so..." She trails off, looking at the grim ceiling, probably imagining silk dresses and silver crowns.

"Shiny?" Noor laughs. "Prince Russel does have a few *special* ladies staying in Kosta, I think. Who knows, maybe I'll meet them today."

"And they'll spit on you."

The other pawns glower at him and begin to trail off in clumps to the door. It's strange. Noor and Ibby are the only ones who talk, but even then, only in a hush. Everyone else seems to be in a trance.

What he means by *special*, I don't know for sure, but I did know Prince Russel. In our childhood, there was only one girl he really liked — this one sassy little duchess from Lusk, Regena Pagele. He would chase her around, smile at her, throw flowers in her hair. He always tried to hold her hand, but she would snatch it away and smack him. He loved the hell out of her.

She was older than both of us, taller than Russel. She wouldn't sit in her room powdering her cheeks.

They couldn't have been more different, back then. Russel, he was an absolute elf, short, pale as a seashell. Regena — tall, with her queenly loop of dark brown hair, and rich, tan skin. She'd sit in the slight sun and read for hours, glaring at anyone who dared to interrupt her — no patience, stomping, throwing, impudent, proud as a princess. And then there was Russel, with all the patience in the world, far from polite but far from cruel. Polite in the way that he would shake your hand too aggressively, but shake it nonetheless. The way he would treat everyone warmly, giving them his biggest smile — that was what drew everyone to him. A genuine prince. The only one.

Us three, we ate sweet coconut buns under the trees. We watched fireworks sprout in the sky. We made up secret languages inside the walls of the palace. Jumped into off-limits water. Swam in the Moonglow lake without permission, got chastised constantly by our parents. We wouldn't let go of each others' hands, though.

But of course everyone found it odd that two princes played around with a duchess girl so much — those disapproving looks, those confused glances — they all told us that it would be better to eat sweet coconut buns with Prince Leo or Princess Stelle, God rest her soul. Our supposed equals. But us children, what did we care if Regena's parents weren't entirely *royal*, or if she was from Lusk? We didn't care for their side-eyed glances. She was the only one who wanted to climb the daffodil hill with us, and she didn't care much about getting her leather shoes scuffed up. She would scream at Russel and punch him in the ribs, spit on his face, and be called filth for it. But then she'd laugh. We'd all laugh our childish laughs and fall into the grass with arrant disregard for everything. Then the rain would start trickling and spilling and falling, but we didn't care at all.

My memories are interrupted by the stale smell of the pawn hall, and again I realize I am worth nothing.

Those childish dreams of saving the burnt world – they evaporate.

Then there's only the dark ache of longing again.

Ibby gets up and stands by a bizarre device on the wall, extending her arm, palm-to-ceiling. There is a faint humming and beeping as a long spindly wire descends and coils itself around her wrist. It stays pressed there for a moment and unwraps itself slowly, then winds back into the wall. She examines her wrist and mutters, "Pawn level bathroom sanitation again."

"It's the inker," Noor explains. "Just hold out your hand, it scans you." He holds his own hand under the spindly inker.

"Oh," I say. The wire stamps some kind of pawn duty onto your wrist — I take a second look at Noor and realize his right one reads *Upper palace kitchen duty* in neat black type. Ibby's reads *Pawn level bathroom sanitation*. I remember Klosswarden's words and figure mine will be bathroom sanitation, too.

Wrong. *Upper palace, Royal Hall sweep.*

This could go very badly, I'm afraid, but I collect my broom anyway.

I walk behind another pawn boy, and all I can see is the Kosta diamond stamped on his sallow neck, burned into the skin.

Silence from every corner.

After a long, winding trip up various Kosta staircases, I'm in the lofty upper level of the palace. As Ibby said, *The Royal Hall, for God's sake.*

It certainly is much more beautiful than the Wickwolf Royal Hall. Warm buttery yellow walls, tapestries hanging from every corner of the intricately-painted ceiling, bouquets and blooms everywhere. A bright canopy of light. It is a golden garden, and I am a foreign weed trespassing upon its loveliness.

Magnolias and marigolds. Royals and palace pawns.

To add insult to insult, there are throngs of richly-dressed aristocrats and royals howling with laughter at some private joke in the middle of the place. Feathery headdresses, pearls, velvet, ruffled collars, curled hair. Pawns line the perimeters — it is so infinitely easy to pick them out, in their dull togs and slippers, their skin lifeless and their bodies small and meager — like a picture frame to this colorful, bustling work of art.

"The gardens didn't grow – they never grow—"

"—yes, thirty of them—"

"*She's* here again?"

"—you wouldn't believe it—"

"—out in Ordim, yes—"

As I sweep through the Hall, I scan the crowds for recognizable faces — the ones I spent long evenings with, surrounded by luxury. Childhood friends, maybe. But most of them are dead.

"Lord Charon, it's just impossible, that's all I mean—"

"Oh, hush, you can't go around saying—"

There's an incredibly pale man – sickly-looking, actually – with frosted buggy eyes and silvery-blonde hair, in Kosta green. A gaggle of Lusk girls surround him, their sentences blurring together and bumping into each other, so I can't get a full grip on what any of them are saying.

"She's an absolute blot, I mean—"

"*You're* an absolute blot—"

And all of a sudden — yes! There *is* somebody! Lady Regena Pagele! With her warm skin and glossy dark hair; it's her! She's different — but I'm sure of it — it's her, from my memory. Finally a familiar face!

But from what I can see of her, Regena is hardly the girl I saw as a little prince. Her hair is cut rather short near her neck, and curled elaborately around her ears— it used to be long and straight. It's decorated with feathers and black-painted pearls, and her ears are framed with a dozen or so studs. She stands a bit above average height, I guess, curvy and round-faced. She's dressed in black and deep violet, the color of Lusk.

Although she's changed, her face still holds that same brilliant fire. The yellow of youth has given way to a scowl – a strangely beautiful scorn, an utter contempt for everyone and everything around here, smoldering in the sharp lines of her eyes.

Regena was my good friend, until the War. Incredibly clever, confident, if a little cheeky; she loved books as much as I did. Four years — it's been that long since I've seen her.

My spirit sinks as I realized a pawn has little to no chance to befriend anyone here. But I'm so anxious to talk to someone I remember, I rush up to her, broom in hand. Poor judgement, but I really can't help it.

Regena seems preoccupied, talking with the brawny-looking chunk of a bastard I recognize as Prince Leo of Lusk. His theatrical getup of white and purple silk can't hide the ridiculous muscles of his arms and chest. Eyes like marbles someone dug into his skull, glittering with aggression, scanning the crowd. A straight, long mouth drawn into a suspicious smirk. He is barely talking to her, just nodding her away — and she doesn't seem too invested in this discourse, either, turning her face to the side every so often. Leo's hair is cut close to his forehead, slicked back into a pompadour, and he's let the bristles on his chin grow out. And hell, the puffed shoulders on his outfit are obnoxious even for a Lusk. Those graying tombstone teeth snarl at me slightly. He was never my friend, even as a child.

"Excuse me?" hums the duchess, darting her eyes toward me. They are caramel-brown and sharp, like a cat or tiger, and she seems to be wearing jeweled eyelashes. She flicks a curl of hair from her face, and I notice the gloss-black polish on her fingernails, marked with gold crests. I've forgotten how extravagant Lusks could be, and how she looked without mud and grass on her face—

I stare at her longer, try to throw her a signal:
It's me! It's Prince Ezra Wickwolf!
Don't you see?
She doesn't. She looks at me with the same contempt as everything else.
Leo chuckles into his knuckle, muttering something about those screw-

loose pawns. Some part of me wants to punch him in the hairy jaw. I don't. He's never outwardly done anything to me — he just sends off an atmosphere that tells me he's despicable, and I can't explain it, but I don't want her anywhere near his smirking excuse for a face.

I should give him a chance. Maybe.

But I'm usually right when I think someone's despicable.

"Well," Regena drawls. Her shrill, childish voice has turned to dark silk, it almost makes you want to shiver. "Aren't you're bold, sauntering up here."

Of course she wouldn't recognize me. The thought was ridiculous.

"Sorry, Lady Regena, I'm so impolite." I accidentally sneer.

I vow then, silently, to steer clear of the palace people from now on. After all, I'm Wick now! Wick! *Wick!*

Who the hell is Prince Ezra Wickwolf?

As I whip around to continue with my humdrum sweeping, I swear I see a glint in Regena's sharp eye. Of what? Contempt? Realization?

No. I won't dare to believe it. I'm done with the royals, the palace people, all of them. Starting anew, and living in the dust. Dwelling in the ashes. Rising from them.

Of course there is June Kinsel, "junior palace handler", on the opposite side of the room. Her hair is tied back in knots and she wears a tired expression. What's remarkable are the dozen or so children that surround her, brushing against her and steering her in every direction — of many ages, and dressed in jewel tones and soft leather shoes. She weaves through the throng of Kosta duchesses – anxiously, as if she could burst.

I see him from the back, standing in front of her. He is surrounded by Lusk nobleladies — Odelyn, Charmaine, and Marie, the triplets — and talking to... June, of all people. A head of copper-blond corkscrews, traced with gold in the balmy light — and I know it's him: Russel Kosta.

Without a doubt, he was my best friend, four years ago. Who I ran with under the castle trees, on visits to our neighboring kingdom. Who I talked to for long hours about anything, whose hand I never let go. Then the War came. I never got the chance to say goodbye, and now he will never see Prince Ezra again. But I'm not sorry. The prince was a coward anyway — never a wolf, always a mouse under the cat's shadow — and I'm glad he's gone. Those memories will be soon replaced with my quiet, undetectable existence as Wick.

But no.

No. I can't.

I dash my way around the room, circling, bounding — this is dangerous. But he was my best friend, and my heart is fried, and even if I was not the *me* he knows, I'll still see him. After these four long years — no letters, no communication, no relation to our enemy Kosta, and now I'm in the center of it all.

No.

I worked to get here. So I stop myself — I slow my pace and continue sweeping as if nothing had happened. *No. Palace. Interaction! Never, never, never.* Remind myself... I've got to remind myself. I have to act like who I have become... the silent boy who sweeps under the radar and kept quiet, keeps quiet, keeps *quiet*.

But then —

"*IT'S YOU!*" blurts an emphatic, shocking, familiar voice. Then I see him again — Russel — his head turned my way, green eyes huge with surprise, his mouth gaping as if in the middle of a yawn. He quickly stops himself, covers his mouth, but he won't turn away.

"A new pawn, I guess," he's quick to explain to his embellished friends, though still staring at me in disbelief. They nod with hushed snickers. As I walk away, I catch a piece of conversation.

"So Russel," hisses a girl whose voice I can't place. Her voice has a distinct squeak to it. "Didn't you hear?"

"Hear... what exactly, Joss?"

Her voice becomes so quiet I can only grasp at bits of sentences. "Prince

Wickwolf ... gone... vanished ... trying to track him ... but ... nothing."

My heart jerks. Now I run.

Hot sweat on my face. A burn in my stomach. *No. No! Let me never be found! Please!* I can't stop myself from clutching my head in my hands, running into the nearest nook, and crouching down in hysteria. I'm a fit. I'm a mess.

Of course my mother would report this. Of course the news would go to Kosta, through the pipes, through dainty lips and teeth. Inevitable. All inevitable.

I feel my skull through my head, struggling to break out. My jaw wrestles with my skin.

"For the love of God, kid, if you don't get back to work..." The person the voice is attached to draws his fingers along his throat.

He's a young pawn, dark and sallow and beaten-down, sluggishly coating the walls with some kind of preservative polish. His skin is covered in deep purple bruises. He calls me kid, but he might be *my* age.

He steps toward me and touches my curled back, like I'm a wild animal or something. I am. Because I lash out at him and hiss, "Go."

The pawn widens his eyes at me, probably thinking I'm insane. Because maybe it's true.

Every muscle in my back is tense, every vein filled with unfamiliar blood. My mind is thrashing. I steady my breathing and add, hushed and pathetic, "Please," and the boy looks back to the wall with unsettled exhaustion.

The laughing, the childhood laughing, the running, the swimming, the daffodil hill, they circle inside my eyes.

And I cannot, cannot, cannot let them go.

As I fall asleep, I think of my mother. And what I remember most are the veins in her hands as she signed legal documents, or painted on canvas. The ink spin of her pen on paper. The book she would always read to me, *The Wolf and the Starling*, with splatter-ink pages. How she barely talked or moved for the last few years I'd known her — paralyzed and lost. And how I will never see her face again or say goodnight.

"Goodnight."

The words were stuck in my throat that night. *Goodnight.* They'd never fly free from the deep pit of my stomach. *Goodnight, mother.*

I'd said goodnight so many times. I had shut my door, the door a few down from theirs. And after, I'd hear things I didn't want to here from their bedroom. I couldn't help but listen, though. It wasn't like fighting, but it *sounded* a lot like it. That was the only time they really talked or touched. In the dark. In their room. They didn't do much of either outside the castle, but when they did, they did it to the extreme. Their words were vulgar, but they were words. And sounds. Not silence. I've always hated silence.

And then there were no words at all. The silence swallowed the whole kingdom.

Snow fell and mixed with the ashes, with the poisoned air. I didn't dare go outside, but I could see its dark glitter through the window. The army men had dismissed all the servants but Emelin, and then the bombs came. Just the army men, my mother, Emelin, and me, a traumatized, amateurish child. The great kingdom of Wickwolf.

My mother's throne was surrounded by an air of agony, so thick I could barely cross it. That snow-smothered night, I approached her and dared to touch her hunched, sleeping shoulder.

No reaction. A staggering stillness.

"Wake up," I whispered, and my voice gained momentum. "Wake up, mother, wake up, wake up..."

She was still. In my memory, everything is still, frozen and lodged and petrified; everything is confined in its glass castle. My nightmares move, just slightly, like jittering ghosts.

"Wake up, please..."

Soon everyone I have ever known crowds themselves inside my head, and says goodbye one last time.

I have no family, no past, and I am no one.

"I'm so tired I can barely sleep." June's voice comes muffled from the other side of the room, all but buried under her blanket. It's incredibly dark — and the kersone lantern has been shut off – but her candle of a voice stirs something up in me that I haven't felt in years. I'm struck by a sudden happiness, an appreciation of her presence, that fills me like helium.

"Yeah," I mutter, trying to get comfortable in the flimsy excuse for a blanket, on this stony floor.

A minute passes before she asks, in a quiet voice, "May I hum?"

"Mhm." My voice is filled with sleep. But I stay awake for awhile, listening to her soft, low humming, a repeating chorus that blends itself into my nightmares. Takes the edge off of them. Turns them into peaceful dreams. Where there is no such thing as the Regicides, there is no missing prince of Melchor , there are no royals and no Pawnmaster Klosswarden and no dead kingdom, just this strange, ghostly girl and me, lying four feet apart, dreaming.

Her hair almost covers the swollen scar of a diamond, branded dark into the back of her neck.

CHAPTER V:
THE CAMPGROUND
OF THE REGICIDE QUEEN

ROUGH VOICES GRATE against each other. Knives are replaced in their scabbards, filthy boots are laced and unlaced. Old blood, human or animal, is scraped off of arms and hands.

There is a clamor about the Regicide grounds, low and rumbling.

"Chief Onderschot..."

"*She* got him. *She* did him in."

"Who?"

"Nox."

"The— the *girl?*"

"Yeah, the *girl.*" The man lets out a low chuckle, replacing the mask on his face. "She's a horror."

A horror without a heart.

Hearts break; bones shatter; lives end; but she does not.

Hearts fail, so she is indestructible.

Hearts burn, so she is impossibly cold.

Hearts fail, always fail, so she has disowned hers. It is a red piece of meat that goes womp in her chest. And nothing more.

Nox stalks through the campground with nothing in her eyes. Blank as ever, in front of the hulking, armed men. Her assistants; her subordinates. She allows herself to think only one constant thought:

I am queen of this operation.

A creeping smile sneaks through her lips until tiny creases form in her cheeks. Her eyes take on a kind of cold blue fire, different from their cool, usual gray.

She might not look deadly, if not for the stark gray mask she carries at her side — an oval, divided in half with a thin line — one side dark gray, the other, white. One black X for each eye. A pristine Regicide mask.

"The long winter of Belvidere has almost reached its end."

"So it has."

Locke kneels before her, his face a cold, pale blood-pink, his eyes sinister and clear. "And half the royals are dead, your grace. It is your triumph that has brought us here."

"Yes" — she licks her teeth and spits out a laugh. The words of victory curl her lips. "Checkmate."

"But not quite, Lady Nox," Locke whispers, not daring to look up.

She clamps his face with a cold hand. "I'll track them all down, I swear to you. Every wretched shining diamond on this god-awful island. First the ones on the pedestals, then the down-lows. They'll be later. Then we'll be the last few people in this world, my Locke."

"*I'll* track them down, you mean," he mutters.

She sends him a lethal glare, disguised by a squirming smile.

"Will you..." She tosses and twirls the gun in her hand. "I think that job belongs to my little silver darling."

"What about the Wickwolf prince?"

"Ah, no. Not yet. That boy... I'm saving him for last."

"Then there will be freedom, my queen – complete freedom, at long last."

"Freedom is never complete," she says, "unless it is stolen."

The camp was quiet that night. The distant cry of black wolves, crickets' bleating, and the murmur in the trees. But no sound from the Regicide grounds. Men without homes or fond memories. Cold hands pressed to guns and swords alike. Thirty-six halfmasks, sleeping like death.

And Nox.

The girl was not yet twenty. She knew death like a friend, kept it at her side as a comrade, threw men and creatures to the ground with a smile. And no one knew, for she was one with the shadows, one with the night. She suppressed howls of laughter that climbed up her throat, but let the low, long grin curve across her face, making cracks in her lips. Then she slunk out, gangly-limbed, hissing, and peeled off her dirty socks. Stole away from the crime scene. There lay a massive slab of a man, turned on his stomach, blood still spreading from his mouth.

An ear-whispered obituary.
"She crept into his bed. That's how."

The night was frigid and empty of stars; it froze her to the bone. It dug the cold into her joints. Chief Onderschot's tent looked like a dark, slow-sailing ship in the deep haze, nearly disappearing into the dark. Not a light in sight. Nox crept in with filthy socks, a cold, malicious smile. As his gaze pinned itself to her — silently, condescendingly — she replaced hers with a feigned, sad-eyed pout.

"The hell are you doing in my tent?"

"I'm cold," she purred, mock-shivering.

"I don't care."

"I'm tired, Chief."

"Leave."

"But I'm — oh, so tired. So tired, Chief..."

The fool who joined the Regicides as a scrawny, homeless little girl. The fool whose hands twitched at her gun. The fool who thought she could become anything like *him*.

He said nothing.

He said nothing as she twisted her arms around his back, pressed her mouth to his.

And died, throat full of poison, in his sleep.

CHAPTER VI:
AS GOOD AS DEAD

THE PAWN BELL rings, but I've been awake for hours. I wouldn't let myself sleep again, for more than a minute, my eyes pried wide open. Somewhere in my slice of successful sleep, I did have a dream – a mild one. My teeth fell out. But my mind is a slippery slope, and flowers can turn to fire quite easily. I woke with a dark song.

King Karan, the Goldenheart,
brought Merris to the door.
He spun his webs from kingly fingers,
And his heart, he tore.
The figures tall and never seen,
had dark deeds yet in store–
King Loupe, his heart of ruby
Stopped beating evermore.
And our dear Queen Gloria,
lay broken on the floor.
Queen Gloria, made all from dust,
lay broken on the floor.

My throat goes dry. I bite my lips raw. I chew my fingernails to the skin. Constantly on edge, with the sick songs echoing. I really am a mess of a person, and I have deconstructed myself so completely I'm afraid I won't be able to pin myself together again. To pin some semblance of myself together again, to grow a lion heart – a human one – to become someone who does not run away from everything. I can't sit still. How can I do that when everything is chasing me?

The cackles don't help, and I hear them too often. The duchesses, aristocrats, nobility, all of them – mocking me, mocking my family, in the lavish clothing I once could wear, in the haughty accent I once could afford. It chases me. They talk in imperial voices, voices that sound like laughter, like eventful days outside the castle, like beautiful sunlit strolls. Voices that say nothing. That lofty, spite-sprinkled laughter in the mouths of the victors, it chases me until I can run no more.

Two aristocrats from Lusk walk by me, ruffling their skirts as they pass.

"...the once-great Wickwolves..."

"Prince killed himself, I guess."

"But there are *no* traces of him."

"Does that rule anything out?"

"*No* traces."

"Killed like his father." She shrugs.

"Shhh! Hush, hush, don't say things like that!"

So I bite my tongue, and continue working, hauling crates for shipment, refilling royals' plates, pouring wine into glasses, acting as a pawn would. I shuffle through my duties as my mother's scream replays itself in my ears, the Regicide bullet through my father's neck.

"The mark of a good pawn," June told me, "is silence."

"What's the matter with him?"

Good question.

"Who?" The high-pitched voice of Lady Joss.

"That pawn boy, sweeping the floor over and over."

"I don't know. He's a little — you know, those screw-loose pawns. He really looks like he doesn't sleep at *all*..."

"Too bad. They could give him something to shut him down for a bit."

"*They* could?"

"The medics."

"Yeah," Joss says, her sickly sweet voice not matching her words. "They'll really fix you up."

"Sure they will," the other girl agrees. "Miss Joss, did you happen to hear about Prince Leo and Lady Regena?"

"Of course. The girl's a madwoman to refuse him. If I wasn't with Russ—" She stops herself and giggles, holding her manicured hand up to her mouth. "Oh, dear."

"Just hold on. He's a little cracked, but I'm sure he's good."

I try my best to bite my tongue. The nerve of them. What disgusting things would they say in total privacy? Though I guess, as they consider me nothing more than the dirt on the floor, this counts as a kind of privacy.

I move on to sweep a larger room. A familiar room, a room that glows with the light of one thousand candles, circular fountains spraying water into unaccepting air, paintings of the royal family strung across the walls by thick, jeweled ribbons. King Karan's painted face registers no sadness, Queen Merris looks joyful as can be, and little Russel is untouched by tragedy. Their eyes are all a bright, startling green. It would create the illusion of happiness, if I didn't know better.

As if on cue, the Prince of Kosta saunters into the flood of light, standing taller than before, pale as a seashell, extravagantly dressed. His curlycues of blonde hair have been styled into curving loops; his green eyes bright as ever; his mouth smiling, enormous and filled with perfectly white teeth. And his electric laugh, born from nothing. Just as he's always been, a revived ghost of my memory.

Then his laughter starts to fade. His feet trail uncertainly on the ground. He surveys the Hall, his eyes too desperate, his face too pale, almost lonely. He strays to the corner.

I see him then, a boy draped in gold and drowned in pills, waving like a diplomat, calling the kingdoms in.

He's like a ghost, I think to myself. A ghost that is happy only because he doesn't remember what he's lived through. I know it – I know. There's something stretched in his smile, and all of a sudden I get the itching feeling that when the day is over and when he's through with smiling, he'll pitch himself onto his bed and cry. But it's only a feeling.

Then I remember there are one million ways to pretend to be happy. And he's most definitely chosen the way of the heavily-medicated smile, the sadness rolling in and kicked away every morning.

Out of the corner of the room, June approaches him, holding the hands of two royal toddlers whose names I don't know. A boy and a girl, dressed in deep silver and green, with fist-sized pastries jammed in their mouths. I inch even further out of sight.

"Angelica." Russel ducks to pat the head of the little blonde girl with a pastry in her mouth.

"Prince Russel," June mumbles, staring down at his feet. He is wearing white shoes with finely sculpted wings at the heel, like the ones he wore as a child. "Can you fly?"

Russel laughs, a warm, appreciate laugh that seems to fill the massive room. He has that unfortunate kind of voice that could make anyone think they've fallen in love with him. "Sadly, no. But that's what they used to say."

"Huh?" June smiles cautiously.

Russel continues on in his loud blare. "You see, I took a huge dive from this *enormous* tree, ages ago; broke both my legs. But some people... some people say they saw two wings sprout from my back." He grins, wide and friendly. "I didn't even close my eyes, was the rumor. These shoes... my mother made them for me."

June smiles faintly, her eyes trailing off to imagine a small, flying Russel with sky-colored wings. The royal children beam up at him, in a daze.

"I've actually broken my nose seven times, you know. The ground seemed to have a fixation with that spot. But it was sometimes my arms, too.. or ribs, or legs–"

"Socked into the ground by your own stupidity," Regena cuts in, appearing seemingly out of nowhere, by the swish of her skirt. Today she wears dark feathers, pearls, and... a smile.

Russel just chuckles, and finally his face comes alive with real happiness. "Reg! – haven't spoken to you in a while. Anyway, they called me the flying prince. So at least I got a name out of my stupidity."

"No one calls you that."

"Must you dampen my mood!" His laugh makes it clear that his mood isn't dampened in the least. "They do!"

"Your favorite line," Regena smirks, "was always, '*WATCH THIS!*'"

"Hey," says Russel, smiling huge and crooked. Suddenly it seems as if they are the only two people in the Hall. "Maybe you'll jump off that tree with me?"

"Oh," Regena snorts, "on a cold day in hell."

There she is. I try to suppress a smile from behind the corner.

"Actually," Russel says, very matter of fact, "hell is cold. It's a big endless cold place where you just sit alone forever, freezing your neck off! There's rivers, but they're frosty and frozen and dead, and full of water demons and whatever else! That's what they say. And I believe that, too. I mean, if you're burning you at least feel *alive*, right?! But cold is just — you'd just be freezing all the time and there'd be nothing. Charming, right?"

His smile stretches even further, but it's not false this time.

"That does make sense," June mumbles, not daring to look Russel in the face. She immediately claps a hand over her mouth, as if it's a crime to speak.

Even now I admire Russel, though he might be an ounce stupid. Stupid has guts. Stupid has adventure. Stupid has thrill. And even though stupid is cocky and half-baked and shows off too much and really, tends to fail — smart forgets to live sometimes.

I see Russel, seven again, shooting down from the branches with an incredible grin on his face as we watched him awestruck. I am starting to wish I had jumped from that enormous tree. Although, I'd never find it now. It's gone with time.

"Hey!," interrupts a shameless voice, as Prince Leo Lusk basically rams into Lady Pagele.

She freezes.

Her paralysis quickly mutates into rage.

She shoves Leo's boulderish form away with her fists clenched. "Leave," she breathes, a cold, violent hiss, ignoring the bewildered look that crosses Russel's face and the unimpressed grin on Leo's. She grinds her teeth against her bottom lip but keeps her eyes directed at the floor. "I told you... I told you to *never* go near me again... you — "

Leo laughs — if you can call that kind of sound a laugh — a gnarled snicker. His laugh violates the very meaning of laughter. His face contorts; there is no sense of depth to his hollow, hollow eyes. "Wasn't that a joke?"

"Go away," she continues, her voice sharper than ever, her eyes wet and chaotic. A fusion of fury and injury. "I *said*, stay the hell *away* from me."

At this point June has retreated to the nearest wall in confusion, holding the hands of a few royal Kosta children, her head in a customary bow. Russel stands.

Leo withdraws from the little battle and makes his getaway, muttering like a misbehaving child.

"It's done, then!" he hollers, his big slick head turned towards Regena. With a malicious, toothy, squint-eyed smile, he is gone. When he's completely out of eyeshot, probably strutting to his guest room, Regena bolts out of the Hall, leaving a trail of purple feathers.

"Hey," Russel whispers, moving his hands as he speaks. "June. You know that boy that just came in? The tall one in black?"

"Y...yeah, um, what about him, sir?"

"What would his *name* be?"

"Oh... Wick."

WARD 1, ROOM 8

June Kinsel has a small collection of things:

Her pawn dress.

A ratty pair of socks.

That strange little ragdoll.

The kerosene lantern.

Her kit bags.

A patchwork pillow.

And the thin, disheveled cot.

Our two small collections form a brown heap in the corner of the room.

I try to detach myself from her gaze. It's as if she has never seen the likes of me before, as if I am some newly discovered species. Maybe she just stares at everyone this way. So I decide to stare back.

Some part of her is always in constant motion – a twiddling thumb, a restless wrist, bobbing feet, the flickering of her fingers over her mouth to hide a lie. She moves in a skittish, light-footed way that suggests she's made of wind, but her face is made of something much more solid and impenetrable.

June has stolen some sheets and books from the Uppers. She tossed the sheets in the corner for later, and she gave up reading the books after struggling with the first few pages.

"Stupid letters all blurred... it's too dark in here..."

At that point, she turned the lantern on, but I could still see the effort in her face to decode the stolen words and their meanings.

I vaguely remember the hundreds of books I read as a child — not their content, but the near-identical look of them. Leatherbound, with huge black type. The smell of them — different for each one, but all distinctly the same, in a way. The smell of words and shelves and adventures I'd never have, heroes I'd never be.

I kept them in the Wickwolf royal library, a room dozens of times the size of this, with no staleness and no rust. Ornate chandeliers and the knowledge of centuries. But that's all over, it's gone — that's what I need to remember.

I'm living in the past, but the past is dying inside of me.

We are in Ward One, Room Eight, smelling of rust and dust. The ceiling is so short that with any sudden movement, my skull would be cracked in half. I crouch into my knees and long for warmth.

June scrapes absently at a long-staying stain on the wall and picks dirt out of her fingernails, still staring at me. Maybe she expects me to say something. I can only think of her face as she watched Russel tell his flying story. His laughter and her quiet observance. Regena and Leo...

"Why do you interfere with them so much?" I ask.

"With who?" She's still searching my face for imaginary words.

"The... the *royals*."

I turn my face to the side. There's something eerie about her eyes.

June ponders this for a moment. "I guess, like anyone *else*, I just want to make them happy." She offers little explanation.

"First you should be happy yourself, little ghost. Stop bothering them." She glares. "Also, I'd recommend not stealing their books and bedsheets?"

"Shhh. Can't have books down here." June chews on her fingers. "*Anyway*, th-they gave them to me. They said I could have them. So I *am* happy. Happy. Happy as can be. And I wish everyone in the whole world was as happy as me." Her expression remains; her eyes flicker nervously, and I feel the forced sincerity in her voice.

"You're not going to accomplish that by ruffling the royals' feathers, you know."

"I'm – I'm just doing my duties. Taking care of them. Serving them. Sending their messages. Junior palace handler. I'm just doing my duties. They don't bother me too much. I'm small... and I bruise easy." Her eyes trail off into the distance, far away from mine. In a low, even voice, she recites, "Kosta is our kingdom. Kosta is our master. Kosta, we must serve."

"So... the royals," I begin, observing the strange, vacant look she has taken on. I have the sudden urge to break the lock on her eyes. "What are they like?"

She still won't look at me. She seems to be under a spell.

"June?"

"They're disgusting."

"Oh."

"They don't do much of anything. Not that I'm any better. I dress them up in the morning and powder their faces, I watch their rotten kids during the day, I clean up after them at night when the party's all over." She wrinkles her nose. "I always mop up Prince Lusk's vomit."

"You could've left that out."

"Why leave it out? He's the worst of the lot."

She curls her arms around herself and soaks in the silence for a minute.

"I've only ever *really* seen Prince Russel and Lady Regena. And Lady Joss, sometimes, because — you know — her and Russel are lovey together."

This really takes me aback. "*Lovey*? The hell?"

"You know. He's wooing her. They're marrying in the summer... flowers and rings and white horses. That whole thing."

Her voice is absent, miles away.

"*That* whole thing... oh," I mumble. But I can't stop thinking of the summer flowers in Regena's hair. The coconut buns. The tallest tree.

Little Lady Joss walked with a pompous, fluttering lilt, the same as her father's. When the headlines came, no tears came from her little blue eyes. I've no fond memories of her at all. And all of a sudden, very quietly, I start to cry, and June finally turns around to face me.

"God, you're a mess."

Yes.

"What? Don't tell me you're jealous or something?"

My face sinks lower into my knees. *"Or something."*

"Tell me you're not in love with Lady Joss."

"*What?* God. No." Perish the thought. "I don't know. I don't know, it's just — I miss home. I miss home." I collapse against the wall. "It's gone."

I can't tell it all to her. I've left myself behind. I can pretend everything will go back to normal. I can pretend all I want, but for nothing. Everything's changed. They're not the same. I'm not the same, no, I most certainly am not the same, and as much as I want to, I can't tell it all to her.

"Yeah," she whispers.

Unexpectedly, June wraps her arms around my neck, and sits her face on my shoulder. Her cheek against my collarbone. At first I flinch, not used to this undeserved affection, but she doesn't seem to mind. We sit still like that for a long time, until I close my arms around her back.

It's the safest and strangest feeling in the world.

"I've never really had a home." She speaks into my shirt. "This is the closest."

After a minute, she detaches herself and covers her face with her hands. "I'm sorry. I don't know — what I..."

"It's okay." I pause, looking at the abandoned book in the corner. It lies, discarded. "Do you... know how to read, June?"

"Shut up!"

"It was only a question."

"Shut *up.*"

"Well, can you?" She won't stop glaring at me with those huge unnvering eyes, too big for her face and too dark for her skin, not blinking as often as they should.

"No, not really," she says, as if this is a well-kept secret. "I don't know how to do much of anything, though. I'm useless 'round here."

"No, you're not. You could learn to read if you wanted to."

"How?"

I shuffle the large book in my hands until the pages whisper and thump.

"This word, right here." *Free.*

"Free. Free..."

"Yeah. You got it, see? You know." I watch her lips move with each new word.

Free thought will create angels or monsters. Be careful with your mind, for it is a precious and ever-changing thing...

"Angles?"

"*Angels.*"

The night grows darker with word after word. By an invisible typewriter, they are pressed into an unseen sky. Somewhere out there in the distance, someone can read the words in the stars. They'll come to rescue us. They'll set us free.

CHAPTER VII:
THE MUSIC OF THE MACHINE

I WAKE UP the next morning alone before the bell has rung, trapped in the empty pawn box, and make my way to the hall. *She leaves early,* I make a note to myself. *Every morning.*

The inker gives Noor another *Upper level kitchen duty* and Ibby *Transportation.* "I'll drive the chariots again," she says with a slight smile. June skips the inker again and heads straight to the Uppers with slippered feet.

"Klosswarden's pet," Noor mumbles through gritted teeth. She says nothing.

This time, it's *Pawn level assembly line* on my wrist.

Straight down the hall is a room of bricks and stone, so long it extends beyond my eyesight. Hundreds of pawns collect themselves on each end. Whirring, buzzing, clacking, and knocking fill my ears and vibrate in my temples. The music of the hideous machine. Pawnmaster Klosswarden sits in a long chair on the edge of the room, in a laced black cloak, this one different from the one he wore when he opened a hole in the gate. It ties at the throat by the green diamond of Kosta, and black strips of fabric form long triangular shapes across the front.

Pointing to me, he says, "Stool 98."

The conveyor belt of metal parts whirs on.

It starts with the guns. The pieces are cold and solid in my hands, the triggers sloping with identical edges, as I struggle to click it all together. My fingers won't move quickly enough. *Pretend they're not guns,* I tell myself. *They are harmless, they are toys, and this is what you are going to do, and you are going to do it right. Or you're out. You're out, you're out.* This mantra rings over and over, and I manage to become consumed by self-hatred by the end of the first minute. After a good hour, the load of guns trickles off, and then comes bullets and caps and clocks and wheels and eyeglasses and copper cables until my hands grow accustomed to the labor. A perpetual motion. The self-hatred transmutes into not even knowing who I am – a complete inability to recognize myself. I'm a cog. I'm a pawn.

I am a piece of the machine for twenty hours more.

◇

A figure in a clean cloak sweeps down the pawn corridor, clutching a basket. Her manicured hand drifts in and out, leaning down to scatter pomegranates on the floor.

She doesn't see her shadow.

June looks at the figure from ten feet behind, tall and with a familiar walk. Someone who stands straight and lifts their feet, whose cloak has no patches or rips.

The figure turns the corner, and June follows. She scoops up a pomegranate, its color red and strange against the grayness. Her hand shaking, she reaches for another. Breathing quietly, making herself invisble, she tries her luck for a third.

The cloak turns around, just slightly. June catches a sloping profile in the darkness, a stained eye glinting gold. The figure turns around all the way, and her voice breaks out of her mouth with a hint of a laugh.

"They're not all for you."

No *little ghost* attached to it.

◇

The galloping of white Kosta horses fills the outer palace streets, now powdered with premature snow. Ibby sits in the front carriage, steering the horses through the maze. Dead silence.

"Would you like to go to the inner markets, my lady?"

Joss fiddles with her muffler and adjusts her fur hat to keep the snow off her powder-white face. Eyebrows waxed to nonexistence, blonde hair bleached off all color, sapped-out skin, an albino rabbit on her lap – she blends in with the snow. "Russel, Russel."

"Yes?"

"How many times around?"

"Seventeen."

Ibby nods in her black cloak, tossing the reins forward once more.

The floor is cold, the air bitter.

She tiptoes up the steps, traces her fingers along the walls, and tries hard to make no sound.

"Excuse me." A door swings open. The girl is tall, regal, dark, her hair wet from a sweet-smelling shower. "I see you out there, you know, even if you're about two feet tall. Is that really your job – spying on people and stealing food? You don't need any more trouble. And to be honest, I don't need any bony-kneed munchkins invading my bathrooms."

"M.. 'm... sorry–" she begins, darting back and forth between golden-fire eyes, deep violet towel, shiny fingernails. The elusive Regena. The missing spot at the table. The clean cloak in the dark. "–Lady Pagele – g'bye –"

Regena smirks.

◇

At the end of the day, Noor follows me through the halls, his hands raw and rough with labor, like mine. I can barely bend my fingers, and both palms are bleeding. June is nowhere to be found.

"Ah, the little ghost's got to be in the Uppers still," says Noor.

A shadow follows us – Ibby. Ibby and Noor head their own way, and I stare at the swell of blood in my hands. In the quietest of voices, they're chattering on about the royals, the missing prince, and bumping shoulders occasionally.

"October 26th, isn't it," Ibby whispers. "That's what Lady Joss was saying when I drove her britzka carriage today. She said it was Prince Wickwolf's birthday."

Right you are. I hadn't remembered.

"Is it?" I ask, startling them.

"Oh, Wick, didn't see y'there," Ibby says.

The rest of the walk down the hall is filled with memories of kingdom fireworks. The last four birthdays spent collapsed in my bed, avoiding the world in the palace library, hiding in the bomb shelters with Emelin and my mother. Dead to the world. Now I am bleeding from the hands, tired, neurotic, seventeen years of age, and more dead to the world than ever before.

My only two friends were at my father's funeral. I remember their hands holding mine, the sky full of swollen clouds. The casket was closed and covered with roses. The rest of the day is a black blur, lost to the rain.

Russel came to my father's funeral, but I didn't do him the same favor.

The first bomb I heard came on my tenth birthday. It was like a hiss in the sky, then the hideous crackling of a thousand fires on the ground. I couldn't believe it was real until I saw another shudder in the shadows. I was crouched in the corner of the shelter, cloaked in the smell of dankness and stale bread. Emelin whispered something to me about the bombs being done soon and the war coming to a close, but there was nothing to be glad about. My friends were a kingdom away, turned into enemies by some giant, invisible monster called war.

My father's voice didn't exist anymore. The books he once read to me would never spill from his mouth like ink again, would never turn down my sleepy eyes and remind me that I was loved. Never, never, never. I had forgotten the color of my mother's eyes, and no hand on my shoulder could fix that.

◇

The tight-walled room called 8 welcomes me with silence. Thoughts and memories collect in my head, and I'm drowning. Then I hear the crack and creak of a door. No eight soft taps included.

June immediately crumples down to the floor, as if she can't bear another step. No greeting, no long sigh, no lantern light, just a tiny collapse.

Happy birthday to me.

◇

Alone in the Ward, the memories flow in again, memories I thought I'd buried a long time ago. The way my father turned the pages of books. The voice he'd use to read to me, tired and casual, completely lacking in the formalities of earlier in the day. His ghost is creeping up on me again.

Nine years ago, he read me *The Wolf and the Starling*, his deep voice spilling from his mouth like ink. He told me secrets that were not really secrets at all, but a child like me wasn't supposed to know anything.

"What are the colonies?" I asked, my head heavy with sleep. I'd heard the word somewhere inside the walls of the castle, drifting around like a rumor. It was a place only addressed with sneers and whispers, with the haughty waves of hands – never one that I could ever imagine to exist.

"They make our food," he explained, pulling the blanket over me, "and help us. Go to sleep, Ezra."

"Then why can't I go visit them?"

He just shook his head. "We are like Jupiter, son, and the colonies are like our moons. It's best to let them alone to shine their light on *us*, yes?"

"But we're not on Jupiter," I murmured, drifting into sleep. "We're all on Earth... and the wolf and the starling met each other... even though they were so far apart..."

That was the story. I always thought of it. The thin black wolf of legend, who slept in the deepest forest in the farthest island, who killed his enemies for sport, traveled to a land where the sun's light refused to reach, where birds sang for the sun. The wolf howled. He howled to the moon, whose stolen light showed him that the sun still shone somewhere. His howling scared all of the birds off but one – one tiny bird, with purple eyes and glossy wings, who lets its notes ring louder than the rest. His journey had made him hungry, but instead of devouring it whole, he let the starling sing him to sleep.

I'm not sure if the story was kept in the safe, dank shelter, or turned to ash by the bombs. Either way, I don't think I'll ever get it out of my head.

KOSTA DINING HALL

The table is long, made of pale green glass, decked with white china-bone plates. Sunlight dances in golden hair, darkness in the corners. Pawns cycle in and out, silent as shadows, carrying new courses in gloved hands.

"The buns are stale." Joss wrinkles her nose and flicks her pastry back to its pink-rimmed dish. "*Russel.*"

"*I* didn't make them!"

"I mean, *Russel*, let's head back to your suite." She shields her eyes from the sunlight with a delicate hand.

Prince Leo breaks into a snicker from across the table. With the sun shining on his back from the enormous window, his face is cast by a long shadow, and his drunken grin looks almost sinister.

"Oh, shut your big mouth!"

"*Ladies* should be seen and not heard, *Joss,*" he drawls. At this, she straightens her back and stares politely into the distance.

"Every room needs a lady," she scoffs.

"A room without women is my own personal hell," Russel says.

Leo breaks into another too-loud laugh.

"Hey, where's Regena?" Russel mutters, biting down into a bun.

"Oh?" Joss drums her fingernails on the glass table. "She's been cooped in her room for a straight month. You didn't notice?"

"...'Course I didn't notice," he says, gazing into the sun.

She gives a small smile.

Leo abruptly lifts himself from the table, sending a few cups clinking and clattering, spilling a bowl of sliced pomegranates. Joss looks alarmed, making swift motions to clean his mess.

"Leaving!" he barks, swinging a lazy fist at the table. "You bloody blonde pricks."

"Goodbye," Joss chirps.

"Can't say we'll miss you, Lusk!" Russel calls out, but he's already halfway down the hall. His shadow looms large. Russel smirks. "What a blot."

"He's only jealous because *you'll* be king in the summer," she whispers. "His coronation isn't for years to come, and he's twenty-two. You're sixteen and you'll be the youngest king in Belvidere."

"But you never know... the poor bastard's like to kill his own father, or he'll drink himself to death." He laughs.

In the middle of the night, I hear it. It sounds like choking, like whimpering, like knots in your throat. A small and muffled sound. At first I disregard it, but it grows louder, to nearly a sob. I guess she can't help it. And I can't stand it.

"June."

"Mhm."

"Are you... crying?"

"Yeah, a bit."

A *bit*.

"Why?"

"You're curious."

"I am."

I see the hint of a smile in the dark.

"I'm sad 'cause some big lug invaded my only room, and he asks too many questions, and his legs take up the whole place," she mumbles. Then she sighs, long and weary. "I don't have any right to be crying, so there's no way I could tell you."

"Is it Klosswarden? Did he hurt you?"

"Not *me*," she says. "I'm fine. In case you didn't get it by now, I kinda got it made around here."

I take this as a joke at first, but she's right. Her hands don't bleed; her bones don't crack.

"It's not that bad," she continues, in a voice now drained of emotion. "Once in a while they'll come down here and give us gelcaps. They make you alright. Give you energy, too. You can feel them in your hands and legs. Maybe Klosswarden will give us some soon. I mean... they'll fix you up."

They'll really fix you up.

I still taste the syrup-sweet voice of Joss Conquin, and it disgusts me to the core. I don't want fixing. I don't want their pills to make me anything. I want to be better, *really* better; I don't want to be fixed by falseness.

Lost in my mind, I turn away from her, tucking my head close to my knees. I can feel the cold air on the back of my neck.

"How many do you take a day?"

"Uh... none. None."

"Come on," I say. "If you're going to be a liar at least be a good one."

"Fine, four. Prince Russel himself takes five."

I knew it – I knew that smile was a lie.

"And where do you get your information?"

"I fill his bottle."

"June, I don't want that," I mumble. "I don't want to be okay. I want to be happy. And if I'm happy I want it to be real."

Maybe happiness is too much to hope for. But I can't help it. I want happiness; I want to want it. I must deserve to *want* something, at least, even if it's a dream made out of air.

She goes quiet for a second.

"Your neck."

I flick my head back a bit, to find her eyes fixed on me — or rather, the back of me — with a look of pure shock.

"What?"

"Your *neck*. Where is it? Where... where's your brand?"

I paw along the back of my neck. "It — must have gone away."

That's when June sits up in her ragged blanket and crawls over to me.

"Don't say *stupid things*," she says, hostility rising in her voice. "Those can't come off." June shoves me onto my stomach and kneels on my back, pressing the heels of her hands into my shoulders, leaning over me. Her knees dig into my spine. I try to conceal a grunt, but her elbows are sharp as living hell.

"Ow."

She takes the ragged collar of my shirt and lowers it, studying the nape of my neck.

"The hell are you doing?"

"There really is nothing," June murmurs, a tinge of embarrassment mixed in with the shock. "Nothing here."

"What?"

Awe fills her voice as she speaks to the back of my head. "*How*? Where are you from? Who *are* you?"

"I'll answer that once you kindly get off of me," I mutter, cheek pressed to the stony floor.

"Really?" she whispers, releasing her hold on me and hopping back to the ground. "You really will?"

"Yes." I sigh, a long, heavy sigh, exhaling my worry. "Come closer, then. Give me your ear."

"O— okay." June leans towards me, tilting her ear towards my mouth.

"Please don't scream when I tell you. Okay? No matter what I tell you. You solemnly swear you'll never tell?" I pause. She nods faintly. "You *swear*?" Another nod, and for some reason I can't name, I trust her completely.

"I'm the missing prince of Melchor."

Everything connected to that title rushes forth in me. The colors return and drown this small world. The Regicide bullet, my father's dead heart, the frailty and misery of my mother, my smoking kingdom, my disappearance and supposed suicide — they spill forth to the floor and into June's ear.

Then into her eyes.

"*You*—!" June shrieks in the loudest voice I've heard from her, shock contorting her face. I press my palm against her mouth. "Mmnmffnffn!"

"Shh," I whisper, muffling her voice. "Please. You promised!"

Teeth dig into my skin.

"You bit my hand...!"

"You lied to me," she mumbles with malice, scowling towards the floor. "You *lied* to me."

"I don't want to *die*, June!"

"Well then never lie to me again, Prince Ezra Wickwolf," June says under her breath, refusing to look me in the eye.

"Don't — don't call me that — "

"You going to kill me now?" she asks, ridiculously serene, but not joking, either. She gives me a long watery look – then her eyes are solid, cast to the floor. I'm a royal to her now. She thinks I'd haul her over the coals if she looked at me straight, and I hate it.

I grip her chin and tilt it up to me.

"For God's sake, why would I kill you?"

She swats my hand away. The quick flick of eyes. God damn it, she won't look at me. "Because I'm rude and little and dirty, and I told you a lot of things. And I didn't call you *your majesty*. And I climbed on top of you. Kill me if you like."

"June—"

"Go to sleep."

She rolls to her side and flicks the kersone lantern off. It pulses and dies.

CHAPTER VIII:
CLAWS OF TOMORROW,
DAGGERS OF THE PAST

RUSSEL WAKES TO the chiming of distant bells and high-pitched, sleepy breaths beside him. The sun is too bright. A white-gold head on his dark-tasseled pillow. A bare, colorless shoulder from under the sheets. A terribly familiar ache in his gut.

The sunlight comes in endless shafts, making the room sparkle.

"Good morning," he says, skimming her hair with his hand. It almost aches to stand as he walks over to his cupboard. Headache medicine, golden combs, hair gel, a tube of her mascara, ten bottles of pills. He chooses the last. Five capsules, no water, a pleasant numbness swallowed whole.

And a banquet this afternoon.

The sunlight has receded to a sleepy orange glow. The Hall is bustling, and the tables are piled high for Prince Lusk, the man in white. Star-shaped fruits, apple juices, pomegranate pudding, coconut pastries, hot chocolate, bourbon cake, steaming sausages, and a giant roast pig crowd the table, framed by smiling people and silver plates. Leo's chin is dripping with golden grease, his arm around Alska and Remsa, roaring with vacant laughter.

Duke Calixte Conquin and his daughter sit straight, surrounding the Prince of Kosta with their pale golden hair and bloodless skin.

The Duke of Kosta extends a hand to Russel. Frosted blue eyes and dark red goblets. "Wine, Prince Kosta?"

"No," he says, staring into the distance.

"Are you in good spirits, young sir?'"

"Sure I am, Duke," Russel says, smiling wearily and taking a halfhearted bite of an orange. "The best spirits around."

The Duke strokes his pale, hairless chin, choosing his words carefully. "Could it be the... the recent passing of the Wickwolf prince? Were you two not good friends in your green years?"

"Good friends? *Good friends?* We were brothers. *Smite* me if we weren't."

"My Prince... you speak so informally still. It's one of your habits. Are you quite – at peace with yourself? Do you wish to be left alone?"

"*Good sir,*" he laughs with sad eyes. "I am never alone."

There are Alexia and Constantine Pagele, entertaining Prince Leo with wine-soaked laughter, the wrinkles in their faces softening. Gold-coin eyes trailing back to the unfilled chair where purple velvet should be, glasses clinking hollowly.

There is an empty spot at the Lusk end.

"Ah – that vacant seat. Your friend Miss Pagele has become something of a recluse, hasn't she?"

"She's in her library," Russel mutters, sinking his teeth into another orange, his eyes darting to the ceiling. "She doesn't like this kind of thing, sir."

"How pleasantly unrefined of you to say that," Joss says through gritted teeth.

"It's okay," Russel says, "I'm *drunk.*"

She is alone. Beautifully, luckily, wearily alone, daring to hum as she tiptoes down the hall. Then a dark figure approaches, stumbling, all shoulders and toothy smile, and her hum drops to silence.

"You're shaking," Leo slurs, though she stands still. His eyes are hollow and intoxicated. "Do I scare you, little ghost?" he says, and lets out a hacking mockery of a laugh.

"No one frightens me," she says, straightening her back. "'Specially not you."

Leo laughs again, lurching toward her and lazily groping her back. "Shhhh." His speech is slurred. "Didn't go to my banquet, did we? Not invited? A pity. A *pity*. " His hand falls. "And your friend, neither? Too good for me. And you're her pet..."

She aims a swift kick in between his legs, but her foot just swipes his inner knee. He clamps a lazy hand on her shoulder, and squeezes to the point of pain.

"*Careful,* little wench." His mocking laughter has mutated to anger.

"It's little *ghost.*" She jerks from his grip and runs as fast and far as her legs will carry her.

He doesn't chase her, so she hums again.

◇

No

    in two pieces on the ground –

    the ribbons running along the floor like little rivers –

No

    "I'll be gentler next time" –

No –

    you smiled –

No.

    "Shhhh" –

    bleeding, crying on the floor. Ripped open, chewed up,

and spit out.

I hate you. You laughed again, and everything was dark.
All but those shimmering ribbons.

Regena Pagele sits in her enormous guest room, the ceiling towering twenty feet above, ornate walls expanding around her. Bookshelves line every wall, absolutely stuffed. An orchestra of notes dance from her speldosa, a tiny golden music box perched between two thick encyclopedias.

She holds her venom tongue in two rows of perfect teeth. To most she's sour, artificially acrid like lemon drops. A mask to hide the soft sweetness below, that tingles on your tongue when you suck all the tart away. This mask she paints on her face daily, covering her lids, drawing an upturned tiger eye. Her cheeks and lips, she leaves bare, and it is always her caramel-colored eyes that she plasters with black. She will not be sweet.

Today her eyes are surrounded, almost swallowed by liquid black. Like two honeydrops in a cup, and shielded by a thick loop of hair.

"You foolish girl." Her mother grit her teeth hissed about the bad name she'd put to Lusk, with sharp, golden eyes. The act of refusal had provoked ill-willed whispers in the gallery of duchesses. "Do you know what you've done?" No answer. No rebuttal. Regena's silence had sent her manicured hand across her face. A loud slap, and eyes to match. "A disgrace, a pure, plain disgrace, and a dishonor to your kingdom. Are you even aware of what shame you bring us? What arrogance your refusal displays?"

And her father, the milder of the two: "You can't stay locked up in there forever, Regena."

"Watch and see," she whispers to no one.

Everyone stared at her with ugly, prying eyes, swallowing her whole, gnashing their sighs and words like imaginary teeth. Like they were doing her a favor by trying to make her break. *Leave me be leave me be leave me be.* Leo down on one knee. The creases in his face showing with that grotesquely insincere smile, the oily, formulaic voice oozing out of him. *Marry me.* Then the most catastrophic word in the kingdom: No.

No.

The golden trill of the music temporarily calms her. It almost makes her forget. But her eyes still flicker upward once in a while, watering, shaking so slightly, only to return to the pages of her dictionary.

Arthroscopy, assassins, assault.

She shuffles the pages in her jeweled hands, pressing her eyes closed.

Ransom, rapacious, rape, rapeseed, raphe, raphide, rapid

Ugly words in lovely type.

And back and forth and back and back.

She slaps the pages over.

Silent, silhouette, silica, silk

Twitching. She can't stop twitching, shaking.

The book flies across the room, propelled by Regena's swift toss. It loses momentum and hits the magnificent wall with a thud. The quick-rising scream struggles against the will of her throat.

She erupts from her plush seat, across the room, tears book by book from her shelves and hurls them to the ground. Each bang is muffled by the thick, cushy carpeting.

Jugo's Encyclopedia, A History of Belvidere, Majestic Creatures of the Lagoon, The Regicide Menace, The Complete Works of William Shakespeare, The Day and the Night, One Thousand Songs, The Wanderer, Ancient Mythology, and Proper Etiquette for a Lady all strike the velvet ground, and more, and more.

Don't you dare fall back to the past, said the wiser voice in her head. *It has nothing left to give you. Nothing left to say.*

But every time, she did.

"King Leocor's son *would* be the ideal choice," her mother had said. "He would certainly add to your prestige." Regena had looked Prince Leo straight in the face. He smiled, long-toothed, over-bleached, arrogant, a smile that charmed the ignorant but sent her guts writhing.

"I doubt it, mother," she said. "He's so... full of himself."

"As you wish, dear." Her face radiated disapproval.

As I wish, indeed, Regena thought as the ceremonies and cotillions rolled by and she was, time after time, shoved into Leo by her eager mother. His eyes said nothing. His laugh was cold. He seemed to look at her with only his teeth.

The rest she pressed down into the farthest depths of her memory, buried under Mourning Balls and Summer Festivals, ancient screenplays and fairytales and myths, dug-up childhood nostalgia, scraps of smiles, decaying forests, rusted laughter. But she could still feel him smothering her in that sickly-sweet room. Clamping one hand over her mouth, concealing her thrashing fist with another. The darkness of the night. A single word repeated. *No*. His hands were clammy, and it was as if his whole body was soaked in liquor.

A voice trapped.

Wrists nailed to the ground.

Rich and beloved and laughing Leo.

Klosswarden returns to the Royal Hall in a composed fuss, cloaked in the ordinary black and trailing behind the statuesque Lady Regena.

He wrenches June's skinny arm from two blonde toddlers. "Help Lady Pagele with her room, girl."

Her eyes stay trained on the floor. "I– I'm a bit–"

"You're not too busy for Lady Pagele."

June looks up, cautiously, sleepy-eyed. She expects Lady Alexia, but it's her daughter – the unseen duchess, the girl with the golden eyes.

"Come on, little ghost." Her voice is a bitter liquid, spilling through the Hall. June scurries behind her, following her violet skirt and listening to its gentle swishing sound.

"Hurry."

◇

The smell of Lusk gold, a duchess, and a silent little ghost.

Regena's walls are intricately decorated, her room velvety and sweet-smelling, but thick books are strewn across the floor.

There's the tinkling of a golden music box on her book shelf.

"Hey, come here, little lemur. Listen. You don't have to be a thief." She hands over a bowl of pudding and a wooden spoon. "Alright?"

June hesitates, tentatively taking the food and placing it by the closed doorway. Then her face lights like a star. She says, with conviction, "Lady Regena, you're wonderful!"

Regena turns her face to the side, her hair shading her eyes. She pats her lightly on the back.

The girl doesn't even bow her head. She looks her in the eyes, she goes as far as smiling. *What a strange little pawn...*

"Get going, then," Regena mutters.

"Yes'm," June whispers. She lifts one book at a time and stands on her tiptoes to reach the shelves, teetering slightly. She resorts to throwing a few. While she is placing a leatherbound encyclopedia on its ledge, she asks, "Lady Regena, are you alright?"

"Obviously," Regena quips, "outside of the fact that this room is a disaster. Why?"

"Sorry, ma'am, your eyes look wet." She decides not to mention the visible trembling.

"Well, I've seen better days. Oh, and enough with the *ma'am*. You're as old as me."

"Would you prefer... m'lady?"

"No. I would prefer Regena."

"That's not—"

"It doesn't matter," Regena mutters. Then her voice starts to burn. "It doesn't *matter*. I'm still a girl and so are you. And I've had it with you being below me. All of you. You're people, too, right?"

"I guess so." June blinks at her fiery face, startled. She has never been talked to like this before, especially by the likes of Regena Pagele.

It's unreal, as if someone has taken her lovely face and twisted it into unnatural, livid expressions. Unreal.

"*You are*!" Regena shouts. "But you can't make a single decision for yourselves, can you? But you're ordered around and abused and harassed, aren't you?" She raises her voice yet more. "*Aren't* you?"

But June picks up another leatherbound book, and replies with even less force than before, "...Y-yes."

"And wouldn't you just like to escape this place and be *free*?"

Free...

The word hits her ears, a stranger. One she's heard of before in whispers, but has never had the chance to meet face to face.

"That's not allowed." June buckles under the weight of a particularly large encyclopedia.

"For God's sake, of course it isn't allowed," Regena sneers, walking to June. That gentle swishing sound again, but fast, urgent. "But it's what's *right*. But it's what you *want*, isn't it?!"

June places the last volume on its shelf, a red leatherbound collection of fairytales. "I— I don't know about that, m'l – Regena."

"Fine." Regena inhales, then breathes out sharply. "Thanks for picking up the wreckage. Your name is June, right?"

June looks alarmed. "Yes, ma'am. June Kinsel."

An exasperated sigh from Regena. "*Enough* with the formalities, I said. So, June Kinsel, will you be my ragdoll for a while?"

"Your ragdoll? I'm your pawn."

"Enough with pawns. I'll let you wear my pretty clothes."

June's entire face brightens, her dark eyes shining, but her mouth opens just a crack.

"Oh, you don't have to do that."

"I don't care," Regena says, taking her arm and leading her to the massive golden armoire. "What colors do you like?"

Confusion knots her forehead. "Lady Regena, what are you doing?"

"Opening the closet."

"I mean — " June looks up from the ground, infinitely confused, "I'm a pawn and you're a duchess and shouldn't I be — "

"Just *stay*," Regena interrupts, letting go of her wrist and shuffling through gown after gown. "I'm sick of those words. Pawn. Duchess. So stop saying them. Oh–!" She pulls out a small, velvet dress. "This one. Dark blue. You like that?"

June reaches her hand out, touching the warm fabric as if it is glass. "Yeah..."

Maybe the rumors are true: Lady Regena is mad. Mad, and holed up in her room, and prone to fits –

It doesn't matter. If she's mad, I like her anyway.

"Well, here, why don't you wear it," insists Regena. "Try it on."

June can't resist dancing, twirling, in the blue velvet dress. "Wow," she says, danger in her voice, "it... really does feel nice."

"I thought you'd like it," Regena smiles, sitting in her enormous reading chair and perching *The Day and the Night* on her lap. "Now go ahead and eat your pudding, June."

"You're the most fantastic person I've ever met in my entire life," says June, leaning down to throw her arms around Regena. She winces slightly at her touch. "What was that for, though?"

Regena pats June on the back, breathes through her nose, and decides to be honest. What has she got to lose?

"I was lonely, I guess."

June just stares, unleashing Regena from her hug. Dark eyes to light. She still doesn't understand. How could someone so adored and beautiful possibly be lonely?

"Lonely? But you're so – beautiful, and..."

"Every single person gets *lonely*, little ghost, in rags or velvet or anything else – okay? Even me."

"Lady Regena," June whispers, "Why don't you... try to talk to the other royals, then?"

Her face is caught. "Like who?"

"Er — um, Prince Russel, for instance? He's always around. And he's always looking for you."

"That magnificent idiot," she shoots back almost instantly, "is hardly worth my time."

"Lady Joss?"

"Are you kidding me."

"O-oh, then, er, Prince Leo? I once ran into him while — "

"Stay away from him!" Regena yells. "Don't even go *near* that awful... that..."

Her expression burns.

Her face stings.

The Day and the Night drops out of her twitching hands.

"You're excused, June..."

"Huh?"

"Go."

She had hoped for loneliness. The light is far too bright in the upper chambers, the people far too many.

On her way back to the Ward, the little ghost girl passes by a clump of nobles and royals.

She collects names. Leo Lusk, hacking in laughter at some obscene joke. Russel Kosta, who looks almost diminutive next to him. Lady Joss Conquin, with the powder face, the pale green corset, the high, sugar-syrup voice.

"It's the little ghost!" Russel calls out, smiling.

She just nods slightly, still carrying the bowl of pomegranate pudding.

"Where d'ja get *that,* pet?" Leo laughs, tensing the muscles in his enormous shoulders.

Stay away from him.

"Lady Regena, your majesty," she says softly.

"Mm, I see." Leo snickers. "Is she always handing it out to the pawns?"

She hears Joss' voice from his side. "Russel," she mewls, in what she assumes is a whisper. "Can we go back to your suite? *Please?* I don't like the pawns. They're filthy." He looks at her, eyes wide.

"Joss, that's — that's not true—"

June hears everything, but doesn't recoil. "I'm sorry to bother you, princess," she whispers, and the little ghost is gone.

She's not really a princess, she thinks. *Not yet.*

◇

"Your hands are bleeding."

I lean against the cubby in Ward One, Room Eight, June propped up against the other side with a bowl in her hands. Mine are raw with overuse, blistered and cracking and scabbed over, but hers are always softer than the rest.

"Yeah, I know."

"Lady Regena invited me in today."

"And brought you pudding?" I stare at the creamy red bowl, not yet punctured by the wooden spoon.

"You share."

I eat a spoonful of pudding and pass it back to June. Palace pomegranates. A small part of me still believe she stole it, but a larger part of me wants to trust her. To trust Regena, the girl from my memory.

"I like her," June says, licking the spoon once and dipping it back in. "She's scary, but she's nice to me. Like you."

"I'm not scary," I mutter, trailing off into my memory, nearly laughing as I see an eight-year-old Regena hurling stones into the mud. Meanwhile, June is wolfing down this stuff.

"Hey, you're sort of ravenous for such a tiny—"

She shoots me a look, handing over the bowl. "Yeah, yeah."

"You look like a vampire."

She lunges for me and mock-bites my neck. Strangely, I don't even flinch. "Then you better be careful around me."

She's shivering harder than usual in this freezing cubbyhole, like an unseen snow is flurrying down on her. She has shivering hands and lashes. She has starlight eyes that long for the sun.

"Cold?"

"Always cold."

"Me too." I wonder if she'll hug me again, like last time, but I realize she's too involved in the pudding. We're both cold, but our hunger greatly outweighs it.

"Least we got pudding."

"God, this is kind of a treasure, isn't it." She nods.

"Not where you've been, it isn't, but it is for me."

"Hey, shh."

"It's December tomorrow," June says, studying the wooden pudding spoon. "That's around when I was born, I think."

My heart stands still. Then I feel my pulse like bullets, one by one. The murder. The gunshot. My father's milky, frozen eyes, his cold skull rolling down the chariot. My mother's scream as she covered me with her shaking body. The fresh blood on her ballgown.

It's all I can seem to think about, my father's skull rolling down that chariot.

Suddenly, I'm all too aware of the skin I'm covered in. My blood runs through me, and my bones are only a weak shield. *No. No. I'm safe,* says the wiser part of me that I always ignore.

My voice comes out shaky and choked. "December... the first?"

"No — sometime later. Sometime in winter, I s'pose."

"You *suppose?*" I ask, willing my chest to relax, my mind to slow — without success. The blood still spills in my memory. Suddenly I'm burning in the cold; my skin is drowning, my fingers shaking.

June's voice interrupts my thoughts. "Well... Klosswarden said the nurses at Kinsel told him, ages and ages ago — they said sometime in winter, but he *forgot.* There's a chance it was Christmas, though, right?"

"*At...* Kinsel?" Now I'm truly lost.

"The orphanage — Kinsel orphanage," she explains as if it is the simplest thing in the world. "It's for pawn export. How I came here. They trained us 'till we were twelve and sent us here, four years back."

"Export..." I can't help my teeth from grinding at the wrongness of it all.

Treated like animals — no, worse than animals. Raised for imprisonment from birth, and lorded around. Stocked in pens like helpless sheep, manhandled by kingly fingers.

This is what I've become. No. This is what I have been all along.

I am the villain.

"No," I choke out. *I am the villain*. I caused this to happen, I sat by and did nothing, as bombs were thrown and towns were blitzed, raided, ravaged, as homes were destroyed and twelve-year-old children were sent to toil, as temples were wrenched from the ground, as innocent people died; as my best friend's father committed suicide, as the kingdoms sunk their teeth into everything. I did nothing. I lay in my impossible, exquisite, godforsaken golden castle and imagined I did not exist. The castle stood tall and proud for as long as it could. It pointed a finger at the sky, as if to say, *this is mine*.

And everything was mine, for no reason at all. I was placed on a pedestal made of ancient names and unbreakable walls.

We live.

It's been months since I saw that old beggar, smoke pouring out of his dry, sunken mouth. His miserable face – dark, wrinkled, centuries old in my memory.

My daughters and sons.

And now her face.

We live.

Full of dreams, and in a similar kind of darkness.

We live in your gutters.

A darkness that swallows her.

You're despicable.

"The whole thing's awful. Pawns. Palaces. Kingdoms. I hate it all."

June seems unsure of herself, squirming uncomfortably, glancing away. She whispers, "Me too." For a moment, she looks incredibly sad, like she's just realized something terrible. Then she glances back up again and tries to smile.

"You gotta try pretty hard," she says. "Your feet can't make a noise, and your mouth can't speak a word, and your hands gotta hold on to someone else's kids they don't wanna care about, or make a roomful of guns, or..."

The lantern gutters out, just slightly.

"I had a dream it was all different, though," June murmurs through her smile. "And I lived in the sunshine. Everything was green, like in the pictures and books." She sighs. "It didn't last, though. It was lovely to believe. But when I woke up, I felt worse than before. It hurt me, it really did, and I don't know why. I wanted to feel like things could be different, but those dreams are liars, aren't they? Dreams are cruel."

"Dreams are cruel," I repeat.

"Yeah. Especially the good ones. You always wake up sad..." She pauses. "The bad dreams might be worse. But at least they're honest. You know, I was such a silly little girl. Always dreaming up dreams with no chance of them coming true."

There's honey-red hair in her eyes, and she won't look my way. She's barely stolen a glance at me since I told her about the missing prince.

"We're the same, you and me," I say. With this, she widens her eyes and immediately returns to the book. There's the ghost of a smile on her face.

"That's funny," she says without laughing. She then sweeps up her hair and turns her neck to me. I can clearly see the deep, swollen shape of the Kosta diamond, burned into her skin.

"We're not the same, though."

"We are," I insist. "We... we are. It doesn't matter if–"

"No. I'm small. I'm low. And I'm filthy. They all think so." She searches my face for words again. "You don't think I'm filthy?"

"I think you're..." – I've been trying not to stare at her face for minutes on end. The sharp white lantern light outlines each eyelash, the wisps of hair falling on her cheeks, her dusk-dark eyes finally looking into mine. It distracts me from everything else. Words, words, I can never seem to find the right ones, or any at all, and besides, there's no words for her. I reach forward and touch her face for no reason but to see her smile again. Some strange gravity tugs me in, and I'm leaning into the wall –

"Uh... uh," she sputters, pressing me back by the chest. "I... please– I, you— ... goodnight." She flicks the lantern switch off.

CHAPTER IX:
THE PEDDLE AND THE PAWN

CORINTH, KOSTA
17 YEARS BEFORE

HER MOTHER'S LAST plate. That was when she broke.

The shopkeepers had no patience for her. In the dead of winter, a fifteen-year-old girl, all wrapped up in patches, holding out that pathetic plate. The one her mother used to keep on the good china self. *Don't touch it, don't touch it. You'll get fingerprints on it, and it's worth one hundred monas.*

"It's supposed to be worth a hundred," she said, so quietly the tradesman could barely hear her. His beard twitched. His eyes focused on her downcast head.

"I'll give you fifty for it." He gave what was supposed to be a kind smile.

"Please. It's a good plate."

"Fifty, girl. Take it or leave it."

Her legs moved mechanically away, back to her frozen home. She counted them – fifty. Fifty exactly. He might as well have broken the plate clean in half, the no-good cheat. She felt the weight of silver in her hand, but it didn't comfort her. The food wouldn't last. The warmth was fleeting, and it never reached her bones. The burnt-down beds, the silverware, the plates, her father's watch.

There was nothing left.

When she closed her eyes, she could still see it.

The snow, the snow.

The snow always pulled on the strings of her memories; it reminded her of that Christmas morning long ago, when her mother handed her that unwrapped stuffed doll. The year even newspaper seemed too expensive, its stories too vile. The year before the war. The doll was soft, raggedy, vaguely the form of a bear or cat, with stringy buttons for eyes. To Jette, it looked as old as time.

She kissed Jette on the head as the light, jingling music played. Her sisters danced in the light sprinkling snow, flakes in their unwashed hair.

"Happy Christmas, Jette."

"Buttons!"

"Hm?" Her mother looked down with a smile.

"I'll name her Buttons!"

She placed it by the weak fire, and sauntered into the snow.

When the snow fell, she thought of Buttons, and rainbow lights, and pine trees. Of songbirds and kindled fires and golden bells. Christmas manifested itself in Buttons and the honeydrop-singsong voice of her mother. Her voice seemed to light up, to float through the air, always singing,

The sun is shining still, out by your windowsill,

when the sun was nowhere to be found.

So with every snowfall, she thought of sun.

But today, as the snow fluttered and fell, all she could see were the white-cold bodies in the streets. The raids. The Wickwolf gunfire. Blood made new stains in old snow, and both the winter and the War raged on.

They stood before her as ghosts. Her mother. Her father. Shelle and Trin, their clothes coated in dust and their faces still covered in sores. Then they disappeared all at once. Right in front of her eyes, just as her arms had reached out to hold them.

For Jette, the world spun in quick circles, jolting her awake when she'd just settled to rest. She felt still the warm, envelopineg embrace of her pink-cheeked mother, her father's quiet smile. She felt it in her skin, always. That happiness, it kept her awake at night. That happiness, it tortured her lonely days. That happiness, it choked her, closed its hands around her shivering face, on those long, still, lonely nights, refusing to let go. And that happiness, she clung to it, curled her legs around its memory, twisted her lips into a dead smile, willed her hungry stomach to settle, and forced herself into restless sleep.

They were gone.

She was a young girl with sad-looking eyes, so dark and large and strange, if you looked at those eyes for even a second you could see her whole life, spilling out before you, a wreck, a catastrophe, a long spiral of heartache just pierced occasionally by the golden ray of sun. A thickly clouded life, but even then, not a hopeless one.

Jette couldn't read or write the King's tongue — never learned how, after her move to the main island. And she was too weak to work in the factories, especially to go to war. She lived in the Kosta slums, in a bare, collapsing shack.

She couldn't remember a time when she wasn't hungry. Her stomach was so hollow it hurt to walk.

"There's no choice left for me," Jette whispered to no one but herself. She believed it, too. Her sisters, in the plague-pits. Her parents, in the War.

A hopeless strength.

"And I... I'll go, too. I'll go anywhere."

The grocer wouldn't take her. The lady down the street shook her sad, withered head. The gravedigger's son, the school on the edge, the shirtmaking factory, no one wanted her. She heard bells ringing, thick and golden and rich. *God... I'd forgotten about him.*

The man who opened the massive door wore a white robe, with a golden collar worth a year of bread. His face was powdered and rosy. She sat, on her knees in a patched shirt, and he looked on her with disgust.

The fancy church door shut on her, and she had sold her last plate.

The Peddles lay on the outskirts of Corinth. The lights blared, garish red and yellow. They looked like warped Christmas lights. She took a small, sad delight in this.

The women all wore bright red. Red, red, red, everywhere she looked, daunting. The men came by the bucketful. Not a home, truly, but a job — a shameful one, but a job nonetheless.

She put on her father's factory boots, weathered and dust-covered, their owner dead for years. Her mother's long pants, because the wind whistled mercilessly outside. An old shirt of her sister's – her mother had sewn a patch where the shoulder had worn through.

The storefronts knew her well. Their shaky collections of colorful goods, their pockets half-full, their stomachs nearly satisfied. She had bartered for months, and sometimes she could hear their murmurs. *The poor little waif. Oh, she's finally done it.* Her face burned more fervently than before. She wanted nothing more than to break their bones on the hard crack of their false sympathy.

As Jette walked, careful, shamefaced and empty-handed, to the Peddles, there was a clamor of whispers. A mob of leering faces. Men and women with their hands packed with shopping bags and tickets.

The nervous shuffle of goods. The malicious trailing of feet.

"*No,* Jette Chajkia?"
"Poor girl."
"Only fifteen, if I'm right— "
"That won't sell, will she?"

But the Pedlar didn't scoff as she came around. He examined her with his small, shallow eyes. A tall, pale man, oddly scruffy but groomed simultaneously, with a bristled square jaw, a crooked smile, and a large golden ring on each finger. He coiled these fingers around a fistful of cigarettes; he liked to keep them loose.

The Pedlar wore long, crumpled pants with a seemingly infinite number of pockets. The peddles could guess, but no one knew what they held – some thought he was a rich diamond miner from Lusk, or some secret mogul. Some thought he was just an ordinary con-man. Whatever he was, his golden hands pulled the strings.

A trail of smoke curled from his mouth, spinning long and lazy into the sky.

Jette was small, unthreatening, bony. The Pedlar gripped her by the shoulders and turned her around, scrutinizing her — her chest, her back, her short legs, her long tangled hair — but not once looking at her eyes. Perhaps if he had, he'd have seen the deep-rooted sadness. The desperation that clung to the air. But of course, he wasn't interested in such things.

"Skinny little thing, you are," he said, lifting the cloth of her sleeves. She tried not to flinch. His hands were large and calloused, and his breath smelled of pure tobacco. "Fatten yourself up, will you?"

She nodded, and didn't dare speak.

He blew another puff of smoke. With gruff finality:

"This'll do."

He took a knife out of his coatpocket and, with a swipe, Jette's long locks lay on the dirt floor. Her hair now reached just her neck, jagged and wavy. She didn't cry for this. Of all the things the Pedlar could've done with that knife, this was not the worst by far.

Then came her new clothes. A red dress with spindly straps, red tights. She slipped them on with disgust, the fabric silky and cold.

It could be worse, she reminded herself, a constant mantra, as she inched into the stale-smelling mansion of the first one, a man of twice her age. It could be worse, she thought, the tenth or maybe twelfth time — she'd lost count. It could be worse, screamed the voice in her head, as dozens and tens of dozens of girls lined the street, on tiny pillars, their faces melting with embarrassment, or hardened from those long years, or plastered with a manufactured, forced look of seduction.

It could be worse, as she received a stale loaf for a long night with a man that smelled like liquor and rust.

And as she curled her legs around another hotfaced, snickering body, she imagined a place. Someplace where snow fell and stayed. Everyday you'd wear your fur mittens. Everyday you'd sleep under thick blankets, calm-minded and warm. Your mother would kiss you on the head and your father would smile at you. And you'd be safe from everything.

The guns. The war. The hordes of soldiers pouring in for a holiday from their troubles, hooting and jumping. The blaring lights of the Peddles. She faked a smile until it hurt.

In the darkest hours of night, she slept in a heap of thin blankets, in the tent closest to the Pedlar by his command. The sick scent of smoke wafted in. It seemed strange, because she wasn't a child anymore – but she kept her old stuffed doll. She hugged Buttons close to her, her last trace of home. Her last trace of Jette Chajkia.

In the morning another girl approached her — black-haired, with dark skin, deep-set eyes, and a floating voice. Her dress was weathered with time, but she filled it out better.

"You look like a scared bunny rabbit."

Jette turned to face her cautiously. "Yeah?"

"That's why the Pedlar likes you."

"You're crazy. He does not."

"I'm Lila."

"Jette."

"You're from Rioghnach. I can tell from your voice."

"My *parents* were," she said, embarrassed. "Not me."

"It's fine, y'know. I'm from Shanta myself." Lila smiled, and pointed to a staggering, blushing man. She got a strange look in her eyes.

"We control them. All of them. You know that, Jette?"

"Huh?"

"We *control* them," she repeated. "That's our power. The men around here, they think we fall to them, but they fall to *us*. Even the Pedlar, if you try."

"But I don't... I don't really..."

Lila sighed. "Don't let him see you cry, though," she said. "Don't you dare," and patted her on the head.

Jette said nothing, and watched the dancing, bobbing silhouettes. Wine red and gold, then the shadows the same black as the sky. *But I don't control anything,* she thought.

But Lila was laughing and dancing off into the flickering yellow lights. She twirled around, as if there was no better place to be in the world, putting on her show for the soldiers and drunks.

On her morning drudge to the Peddles' compound, she caught his eye, a seventeen-year-old boy wandering by. Absolutely terrified of the Peddles.

It was an alarming place in his imagination, full of large, naked, paintfaced women. In reality, it was mostly girls. Some smiling through a layer of makeup, and when no one was looking, turning their heads to cough. Some small, some with makeup lines etched into their face. Some without shoes. Some barefaced. All barelegged under cheap red cloth and nylon.

He wore a slippery blue jacket and a terrified look. He walked through with that same unfaltering expression – eyes wide, chin pressed to his chest. His hair was fluffy, blonde, and standing on edge.

Jette sat at her post. Her sign read 10 copper monas. She poked secret eyes of envy at another girl's 20 monas, but who was she to complain?

"You come for one of 'em, boy?" Jette heard the Pedlar grunt.

"No, no, no," the boy insisted, shrinking into his shoulders, "simply coming through. No. No, no, very sorry, no."

The Pedlar snorted and blew off smoke. "As'ya wish."

Suddenly he saw her, bony and redfaced, shivering in the blaring light.

The boy tugged at the Pedlar's vest.

"Wait, actually," he whispered, pointing weakly, "her."

Another rude snort from the Pedlar. His breath was heavy with smoke. "Oh, that tiny one. Seems right."

He stared into the callouses on the Pedlar's palm. His hand stood there, empty and expectant. And after a nervous shuffle of coins, Jette was his for the night.

Usually the men groped her by the back as they led her away, but this boy did something different. Quietly, wordlessly, he took hold of her shivering hand. Jette lifted her face, struggling to remain expressionless.

"Where are you going?" she whispered.

She did not want to look at his face. That usually helped her forget.

"Other side of town." His cheeks were pink from the cold, and the red from Jette's dress seemed to reflect back on his clothes. "We'll catch the nightbus."

The other side, Jette thought. *Where there are schools and hospitals and playgrounds.* Through her mind ran images of clean jackets, ink-pressed paper, beggarless streets. She allowed herself to shiver with the thought of it.

Nervously, he wrapped his white-collared jacket around her shoulders.

Nightbus — the word was unfamiliar, but she wasn't supposed to talk too much. The Pedlar had made that clear. No small talk, no questions. But now, she had only one.

She gulped back her question: where will it take me? She imagined the alleyways, the mansions, the slums, the village homes of previous users. Their sick collections. Their sick words. They squirmed in her mind as she gripped the boy's hand tighter by mistake.

It was an enormous blue metal tube, slick and rickety, with rolling silver wheels. The jingling of the bus, the roar of the wheels, barely allowed quiet conversation.

More than anything, Jette wanted to say, "Let go of my hand." Other men would paw around her and treat her like a limp doll. This was worse in a good way. His warm grip seemed to guard her — it made her feel strange, sent something stirring in her chest. That wouldn't sell well, though.

He finally spoke up. "You smell like smoke."

"Secondhand."

"Ah."

She looked down in embarrassment. How revolting her life must have seemed to this boy, with neatly-combed hair and neatly-bound books. A long pause, and the racket of the train.

"I'm Cole Gretling," the boy said suddenly, drawing his hand away.

"Jette..." She paused, nearly forgetting her last name. "Chajkia... How old are ya, anyway? Why aren't you in the war?"

"Ah... university. Exemption. Also, my eyesight's not too great."

"Oh. That's– that's good."

"I'm not going to do anything to you."

"What?"

"I said, I won't do anything to you. I didn't mean to."

"Oh..." Jette sighed. "You're lying."

"I'm not. I swear I'm not. I got nervous. The Peddles are scary as hell, I was only there 'cause I took a wrong turn. And I saw you. You looked so damn lost, sitting there alone — and I felt..." He buried his face in his hands. "I felt awful. You're not old, or anything, you know? You should be in... in *school*, or something. You should be with your family or... or... But instead..."

"I'm just poor," Jette whispered with her head down, eyes watering. "That's all. I have to. So it's... okay."

"It's not okay!" Cole shouted. She winced in her seat. "Goddamnit, it's not okay at all."

Jette's cheeks burned like a fever. "I can't *do* nothing about it."

Cole paused a second — then whispered in disbelief. "Don't say something like that."

She had no words. So she spoke to him the only way she could think of — nervously, she wrapped her skinny arms around him and squeezed, felt the cold jostling of the nightbus, tried not to remember a single thing. He didn't protest.

"I've got a couple pounds of fish at my loft," he mumbled. "You could have some. And you could stay for a while... and get a good job. Or... you don't have to. I'll help you. Don't say you can't do anything about it..."

He was a small, bearded, unbelievably drunk man, and he had just shambled off the rattling nightbus.

"'Ey, kid," he sneered, "you rented one of them, huh?"

Jette's face blazed with shame, the scent of liquor floating towards her, from his yellow bottles and yellow teeth. All too familiar.

"How about you go to hell." Cole gripped Jette's hand again, about to lead her away.

"No, kid," the man hissed, "I expect a show." He removed a long knife from his back pocket.

The glare of the knife in the snow-cold night, the shaming smile of the man, they shone inside Jette's sad-looking eyes.

"Don't," she pleaded.

He looked to Cole. "Do it, boy, do it or I'll do it myself."

The knife shone. His greedy laugh folded into itself again and again. It unraveled into the sky as they undressed in the snow.

◇

THE GRETLING APARTMENT
CORINTH, KOSTA

"I'm sorry," Jette whispered finally, to Cole's back.

But he wouldn't look at her.

"It's not your fault."

Please.

The jacket was covered in snow. It sat thawing on the wooden apartment floor.

Please—

"It is."

Please look at me.

"No, it's that man's," he said in a trembling voice. "He had a knife."

"I'm sorry."

Look at me.

"Me too. I felt disgusting the whole time. I'm sorry."

"I always," she gulped, "feel disgusting."

Don't look at me.

"It's okay." She turned to him, trying at comfort – for him, for herself. "It didn't hurt."

He looked at her, through her, and started to shake.

"I feel sick," he squeezed out, "I'm sorry. I promised you. I said..." His voice broke, and he buried his face in his hands.

She decided not to touch him, though her hands fought against her. Everything she touched turned to dirt and sadness and hunger. Everything she touched crumbled in front of her; her gentlest touch destroyed.

I gave my hell to you, she thought.

◇

"I want to go." Her voice rose in her throat — choked to tears, burning, horrified. "I want to go home. I want to go home."

I want to go home. The more she said it, the truer it became.

"I want to go home! Bring me home!" she screamed as she bounded into the tent and pounded the Pedlar's chest with her fists, imagining each blow would bring her closer to home. Whatever that was.

If her gentlest touch destroyed, what would violence do?

Her punches became weaker and weaker, but her anger only grew. Jette struggled free from his grip on her shoulders – she extended a hand and reached into his pocket, drawing out a long knife. Clean, silver, shining brilliantly within the smoke and grime of his tent, shaking in her hand. In that moment, she wanted to do it. She wanted to hurt him, make his body go limp on the floor, make him feel for even a second how she felt every day.

"What the hell d'you think you're *doing?*"

The knife clattered to the ground.

"*I want to go home!*" Jette screeched, clenching her teeth, clawing at his face with her overgrown nails. She broke skin and felt a small satisfaction. "Let me go home! Please, let me go... Let me go home, you horrible, horrible — "

One motion and the Pedlar had her tacked to the filthy floor. She could feel the weight of him, the ground against her back. She could smell the cold, solid gold rings on his fingers, clenching her shoulders. Then ashy breath, snaking through his teeth, onto her cheek.

"Shut up."

◇

Home was nowhere, and she lay backwards on the ground.

She missed the boy with the neatly-combed hair and the clean apartment. All she had was a filthy tent, a world of dust, and a torn-apart dress.

Don't let him see you cry. She gulped down the tears, and they tasted bitter.

She cried, rising and falling on the ground.

The tears – no. *Don't let him see you cry. Don't you dare.* They came anyway, heaving sobs. She looked at him, expectingly. Dreading it. What would he do now? What could be worse than what he'd just done? He could kill her. She hoped for it.

"Sorry, girl."

The Pedlar buckled his belt, tossed her a coin, and walked out of the tent.

◇

Jette gathered her trembling knees to her chest. She worked up the courage to pull herself from the wet ground. His footsteps were gone, his breath on her face.

She bolted. To her tent, to her pile of dirty blankets, a loaf of bread set aside, and that damned bear. It smelled like home. It smelled like nothing.

Jette clutched Buttons as she ran. One of his stringy button eyes had popped out. His fur was fading to a dust brown.

She dodged bullet stares and wordless thoughts. Kids she knew, kids that crossed the streets and markets with stolen cash, sprayed decaying buildings with cans of paint, kids who lived in houses instead of tents and had mothers instead of misery.

Don't look at me.

Her face was filthy, her lips swollen, her dress torn in a dozen places.

Why?

Don't you dare say my name.

"Jette?"

Why?

No, remember, it could be worse.

A stringy-haired woman sat huddled in the cold, jingling her coin cup. A dark wisp of a boy shivered next to her.

It could be worse.

It could be worse, it could be worse, as she vomited onto the street, staggering into the nearest chapel.

It was a small wooden place. The decrepit walls slung clumsily into and over each other; the floorboards were filled with rusted tacks; each delicate icon painting had yellowed and curled with age; and the few panes of stained glass looked frail, ready to collapse, casting golden and red reflections in the snow.

The sign simply read *Father Lot's Chapel*, but Jette just squinted at the strange, curving form of the letters, with no shadow of knowledge to what they might mean.

As she entered, the Virgin Mary stared at her from her place in the painting with downcast, smiling eyes. Her hands were clasped to her heart.

Nothing else looked at her, and she liked it.

"Empty," she whispered to herself, crawling into the wooden hall.

She slept in the back pews, restless and jerking, but still some of the best sleep she had gotten in years. The wood had collected warmth from the hidden sun.

When she awoke, the sun slapped her on the cheek.

The iced-over sun.

Frost gathered on every surface, every corner of the village, from the steaming factories to the frozen cottages. From a distance, Jette could see the peddles compound, glaring like a ghost — the gaudy, flashing orbs of red and yellow like snakes' eyes. Shining like the drunk man's knife. It hurt her eyes, and she fell back onto the pew.

"Good morning to you, visitor."

A voice. Deep, ancient, and warm. The sound of it welcomed her.

"Why did you let me in?" she cried at the dark-skinned, bearded man that appeared, looming large before her. The man smiled, with warm golden eyes and long, clean white robes.

His hair was bushy and sparse, his skin a dark cinnamon brown — the black of his hair was fading to a silvery gray. His shoulders were hunched with age, and his eyebrows were thick and coarse, but, oh — his shining eyes.

His eyes were the deepest, most vivid shade of gold she could imagine, and shining with an ancientness that retained the glow of youth, the glow of centuries.

He looked her straight in the eyes, then closed his own.

"Everyone may come," he said finally.

A timeworn smile.

"I am a peddle, you know," Jette whispered, waiting for the creases in his smile to disappear.

"I know." He left it at that, and a long silence settled around the wooden walls.

"What's your — what do they call you?" Jette asked, rubbing her tear-stained cheeks.

"Father."

"Just that? Father?"

"Lot's my name, but not many use it."

She stared at him for a long moment. When she looked at him, her stomach settled. He seemed to radiate light — but not only light, warmth. He remained still, constant.

Watching. Glowing.

"Father Lot, you're like the sun."

"The son?"

"Up in the sky. That sun."

He nodded, smiling that smile of long ago. "Ah."

Father Lot and Jette.

They were like the sun and the moon. He radiated his golden light onto her, and she glowed. Her moonchild eyes took on a strange, familiar, ever-ancient warmth. Each scrap of pantry bread, each smile, every word he spoke. He lay a woolen blanket on her at night. He was the center of everything, a breathing, wrinkled ghost of never-dying light; untouchable in his majesty. She felt that if she touched him, her hand would be set alight. So she circled on her own earthly axis, catching his beams.

But he couldn't heal her completely. Her thoughts were attacks, coming all at once, kicking and clawing.

Forget them all, she thought. *All of them, every single rotten one.* Take the memories and mind-pictures and bleach them out. Mother. Father. Shelle and Trin. Ari. Their faces cold and placid and dead on the ground. The Pedlar. Lila. The people, the people, and their horrible stares. The men who ambled in. The man and his knife. Cole with his books and bags, and that coat still thawing on the floor. Forget all of them, they're gone. Yet, that terrible song still danced in her head. *The sun is shining still...*

She knew full well the sun was darkening every hour.

On the Wednesday that she arrived there, Jette thought she was the chapel's only visitor. But when Sunday came, she was surprised to see a small congregation tiptoeing in, dressed in the darkness of the winter, heads sprinkled with snow. They seated themselves on the pews and the cold sunlight washed in.

Father Lot's voice changed when he gave a sermon; it had an ancient rumble to it, and lost its lightness. Jette sat in the very back, hoping the red dress didn't show through her chapel robe. She didn't know the words to the songs and the prayers, and felt her cheeks heat when the people began to speak again. The words looked like black-ink nothings. The letters started to blur.

When they had reached the end, she ran out into the snow and vomited. An unusual nausea was creeping through her, and it had nothing to do with the sermon and everything to do with the past creeping its way back into her.

Her stomach was swelling.

Jette stayed at Father Lot's wooden chapel. During the day, he let her eat from the chapel kitchen - just a collection of old soups and jars. She ate everything she could get her hands on, and tearfully thanked him each time. At night he gave her blankets and pillows to sleep on, and let her wear a white acolyte robe instead of that red dress. Her hair had grown long and curled at the edges again.

She wouldn't stop vomiting, though.

A cold morning came, the sky lightening with snow. A lovely, quick-falling flurry. Sludge lined the streets, rotten and gray, and Jette leaned over the toilet bowl, incredibly ashamed.

"You're... with child," said Father Lot, neither a statement nor a question.

Jette started to bawl, howling into her hair, refusing to say yes. But it was true.

She shook her head into the toilet.

"I'm sorry to bother you, by staying here — I could go, if you don't want

me. I'm a lost cause. I have... I have nothing," she sobbed. Each word felt heavy.
"I'm a lost cause. No job, no home, no family..."

She looked up to see two warm golden eyes. They seemed to catch the
sun and hold it.

"You're only lost, not gone."

She looked down and nodded, smiling a bit. "You'll let me stay?"

Father Lot patted her on the head. "All may stay. And you can be my
child now."

There were times when she gave up, when the crowd at the sermons
made her ache for a home that didn't exist. There were times when she wanted
nothing more to be with her mother, sleeping underneath the snow. But the life
inside her kicked hard at her stomach.

"A child's child," Father Lot called her.

◇

The baby was born outside of an orphanage, pale and frighteningly small
— but crying, breathing. Shivering and weak, still holding her precious Buttons,
Jette carried her child to the hands of the orphanage. Each step was a labor, but
she reached the door and twisted the creaking handle. She staggered in, though
her legs couldn't stand another step, and extended her shaking arms. The baby's
cry seemed to pierce the wooden ceiling, but the nurses didn't flinch. They
wrapped her in dim-green blankets and gave her milk.

"Thank you," she told them, trying her best to smile.

"What'll her name be?" A tall female nurse glared down at Jette, whose
red clothes showed through the gap in her white chapel robe.

She realized now she had never once thought of the name — the name,

the name, the name! — such an indispensable part of the child, but she'd given
it no thought. Above all, she decided, then and there: she wanted it to be warm.
A honey-colored word, a golden sun of a name, a bright beam through the dust
and snow. She thought of Father Lot. She thought of the iced-over sun through
the chapel window, and the first month of a summer that seemed impossibly far
away.

"She's June."

Just as the nurse turned to carry the child away, Jette grabbed hold of her
slick plastic gown. "You're June," she whispered to the baby, her legs failing her.

The irritation in the woman's voice grated against her, the questioning in
her sharp gaze.

"Would you *please* lay down somewhere, child—"

"M-may I sing to her?"

"N..." The nurse looked at her with mingled pity and disgust. For the red
dress glaring through her robe, for her child, for her age, reeking disgust and
pity all the same. "Fine."

She tried to smile, but just awakened new tears in her eyes.

Jette lay on a wooden bed and stared into the eyes of her child, squinting
and pink-rimmed, watery like her own. A peculiar blackish blue, very much like
a painting with too many colors, like an unlit corridor, like the dark side of the
moon. She stayed in those eyes for as long as she could and let her voice follow
them.

> *The sun is shining still*
> *Out by your windowsill*
> *The angels sing their song*
> *Quiet, low, and long*
>
> *I love you still today*

Don't ever go away
My courage reappears
Whenever you are near

Your face is like the sun
The day has just begun
I'll always be with you
The song I sing is true

She placed Buttons next to June, and felt her words shake as the music spilled. Her body felt ready to collapse.

The last glimpse she saw of her daughter were those two eerie eyes, large like saucers. Her feet started to trail out of the orphanage, with automatic gravity. That's when a rough hand, cold as gold, clenched her hard by the shoulder.

Jette was dragged away from the Kinsel Orphanage by a tall, pale man. His golden-ringed fingers gripped her shoulders once again, tossed her over his arms, and hauled her back to the Peddles, carrying her like a doll.

"Please, you've already stolen her."

"*I* didn't take your worthless kid," he hissed. "You stupid peddy, you can't just quit as you like. But tell me, if y' don't mind," he licked his teeth, "whose it is."

She thrashed around in his grip. "I don't know, I don't know, I don't know, *how* could I know?"

"You're all the same," he mumbled. "Stupid as hell."

Jette choked back tears, aching in her legs, aching in her gut, aching everywhere. Her daughter was gone – she could still feel the motion of her hands as she was given away. She was being forced back into the hell of the

Peddles. All of those faces she'd erased would resurface, and she'd be pushed down under again. The brothel, the bars, the alleyways, the whispers passing by her, the parade of jeers, the racket of the bus. She didn't miss any part of it.

"You're awfully quiet, girl. No spark left in you?"

"Let... me *go*."

He jerked her up farther on his shoulder.

"Let me go!" Jette shrieked. "The chapel, drop me at the chapel!"

"The holies don't need you, dear," the Pedlar sneered. "The Patron Saint of Peddles?"

"I hate you," she spat, dragging a weak hand across his face, but her fingernails didn't break skin. "Let me go."

"Fine," he groaned, "I won't feed you to the soldiers tonight."

She was worn out, and so tired — and he was too strong. His smog breath nauseated her, his ashy hands cradling her like a worthless doll. She fell in his golden hands and was dragged away from Kinsel Orphanage, with nothing to call her own, her mind rolling through her long list of names and faces.

The sermons were wrong. She decided hell was not a place to be escaped from, but a burden. A virus whose talons clamped into your skin and sucked out your love, made you its own.

His face was smug and smoky. An obscene curl of the lips, but he didn't know.

You are carrying hell.

The others were faceless. Those ones, she had successfully bleached out.

He was the only one she could attach a name to. The only one that made her heart stir.

"Cole."

Fog shrouded the young man, but Jette could see the translucent skin, the angular shoulders covered by the same collared jacket that kept her warm that long-ago night. He had a pack slung over his shoulder, stuffed with books. The wealthy, trembling kid had become a full-fledged university scholar. She saw a large brick building in the shadow of the military academy, in the shadow of the factories, and imagined him weaving through it. Living a life that shamed hers.

She remembered her misery.
Did he?
Look at me.

Cole Gretling stared back at Jette, a young, pale, exhausted face. Those familiar sad-looking eyes, the pupils small with fear. She wore a short red dress, and her knees knocked together in the cold. He immediately averted his eyes, focusing on the enormous clock in Corinth Square.

It ticked away and drowned her in time.

She decided it was less like a nervous tick tock and more like the sound of a gimlet, drilling and drilling away.

Four large words. "I had a baby."

Still, he did not answer. He turned his back to the girl.

The ticking of the clock. Its round face, white and bulbous and speckled with snow. Its large hands twisting and spinning so agonizingly slow.

"Cole, can you help me?" Jette felt her voice rising with each word, trembling with the cold.

"The hell are you talking about," Cole grumbled finally, flicking his head back to look at her. His eyes were bruises, and no matter how much venom he tried to inject into it, his voice was as calm and kind as it had been that night nine months ago.

"I had to give her up," Jette continued, lowering her voice to a hush. "The Pedlar — I couldn't keep her — he said, he said, he wouldn't let me leave.

Kinsel... I gave her to the orphanage. Kinsel. You've heard of it, yeah?"

"That's pawn shipment," muttered Cole.

"P... pawn shipment? What is..."

Cole's lip twisted in disgust. "They're boxed off to the palace, all those kids. Baby underlings, you know, slaves for the King. Pawns. Don't you know anything?"

"Pawns," Jette murmured, and without warning Cole began to walk away.

"*No!*" she cried. "Please, you're the only — "

She couldn't finish that sentence.

Not because of inhibition, no — she simply couldn't find the word. The word. Nothing fit. Nothing seemed right at all. What she lacked was words: the words for his hand, his jacket sitting in the snow, the salty taste of her tears, the dozens of textbooks in a language she couldn't read and his lips never meeting hers.

Jette held tight to the front-collar of his shirt, staring into him. Making him gaze into those sad-looking eyes, trying to make him see.

"S'probably not mine," he mumbled, looking absently at her. "You know that, right?"

"Help me. One more time."

"How could I do that?"

"Take me away," she pleaded. The words came out slippery, garbled.

Cole paused. "Where?"

"Anywhere but here."

Tears came and rolled, but the snow only swept them away.

CHAPTER X:
THE MOURNING BALL

SILENCE RESPONDS TO silence, and silence whispers back.

December the 1st. Today the Royal Hall is draped with black. The warm golden walls are shielded, like an enormous storm-clouded sun, like spiderwebs in a dead sunflower garden.

A white mist waltzes in the air outside, but it is the only one dancing.

In the upper hallways, the royals line up for vaccinations, the palace medics in a perfectly straight line. Lusks, Kostas, and medics, all in black. Silence. A forced and complete silence. Even the incessant chatter of the triplets has stopped.

"It's just a tiny jab, Reg," Russel whispers. She lifts a defiant finger to her lips, and mouths "idiot".

Russel laughs, and a dozen stares are directed towards him.

"It's for your parents we're mourning," Regena whispers, looking pained, "so don't be so damn cheerful."

"Don't *talk* to him that way," says Joss, not caring to lower her voice and pressing her pale face forward. Russel holds her back by the shoulder.

Drunken quiet. Painful quiet, quiet you could swim in. They stand in silence until the last needle is pressed into the last arm.

In my dreams, there is a dark, endless mist, an impossibly thick forest. Devoid of life. There are no scurrying animals, no ambling drifters, and no trace of sound. Just gray air and dying branches. Until.

Out of the trees comes a spidery leg, dark pants loose, but choked with bandages. A white shoulder. The forest can't hide the glare of her skin, pale and sunless in the dust and mist. Dry, blood-caked bandages curl around the thin muscles of her arms; her hunting clothes have decayed in this dying piece of forest. Her hair is black and matted, her hands are red with blood. Carrying a gun, finger on the trigger.

I stare into the hell-cold face of death. I immediately pitch backward, thrown by my fear and paralyzed by the sight. Her eyes are perfect cloudy blue, with dark eyelashes, bruised violet crescents of sleeplessness underneath. Black eyebrows with a perfect arch. Sunken, bone-hued cheeks. Deep, dark pits under her eyes. She is very different, but at once, something about her reminds me of myself. The sleepless decay in her eyes. The fury.

Her lips curl, showing small, jagged teeth. The voice that greets me is achingly, eerily beautiful, light as air, with a demonic tinge. "Your sister, your sister is here."

I stand perfectly still, staring into eyes made of emptiness.

"My sister?" I say, and my voice trembles. "I have no sister."

"Oh?"

She laughs, too long, too high, too much. It is the loveliest, most hideous sound I have ever heard; I want to run. I want to stay. I want to hide. I want to throw my legs straight into the forest and never come back. I want everything at once. Suddenly, the spell breaks; the mangled song of her laugh ends, that vile, hideous sound. I will do anything to never hear that sound again.

"Dig two graves, Prince Wickwolf."

With that, she pulls the mask from its hiding place and her face is hidden from view.

She retreats to the forest, and she's gone from my dreams.

The ground is cold. The dream was real. More real than all the others, where clocks melted and floors shook. It felt like my body had broken off in two and wandered off to a forest at midnight. A forest on the outskirts of Wickwolf, a forest thick with dreams. But then I wake, and my two bodies are together again. I wake and reach my arm to the side, but June is absent from her spot on the floor.

The anniversary of my demise.

◇

The pendulum swings and echoes through the hall.

"Prince Russel and Lady Joss, how lovely!" whispers a shrill, lovestruck voice, attached to a woman in black.

The Duke of Kosta holds a straight, urgent finger up to his mouth. There is no talking today.

Lady Regena whips her head to her side and sees the two, dressed in black, pale hands entwined. She can't hide the small sadness that creeps onto her painted face.

Joss is just sixteen, a dainty bird of a girl. She shies away into the corners, but when the time comes, she will make a parade as good as anybody. Her long, butter-blonde hair is intricately braided and twisted and decorated with black ribbons and lace. Her face is powder white, no blush-pink cheeks and lips. A black corset strangles her small waist.

Today, she's lost her smile.

It's odd, seeing Russel's cheerless face. The color seems to have drained from it — he wears a surreal frown of a mouth, and real sadness turns down his eyes. Joss turns to kiss him on the cheek, but he turns his head to the side.

The mourning bells sound, soaking the Royal Hall in grief. There are no words. Today, no one makes a sound; faces speak louder than all. The pawns are more silent than ever. The usual sinking of their shoulders does not compare, for this is their misery too.

    Regena watches. She imagines.

    She wishes she could extend her arms and dance. She wishes that the sadness on the faces around her would melt and disappear – that she could have nothing to do with this, all of this, and all of it would end.

    But the pendulum swings, and there is no brightness to the room. Joss still leeches to Russel's side, their skin halfheartedly brushing. He is a painting, she is a watercolor, both melting away. Her father stands at the end of the room, the war hero, the triumphant, who in a fit of desperation killed an entire troop of Wickwolf soldeirs. War did not harden him, she thinks. It made him fear the very act of living. And her gimlet-eyed mother, so quick to rise to the top – the force of her stare against the struggle of her will – those eyes like freshly polished gold coins. *Please don't make me go near him again. Please, not ever.*

    Her father, a war hero, a badge to be worn. He shakes hands with Leo, respectfully quiet. The gallery of noble ladies silently swoon.

    One part of her would like to join the black-cluster crowd, knit like a cobweb, and dance without a thought, interrupt the heaped-on misery and the choking stillness and the lights dimmed like lost lives. Another wishes to disappear completely.

    Disappear. Please disappear.

    She stands perfectly still, but she is spinning circles in her imagination.

    I watch the colorful shadows and their slow dance. They spin in circles, a twisted mix of sadness and happiness. Most of them dance like stiff little leaves, both partners trying to lead, or neither.

I sweep around the corner into the feed.

My right wrist reads *Royal kitchen duty,* much to Noor's excitement. He says nothing, but I see his face light like a match, his mouth suppressing a grin.

The feed — that's the pawn name for the neverending parade of sudsy sinks, eleven-foot shelves, and gaping cupboards that comprises the Kosta kitchen. We wash clean-licked dishes in silence, and I see Noor's hands cracking raw under layers of soapy water, and hand him a worn pair of gloves. He smiles again.

We'll be at this for twenty hours more.

Even from the feed we hear the mourning bells' long, low trill. Their moaning note seemed to come from the heavens. Or from hell.

There is a pool of light in the middle of the floor, and only four dare dance in it. A hulking, towering prince, shading her from the light. A pale flutter. A boy with dark wings at his feet. The rest shy away like spiders.

Leo's hair shines, dark and golden. In all black, his eyes are especially pale. He looms and laughs at nothing; says nothing. His drunken stupor terrifies her.

He takes her hands and doesn't notice their tremble.

Joss and Russel are a flurry of light in black clothes, flitting across the dance floor. He leads, somber as he should be. She follows, a white butterfly with black wings. *The infinite waltz of mourning. The lost-love that never ends. This is our day in black; this is our lifetime spent.*

A green-eyed glance over. Quick, but she sees.

He is all shoulders and teeth, smiling lazily down at her, his eyes blank and drunk.

Russel hates it.

Joss halts their dance. He misreads her strained smile as *Go, if you want to*

– spins them around, and lets her hand go light as a dove. Joss furrows her
bleached eyebrows, but he has already crossed the floor on winged feet.

Russel raises an eyebrow at Leo, a question that he won't give him time to
answer. He's still spinning, sweeping Regena up into a waltz, as if the wings on
his shoes are real.

A smile, rare as a summer snow. Hands warm and soft and smelling like
the pages of old books. Round cheeks, scornful eyes. Eyes made out of amber—

Pale blue eyes.

"Russel?"

So the dream disintegrates, and nothing is as he wants it to be. She is still
halfway across the room, and another man is gnawing at her in his imagination,
and the world doesn't smile at him like it used to. He is not a hero.

CHAPTER XI:
THE MARIONETTE
WHO CUT HIS OWN STRINGS

QUIETLY, SHE WAITS.

The girl is interested in nothing but destruction. The opportunity will strike soon, soon, soon enough. One more time.

Once more.

She wouldn't look much like a demon if she ever slept. If she cut her ungroomed hair once in a while. If she ate more, perhaps. But it is not her looks that truly terrify; it is the darkness that seeps out through their cracks.

If you would like to imagine the feeling of laying your eyes on her, imagine a tundra. Imagine the frigid face of Neptune. Desolate but sickly, fascinatingly beautiful.

Long, tangled black hair billows behind her like a storm cloud, rolling down her back in a slow, lovely way. It slopes and turns, a twisting river of black oil. Spare locks fall from her face to her legs. A lock of black snakes down her chest bone – a body like a deer, long and bony. Her gangly arms are wrapped in gloves and bandages, her spindle-fingers a mess of dirt and dry blood. Her shoulders like brand new blades protruding from her, sheathed by hair. High-laced boots caked with dirt are stuffed with thin black pants.

It is her expression that terrifies. A nightmare siren. A wolf in wolves' clothing. Lips that twist and laugh. Eyes that know bombs, sink bullets, crave blood, eat terror. She thrives on misfortune, sinking souls into the ground. Beautiful pain. Beautiful death.

She does not sleep. If she does, she will be destroyed.

Quietly, she waits.

Dear Chief Onderschot was long gone; she stole his grimy throne by the poison in his throat. *She stole his skin and then his life,* Spindel would whisper, but she would not listen.

The group cowers, with ferocity. They answer now only to Nox.

Shred was a scrawny, pale little brute when he joined the horde. He had baby-pink skin, whitish hair, and a vicious smile. He was known for his blades and the severe structure of his face, as if he had carved it with his own knife. Each cheekbone buldged with a low grin. His teeth were tiny knives; they glow with a sick sunlit luster.

Spindel came from the other side of town. His violence was more routine; he dealt with fists and guns. He spat at royalty. He spat at the law with a snarling mouth, and he never lost a bet.

Then came Locke Cielarron, the Kostan scholar. No one could guess the path he took to end up an assassin, but none questioned it. He had neatly-combed black hair and wide, trustworthy eyes, and he was an indisputable genius. Quietly, flawlessly, he formulated each and every attack, right down to the centimeter, the bullet's path, the position of each royal. He satisfied; he succeeded, and demanded no credit for it. Nox took it all.

The Regicides were now thirty-six jaded men and a young girl. During the day, they were slick assassins, and they would put on a show of righteous violence. They would shout, they would curse the world and the king and themselves and each other, they would explode in violent fits of hatred. But at night, they all went back to avoiding glances, keeping their secrets, hiding their skeletons. Their rage was nothing compared to their sick dreams.

Any way you looked at it, Nox was a girl against thiry-six men. Small, hungry, and young. At first glance, she was their tagalong, their plaything, their twisted doll. She knew the taunts would never end, but her apparent weakness held no candle to her cold fury. They could put on their show all they liked, but at the end of the day, they were weak, cowardly men, and her finger at the trigger scared them just as anybody's would.

They started with the princesses, the easiest kill, and the kill that would erupt the quickest and most plentiful outrage. Cries of disgust went out for Princess Krysanthe, then little Oriana. Newspapers screamed: Uppica's Princess Fey was shot not in the public square, but in the safety of her bedroom. Little Eris and Stelle were murdered together, by none other than Nox. Her bullets did the trick, and the newspapers thrashed with rageful mourning.

The kingdom headlines all roared. The cities howled, and radios murmured with fright. The near-incoherent cries of the kingdoms, knotted together by desperate fingers, by men who secretly savored each impossible word: *THE KING IS DEAD.*

Blood and ink spilled together.

    ANOTHER PRINCESS DEAD
    UPPICA IN JEOPARDY
    DANGER FOR THE KINGDOMS
    LUSK UPS DEFENSE
    WICKWOLF RIVALRY?
    REGICIDES STRIKE AGAIN

Little Prince Russel had declined the invitation to the Palace Circle Parade that day, four long years ago. He had a procession of excuses: his stomach was sick. He had sunburn on his neck. His eyes stung. His ears rung that day. Perhaps the howl of the headlines had gotten to him and squeezed the health out of his skin.

King Karan nodded and whispered into his son's forehead, which did seem quite hot. His dark yellow twists of hair fell to his face. "Take care of yourself."

"Okay, Papa."

A whisper was met with the headlines' roar.

KOSTA'S QUEEN SHOT
QUEEN MERRIS DEAD
REGICIDES ESCALATE
GOD SAVE THE QUEEN

"Papa?"

The King came home carrying the corpse of his queen in his eyes. One long look and Russel could see, but could not understand.

He could never understand.

The headlines were blurred and scribbled and stamped out. Most were blackened before they reached the child's eyes. Lies! Gone! Slander! Done with!

This did nothing to quell his childish grief. He saw, he knew. She was here. There. Everywhere. In the air, under the floor, smiling at him from the moon.

The ghost of his mother sat on every corner, on everything. She laid down in a pool of air and made herself comfortable in the yellow glare of each palace room. Her lovely light green eyes became bulletholes. Her skin became dust and silk. He could see the long veins in her arms, the bones behind her face. An elegant skeleton.

Her hair billowed out just the same, a heap of hay-yellow curls. Karan reached for her, to stroke her floating face — and she turned to dust and petals in his eyes. Her mouth opened wide, a perpetual yawn, and she disintegrated. The dead flowers, the gray ghostly breath, hovered and sank back into the floor.

Little Russel had gone mad with grief, was the constant murmur of the castle. But his childish turmoil could not hold a candle to the King's despair.

His eyes had buried a deep black grave and dug themselves into it. He wailed. He paled. He screamed in his dreams. The yellowness had drained from his hair; it seemed to turn gray overnight. The soul leaked out of him swiftly.

The liquor didn't work. It dug a greater emptiness inside of him, pulled him farther away. He could not take the look in his son's green eyes — of curiosity and shock and confusion and sadness and questioning and guilt and every pain a child should never experience, stained onto his face. He couldn't take it. He couldn't take the quivering, questioning chin.

In the quiet chaos of his bedroom, King Karan took a knife to his own throat. He had let go of his own strings. The Regicides had climbed into his skin, his eyes, his mouth and veins and hands, and pulled him like a puppet, a royal marionette, in their own vicious intent.

The air around him was still, as if frozen in time. The perfumed air, the low song of trumpets and tinkling of bells, the ceremonies carrying on. The knife shining like a malicious moon. His chin trembling, cold tears jittering on his face, his heart pounding as if racing to the end.

The last words of King Kosta, shot into an uncaring sky:

"You forced my hand."

The King becomes the Regicide.

THE KING'S SUICIDE
KING KARAN KILLED BY HIS OWN HAND
ANOTHER KING LOST

Everything seemed to move in slow motion. The confetti of winter petals, falling agonizingly slow, mixing with new snow. Everything was melting.

"Be quiet, Russel" —

— the only three words that nurse said to him as he whimpered in his seat. His over-white, bleached-out medical throne. He sat with fervent sickness. The palace medics compiled their tools, their white gelcaps and clear serums, gentle drugs.

Soft. So soft. Everything is made of clouds. There is nothing to worry about. There are lilacs in the sky. They will take care of you. The General will take care of everything. The General and the Duke and Pawnmaster Klosswarden, with their big white teeth and smiles. The men in stars. God save Kosta. There is nothing to worry about. Smile, little prince.

His sleep lasted as long as it wanted to. In his state of miraculous sedation, he missed the headlines.

They rolled on just the same.

PRINCE JORSON KILLED
REGICIDES RAGE ON
PRINCE CLAYR DEAD
UPPICA ATTACKED
QUEEN AYANA KILLED

Worse came to worse came to worse. No one could find them. They appeared like ghosts — invisible and mute — and left their crimescene in a hurry. They left behind nothing of themselves.

All they found was a single mask with a knife driven through each X. A warning.

WICKWOLF KING DEAD
PUBLIC SHOOTING OF KING LOUPE
THE REGICIDES STRIKE WICKWOLF
WICKWOLF IN DANGER

My mother's misery, my father's grave, my terror and trembling and pain, reduced to a headline.

◇

Everything was white, violently white, when I woke.

I smelled velvet, vomit, ambien.

You killed God.

"The light," I tried to say, but my mouth was dry as dust. *Make the light disappear, make it go dark again, anything to stop it, anything—*

"He's awake," said the shadow of a voice, and my stomach lurched with everything I remembered. *No, no, no. I wish it was me instead. I wish I was dead. I wish I was dead—*

I vomited into the bucket they held out to me.

The next time I woke it was dark again, and I thanked God once before remembering what he had made happen to my father.

I spoke it aloud this time, in a voice weak with sleep, but loud enough for the shadow of a voice to hear. "My mother."

The shadow woman turned around. "She is alive," she whispered, but shook her head. "She saved you."

My face felt hot and wet, and I realized I was crying, and I didn't want to her see, so I shook my head until it hurt, and suddenly everything was shaking along with me.

Please please please please—

No.

"Where is she?"

"Your mother's asleep," she said, her voice breaking, and I knew it was all a lie. She would see me. She would come and see me if all was well.

"I wish I were dead," I said, aloud this time, the tears making my voice twist and drown. I choked on the smell of the room, the horrible emptiness of my stomach, the taste of salt. I almost expected her to say what anyone else would say – *don't ever say that, don't you know how blessed you are, don't you know how much life you have left to live* – but she didn't say a word. I thanked God again, though I wanted to reach into the sky and scream at him, or climb to wherever my father must be, or sink into the snow until the warmth was sucked out of me, or stop existing for even one second.

No. I don't wish I were dead. I wish I didn't exist at all, didn't exist anywhere.

◇

Buried deep in a Kostan forest, they sit cross-legged and shaded by dead branches. Locke writes with a heavy grip, and Nox spits words at him.

"What is done out of love," she says, "will inevitably end in failure."

"Yes."

"What is done in darkness ends in light."

"Yes, Nox." He nods on. Another whispered tirade, another stolen pen scratching at nothing.

"And I will conquer the darkness."

"Yes—"

"And the light."

"Yes, Nox."

"You doubt me."

"No, no, I—"

Her heavy-lidded eyes bulge at him.

"I'll track them all down, I swear to you. Every wretched shining diamond on this god-awful island. First the ones on the pedestals, then the down-lows. They'll be later. Then we'll be the last few people in this world, my Locke. The last *good* people."

He dares to ask again. "What about the Wickwolf prince?"
"Ah, no. I told you. That boy... I'm saving him for last."

CHAPTER XII:
THE SUNSHINE
SLUM SONG

THE FLOORBOARDS WERE delicate, the food was plain, and the water ran cold. The winter wind always found a way to whistle in one way or another. But she knew it wasn't the worst place in the world.

The orphanage stood at the edge of Kosta, on the brink of the city slums, and it certainly *wasn't*, by any means, the worst place in the world. Not with bombs being hurled at Wickwolf's capital, not with bullets being shot left and right at queens and princes and peasants and undesirables. In the orphanage, at least she was safe and she had a future to look at. In her dreams, she would become the queen's best little friend. She had never seen the queen, but she imagined she had curly hair, long eyelashes, and a ridiculously large, twinkling crown. Merris Kosta would brush her hair and sing her songs and read her stories, the ones she never got to read. One day the headlines told of the queen's murder in the center of Ordim city – large black type on a scrumpled-up sheet, screaming at her from the page. June started to cry for someone she had never met.

At night, she'd look out the crackle-wood hole in the wall at a sky whispering with stars, feel the wind through the orphanage window – on her skin, blustering through her white nightgown. She wished she could steal into the night, explore the whole of Kosta, see everything there was to see. A swift little girl with nothing to lose, running as fast as her legs would carry her. But her wish died in her eyes as the sky darkened, as she heard noises from inside.

"Where you off to, June?"

It was Ibby. A soft shadow, in her identical nightgown, with her little voice. Her big brown eyes were scared, but curious.

"Out." She took her hand and crept out into the darkened street, but Ibby jerked back into the slight warmth of the orphanage.

"I didn't say I was coming."

"You didn't say you *weren't*." She paused. "Well, are ya or not?"

"Where?"

"Just out. The shops, maybe. Explorin'."

"Mother Waise says the shops are dangerous. She says there's dirty women there, and dirty men."

"There's dirty people all over the place. You coming or what?"

"What're you gonna do if we get kicked out, huh?"

She shrugged. "We won't."

"Cause you're always so *innocent* when the big ladies are around. Cause they all feel *sorry* for you, 'cause you're so little and sick and—"

"Hush up." June pulled Ibby down. "Nevermind... thought I heard something..."

They walked further and further down the filthy cobblestone road, June kicking discarded cans, Ibby making sure to keep quiet. June brought them to a halt at the grocer's, a brown building completely bare of all light, surrounded by full-to-the-brim trashcans.

She picked two apples from one of them and handed one to Ibby. "See? It was a good idea."

Ibby stopped and glanced down at the cobblestones. Right next to her feet was a spot of blood. She hopped back.

"You're not scared or something, are you?" June asked, far too casually, and far too loud.

"Shhh!"

Suddenly, there was a glaring yellow light, pouring like fire from the door. Out from one of the shops staggered a tall, stooping man, holding a whiskey bottle with one hand and waving a thick, ancient newspaper with the other.

"Little bugs!" he spat, but they were already on the run.

One morning, Sister Waise called her over. A nun who volunteered at the orphanage, she had a sharp face but a soft disposition. June walked toward her, nightgown still on, head bowed.

"Little girl," she said, adjusting her thick-rimmed glasses, "you are one of the better-behaved children, aren't you?"

"I — I'd like to think so, Sister Waise..." Her eyes flickered nervously across the wooden room. She hadn't always been that good. Apart from the sneaking out, she'd stolen a packet of crackers and an apple from the corner shop. She'd kicked a boy in the shins when he taunted her. But she wasn't about to let any of that out.

The nun walked her over to the very front of the orphanage, and at first June squirmed. *You're kicking me out,* she thought. *I didn't think it would be so quick.*

But no door was opened, no draft poured in, no pointing fingers or shoving. The front room was full of swaddled babies, milk, spoons, and needles. It smelled of wood.

"I'd like to assign you with the littler ones."

Each morning, June switched out of her nightgown to a high-collared robe. She reveled in her privilege to help the nurses, even if they looked at her with narrow eyes. They didn't trust her with the babies and handed her a sewing kit to patch up the blankets, which were all but washed to rags. Most of the nurses held her in vague contempt and glared down at her with tired hostility.

They grasped her fingers roughly when she held the needles wrong.

All but one.

This nurse didn't wear the same exhausted look as the others. Her skin was warm and brown and her hair was often loose. There was an air of sterilized sweetness around her. Sometimes, though, she'd look out on the city streets, and her eyes would grow distant and sad.

Over and over again, with no regard for the dagger stares of the other nurses, she'd sing. A simple song about the sun. She'd look out on the sky, bleak and sunless, and then her deep-set eyes would trail back to June.

"You're off to the palace soon, dear?"

"Yes... I'm twelve in a bit..."

"How long?"

"I'm not sure — we all go at the same time, you see."

The singing nurse looked back on the bottle of milk she was filling and sighed, almost happily. June whispered over the cry of children:

"Could you sing your song again?"

She smiled, and this time the little girl sang along with her.

"You have a nice voice," she told her, looking up from her needles. "You really do."

The sky was cold, the air dry and unwelcoming. The nurse waved her a quiet goodbye, voiceless – and on the wooden chariot rolled. The wheels bruised the road, spinning violently.

Goodbye.

Its rigid driver cursed softly under his breath.

She was alone.

She breathed it in and savored it.

The dank smell of her room. The walls made of concrete and stone. The floor relentlessly cold.

She breathed it in until she couldn't stand it any longer. Then her feet moved on their own, her eyes lifted to the ceilings.

It was dark, and she ran as fast as she could up the stairs. Her legs started to ache, but she went on. It was a beautiful, velvet-textured ache. She ached like freedom, like weightlessness, like hope.

And the stairs finally ended, giving way to a dark wonderland.

The Hall had lost its daytime glow. Empty. The heavy velvet curtains were closed.

Then, a footstep in the darkness.

Suddenly, a bright light was in front of her eyes, bringing her face to life. Artificial starlight.

Two childish gasps.

The living son of the dead queen —

His perfect, tragic, lamplit face. Green eyes turned sharp yellow by the glare, a gaping mouth and a single curl of hair, twisting innocently between his eyes.

He screamed.

She scampered.

You're a wanderer, too. You're an orphan, like me.
The little ghost walked into the darkness again.

Sixteen, and she wandered again. The castle had grown grimmer, darkness creeping into the dust-filled corners.

Golden-plaqued rooms, tapestries of fine thread, the lull of sleep pulled over like a canopy.

Softened screams from the hallway.

The sun is shining still
Out by your windowsill
The angels sing their song
Quiet, low, and long

In passing, I hear June's voice, drifting, spilling out of the washrooms. Singing an unfamiliar, ancient tune in the female communal shower. It must be native to Kosta, because I've never heard it once before.

I love you still today
Don't ever go away
My courage reappears
Whenever you are near

Your face is like the sun
The day has just begun
I'll always be with you
The song I sing is true

The sound of it heals me. It warms the sickness in my heart.

I see her trail out of the stalls, still humming that strange chorus, but at the sight of me, her voice drops and hardens, loses its song.

"Huh? Wick?"

I'm at a real loss for words, so I choke out: "Your voice..."

As she takes off, she crashes into me. I feel the dig of a malnourished elbow, the rush in the dry air between us. Now she runs.

The rest of the female pawns trail out in dull, silent clumps.

So much silence. I'd rather have song. I'd rather have screams.

The mark of a good pawn is silence.

All the while I am left thinking, where did that song come from? Where did she learn it? I have never heard a song in the gutters before. Everyone shuffles through, ashen-faced, straight-mouthed, except maybe Ibby and Noor. Sure, their faces occasionally brighten and move. But they never *sing*.

And then a thought smacks itself across my face.

June hasn't seen the sun, real, strong, warm, in front of her eyes. None of the pawns have. Their whole lives, they've been slaving for Kosta. Slogging away trapped in walls. They don't remember, don't know what sunshine feels like, beating down on their skin.

So June sings of something she's never seen, at least not in many years.

I watch her run clumsily down the dark corridor, and before I can help it, a deep ache overtakes me. Suddenly, it's all I want to tear down these walls. I want her to feel something beyond these stones and dust and metal bars. I want her to hurt me. I want her to make me accountable for stealing the sun.

She doesn't know. None of them know.

Ward One, Room Eight is freezing cold in the night. I can see my breath bloom out of my throat, dry and heavy; it makes me long for the sun I will never see. June finishes her tasks later than usual. She tiptoes into the pen of a room in a heap of a cloak.

"C'mon," she says.

"Huh?"

She wraps a hand around my wrist and tugs me out of the room, taking the lantern along with her into the dark.

The halls are filled with silence and darkness, and her cough seems to scatter the dust in the air. She leads me up the stairs to a large, creaky door that she's careful to open slowly. I follow her in to find a night-darkened broom closet. In the corner, a mirror gleams. Then I see other strange little things – a pile of apples glinting red in the dark, the outline of what looks like a giant, leatherbound book.

June picks two apples from the floor and hands one to me.

"My stash."

"Ah."

We walk back into the darkness of the hall.

"I'm sorry — for before — " I begin.

For hearing your voice. For stealing your sun.

June interrupts. "I was just embarrassed."

"No, you're a very good... I mean," I clear my throat, "your voice is beautiful."

"It really is? You mean it?" June hides the beginning of a smile with her forearm.

"Smite me if it isn't." I smile back.

"The — THE CORNERS OF YOUR MOUTH ARE TURNED UPWARDS! WITCHCRAFT! SORCERY!! A TRICK OF THE LIGHT?!"

I let out a laugh. "What light would that be?"

"Oh, I don't know," she says, and flicks the lantern on. "Hey, you should smile more. Y'don't look half as grim."

"You don't smile."

"I do, though!" she protests. "And what's that got to do with anything?"

Suddenly all I can think of is sun.

We walk back down the stairs, her scampering to keep up with me, tugging on the too-long skirt of her robe. She finally takes hold of the back of my shirt. "Walk slower, you overgrown—"

"Sorry."

Ward One welcomes us back with a silence that swallows everything, even the darkness. June kicks open the door and chomps her apple.

"Oh," She tugs off the hood of her cloak. "Your hands are bleeding again."

"Yeah... it's not bad today. I gotta go to sleep."

She touches my hand, saying nothing. Her fingers trail along my knuckles and finally grab hold of my hand, a touch that seems to invade my veins. Fairies in my gut. She turns my hand over in hers, and my goddamn blood is on her fingers.

Oh, God. Please don't, for God's sake.

Say something. Please say something, anything. Call me a name, yeah, insult me. For God's sake. Crush my hand. I can't handle your damn painful silence or your soft hand on mine.

Her hand, the purple bruises on her arm, the inky eyes.

She lets go of me.

"I think I..." She pauses, scanning my face as if there might be words printed there for her to recite. She wipes her hand on her cheek, smearing it with blood, but she doesn't seem to notice. "I might..."

"You might?"

She jerks her head away. "...need some sleep, I mean. Nevermind. Nevermind," she says, curling into the ragged blanket.

I see no sun. I see no windowsills, only hard stone and concrete.

I have no courage.

No always, and no truth.

I hear no angels, just a little ghost that comes close.

"Sing again."

"Huh?" June sits up.

"I said, sing."

She sighs. "Only if you do, too... the Kosta anthem."

O Kosta,

My Kosta,
I pledge my life to thee.
Your vastness,
Your courage,
Your generosity.
I live to serve my kingdom,
My motherland and home.
O Kosta, my Kosta,
I'll never walk alone.

There's no grace to my voice, but I have one, at least; I haven't lost it. It spreads through the tiny room, mixing with hers.

"Not bad," she says, snickering into her hand. "Now you gotta do something for me. 'Fore I fall asleep."

"Huh? What?"

"Tell me a story."

"Okay..." I sigh. My mind is in the bomb shelter. The shelf. The ashes. "Once there was a wolf who lost his pack. There weren't any more animals in the forests. His pack had killed half of them, and the forests fires had done the rest of the job for him. So he went looking for his pack. He couldn't hunt without them, 'cause his leg was broken. He was starved, so he limped on his three good legs to find a place where he could live. All he could find was an island of birds, singing carelessly. Most flew away from him. Then he found the starling..."

"A starling is a kind of star?" June mumbles. "A little star?"

"No, a little bird. He couldn't bear to kill the starling. Its song was too..."

I can't find the word. What word did my father use?

It doesn't matter. June's eyes are flickering shut. Her head is bobbing unconsciously towards my shoulder, then flitting away.

"It's fine."

She looks up at me with half-closed eyes. "You'll crumble if I hold you."

I have no idea what she means, but in a second she's asleep. Breathing into my neck.

The darkness closes in on us. The lantern gives a sudden flash, and the wall is illuminated again. Now I see the tiny pinpricks of her handwriting, one word over and over.

Free.

CHAPTER XIII:
A COLD SMOKE RISING

BORN TO A widow, into a home of dust, into a shack of sickness, it seemed as if she had no choice but to go mad. To take that final plunge into mania. Perhaps that was true, but the madness grew inside of her still. Not a hot, jolting, or electric kind of madness — the kind you hear about in stories — but a cold fire burning, a cold smoke rising. Rising, rising. Rising still.

It doesn't matter what her name was before, because before she was not Nox. She never cursed in school. She kept her hands to herself. She was a rather ordinary little girl, who didn't quite understand what anything meant around her, why people were the way that they were, why anyone cared, or why anyone even bothered. She just became the girl threatening to break through from the mirror. She became Nox, or rather, Nox swallowed her up. But rarely do these things happen overnight.

She didn't understand how someone could be so sad, or why. Why her mother pounded walls and swallowed pills. Daddy was gone, but he was always gone. Since she was born, and even before that. Away, always.

The war was okay to her. It was a distant, make-believe, empty word – but then some string made a knot inside of her, and it was the reason he was gone.

And she knew that sadness didn't belong to her. But it seemed like the right thing to do, so she cried anyway, and that was the only time.

The tears took a while to form and shove out of her eyes, but once they came, they satisfied. Crying was weak, sadness was weak — even when she couldn't put it into words, her childish mind held that sickness. That indifference that glowed in the dark, that darkened every glow. Emotions didn't interest her. Smiles did not move her, the cries of others meant nothing, just wet twists of the face.

All of them. Pathetic and hopeless. Emotions reduced them all to sniveling wrecks – but she, she was stronger — nothing stood above her blank-faced domination. That subtle sway of her ever-gray eyes as they followed the strange words that leaked from others' mouths: *Love. Hate. Heartache. I feel.* What were those but words? But letters thrown together?

She did not need love. Disposable love. Drowning, worthless, crack-away-at-the-edges love. Even hate. Hate was an infection, a virus, a disease; and so was love.

Especially heartache, the weakest of them all. She wanted nothing to do with it. Loss, goodbyes, fists pounding on walls, crying lunatics who longed for, longed for, longed for. Her heart did not ache. It sat still in her chest, and beat only when it had to.

"Sick in the head."

Her mother dubbed her as such in the middle of a crying fit. Nox sat still, didn't offer any comforts. At one point she had let loose a tiny snicker as her mother cried.

The tears twitched on her face.

"God dammit, why'd you have to be born like this?"

She agreed.

Why did she have to be born at all?

"It's your fault for giving birth to me." Her mother's face convulsed at her words, but the girl wanted nothing to do with it.

Her mother gritted her teeth and took her by the head, slamming her against the crumbling kitchen counter.

"Get the demons out of your sick head," she hissed. "Something's broken inside of you, wicked girl. Something's *wrong* inside you. It's all because of–"

Her mother didn't finished her sentence. She staggered into her room until Nox could only hear the muffled sound of sobs.

The side of her head throbbed. No demons escaped, just sick, swelling blood.

To say something broke inside her would not be quite right. It was more like a string unraveling – slowly, over time.

She did not hate the Wickwolf King. She did not hate any of the royals – or anyone, for that matter. Perhaps she was incapable of true hate, of emotion of any shape. Emotion was a disgusting thing. But in her gray heart lay a cold, logical vengeance. Not against anyone in particular, but *everyone*. Her family; every royal; every human. The secret sat under her mother's bed: a Wickwolf royal note, half-burned, half-trampled — but not enough. The letters did not match the scrawling charcoal loops of her dead father; they were written in quick quill, and spelled out:

This is the last of it. It has to end.

Who could it be?

She reached under the bed once more to find wilted red roses, a rusted golden ring attached to a long chain, a dozen dark secrets piled on top of each other. Secrets meant to be hidden away for good. A long, emotionless smile crept over her face, and an ancient malice snuck its way into her childish eyes. The rich ink of the page seemed to float off and coil around her hands, squeezing vicious strength into her.

"Yes," she spoke aloud, only to herself. "This *is* the last of it..."

Her mother sat in her broken old chair, spinning smoke into the sky. She earned just enough to keep the wolf from the door. She no longer cared if her daughter wandered into the bad part of town, so she did. It quickly became her favorite part. There was no one to wave at, no smiling faces and yelping voices from school, no one to exchange polite conversation with. Grown men stared at her wearily – a strange girl, with tangled black hair and skin as pale as the sky, walking through a Southern Wickwolf alley as if she belonged there entirely.

They assembled in the slum cemetery, shaded by hunched black trees. The tombstones stood, planted like teeth in a jaw. They were rotten, ready to be plucked and discarded, their names lost to years of dust and decay. No one would visit these graves.

The whole gang laughed at her when she first came through.

"What could you be here for, girl?"

She set her eyes on Onderschot, whose eyes remained black and empty, focused on his knife.

"A job."

"A scrawny lit'l girl like you, a bloody killer?" spat a man with a gaping hole in his cheek, roaring, laughter shaking his Regicide cloak.

"You think you could take one out?" another screeched, clutching the sheath his sword lay in and chomping on stolen fruit. "You think so?"

"I know it," she murmured, then rose her voice. Her thin black eyebrow twitched at their spite-spat laughter. "I know it! Just give me a gun. A bow. A spear. Just give me anything, I'll prove it to all of you."

The bullet made a neat hole through the half-eaten apple on the tree. Another apple. Again and again and again.

She proved it.

She watched their faces grow still, and they watched the smile spread on her face. A crescent moon.

The hulking, leathered man sat hunched, looking at her like a piece of meat. Spindel nodded, and Onderschot grimaced into the glare of his blade.

"We'll humor you, girl."

She became Nox.

The bullet-crusher, the venom-spitter, the ice-gazer, with a loaded gun and a Regicide mask to match the rest. But she knew she was above them, far above them. No one could reach her – they all carried something. Things she learned in the dead of night, when they all lay clutching their weapons in tight fists, whispering their agonies into the sky. A lost mother. A dead little sister. A starving family. A shameful secret. A personal vengeance against the throne. Their pasts were chained to them – but could they not see? Could they not understand the simplicity of unhooking the clasp, of tossing the sickly metal aside? She did it without complaint. Her mother was a crack in the ground; her father, dust fluttering away in the wind. She carried nothing of them. She had dropped everything to the ground, everything but the gun in her hand.

She hit the target every time. Cold precision, deadly aim, and a girl marching coldly forward.

Her next target was King Loupe Wickwolf, the man whose pen was hurried and graceful, the man she now thought she could see in every shadow, the man who hid under her mother's bed.

CHAPTER XIV:
THE FOOL

FIVE YEARS AGO

"YOU WILL KEEP your end of the bargain, won't you?"

A man with bloodless skin sat at one end of the sprawling white table, drumming his fingers against the porcelain. At the other end was a girl of fifteen. She was scrawny, filthy, devious. A smile that could stamp out the sun, and a fully loaded gun.

"Of course, Duke."

She was already hatching the plot in her head — and planning to consult Locke the scholar before it was carried through. But she was all too aware that there was another plot spreading its roots across the table.

"And will you keep yours?"

"Yes," he said, pale eyes darting away.

Nox ambled around the table, dragging her dirty fingernails around its edge. Palace porcelain. The Duke visibly squirmed. Slowly, she reached him, and leaned to whisper in his ear. "Then when it comes time, I won't kill you, or your daughter." She paused a second. "Unless, of course, you fail."

"I won't fail."

She smiled again, the sun heatless and dim against her back.

"You *can't* fail."

◇

Everything is falling apart in front of me, and no one has anything to say about it. Silence and hacking coughs. Bruises that multiply. The gutter's getting colder, and the royals are sharpening their knives, their tongues, their eyes.

The hall is dry tonight, the color of rot and dust.

I watch blood drip down my hand, mesmerized by the red dots on the floor.

Two small shadows approach from the darkness, small-shouldered and soft-footed. Ibby and June. Ibby staggers down, barefooted, trailing a long line of blood behind her. Biting her lip to keep from crying.

"What the hell?" Noor hisses.

"I spilt the glass," she explains through tears. "They made me walk through it."

"*Who?*" Noor's fighting to keep his voice down, but Klosswarden is nowhere to be seen. He rushes over, clutching her by the shoulders.

She keeps silent, still biting her lip.

I help her to the floor and frantically rip off pieces of sleeve to stop the blood, but June's already made a run for it.

"Little ghost's not scared of blood, is she?" Ibby sniffs. "She gets all the cushy work..."

But June comes back carrying a roll of bandages and a bruised apple.

NO PAWNS PERMITTED, reads the towering white label on the uppermost doorway of the palace.

It soars hundreds of feet off the ground, and inside lies what seems to be a peek at heaven, a glimpse of one of Eden's shimmering rivers.

The Kosta palace pool gleams — surreal, enormous, the brightest shade of turquoise you can imagine, the shade of turquoise you'd imagine sirens' eyes to be. Square stone barriers surround it, hugged by metal rings. Spikes of pearl-white poke at the ceiling. The walls glows, aquamarine, emerald green, and pure iridescent white. Fluorescent paradise, complete with chlorinated water pumped in, warm and clean, from the walls. Dozens, hundreds of blue-glowing lanterns surround the perimeters.

A rolling, weeping music rumbles through the fifty-foot pool. The sun glances in through the fading noontide, and spreads itself throughout the vastness of the room.

Russel Kosta is the only one splashing.

Duchess Joss Conquin seems to prefer not to go in; instead she sits on the glittering poolside, skimming her pink-painted toes through the water. Regena sits far off, wrapped in long layers of dark purple cotton, nose buried in a book of poems.

"Why so swaddled?" Russel directs the question to Regena in honest curiosity. She grunts in response, and he swims over to her chair.

"You're not coming in?" he asks, shaking the water out of his hair.

"I don't much feel like it," she mumbles, distracted. "Why don't you ask your pretty little girlfriend."

"She doesn't like getting her hair wet." Russel glances towards her, smiling ceremoniously. "I thought you didn't mind getting your hair wet, Reg."

"I don't," she grumbles. "I mind you."

His reply is a sad, glowing laugh. "Okay... have fun."

Joss is still perched like a pale little bird on the poolside, her powder-blonde waterless hair tied into two braided loops. Her feet trail along the water. She tilts her head to the side with a pastel pout; her faded blue eyes are still fixed on Regena.

"Russel," she whispers, "stop that... with her."

He falls silent. A strange, foreign silence, without a splash or stir in the palace pool. Regena's eyes are pressed into to her book, and Russel's are fluttering anxiously.

"Are you kidding?"

"I feel a bit *slighted*, you know. Of course I do. I know you used to love that girl," says Joss, in a delicate, soft-hued hiss of a voice. "Don't try and hide it, Russel. I know you loved her for a long time."

"Joss, you've got the wrong idea."

The twitch in his laugh betrays him.

"I'm not an idiot," Joss says, "please. Is that too much to ask?"

Yes, he thinks. It's almost comical. But her pale blue eyes glitter with anger, and Regena sits still, placid and focused, her legs crossed in front of her. He redirects his stare, and her face has knotted even further with envy. He wants to say a million things in his defense, but none of them suffice.

Instead he whispers, "Whatever you want."

◇

The day he first took flight was full of yellow air, full to the brim with sunlight, his overgrown kingdom in full bloom.

The forests that guarded the palace were much brighter in his child eyes. The trees had lost much of their color, much of their size as he grew older and trapped himself in his castle. His whole life had drained itself out when he lost his mother, his father, his best friend.

The swift, sudden pull of fate, and the rug out from under him.

His childhood still shines in his evergreen eyes. A history of trees, lakes, and luxury. Of fireworks and ceremonies. Of sweet coconut buns and contraband friendship.

◇

NINE YEARS AGO

It was a particularly humid day in July, the kind of day reserved for staying indoors and waving a fan at your face, pomp and pampering. The day of the Summer Festival, and no one would venture into the sun. Russel Kosta passionately disagreed.

The Wickwolf and Lusk royal families and aristocrats had retreated from their furiously hot kingdoms to the "safe, mild" haven of Kosta. My father and mother sat stirring the ice in their water. The Lusks were arranged in gold-and-purple clumps of extravagance. All but one.

The Duke of Lusk's daughter sat at the corner of the room, hands clasped to a black book, legs crossed in front of her. Her skin was deep brown from the glaring sun; her eyes pierced the pages.

Her sidewards glance set light to Russel's seven-year-old face.

A startled smile from the smart little crisscrossed girl. I watched them watch each other. In the time where my smiles were much less rare, I couldn't help but laugh at their little spectacle.

If there was ever anything to make a kid believe in love at first sight, this was it.

Russel grabbed hold of my hands and started to dance wildly, spinning me around in circles. Confused, my feet stumbled along. His eyes were focused on her.

"You court fool," I whispered. "Is that some sort of mating ritual? Do you really think she'll come over here — "

The little duchess girl sat her black book on the floor and performed an elegant kind of scurry over to us. Russel dropped my hands and stared at her with a smile.

Her first words to the jester prince: "Are you crazy?"

A stupid smile. "For you, I am."

"You don't even know me." She had a small, sharp voice and perfect teeth.

"You know *me*. I'm Russel Theodore Ruben Astor Kosta!" he blurted, in some sort of trance, with an eager smile and wide eyes. "Prince of Kosta."

"Obviously. I'm Regena Pagele."

"Charmed." He grabbed her small hand and began to run. "Quick quick quick! The forest! Come on! The *forest!* You, too, Ez!"

Russel chased on over to the small golden door leading to the Green Garden. Far out from the garden was the forest — the most mysterious, enchanting piece of earth Russel could think of, where vines looped their way around branches, where trees stood like giants, where he swore we could hear the chiming laugh of fairies.

None of the adults were paying us any mind.

Regena Pagele looked back at me, baffled. She had eyes like amber stones, sharp and warm. I smiled and started to run into the light, into a day that could not be forgotten.

We ran all the way up that beautiful hill, picking dandelions and daffodils as we passed, and toppled each other over as we crashed to the ground. A heap of extravagant clothes, laughter, and dirt. When we'd finally reached the top of it, though, we discovered there was nothing to it. It was an ordinary, weed-ridden hill, no magic or lushness to it. We must've added the magic ourselves, with sprinkled laughter and stomping feet. But I guess we've used up our supply.

We were so high above the world, the world we insisted we never belonged to, Russel higher than the rest. That's how it goes. You are so high above the world, the bright endless world, so high you don't even know it until the colors of the sunset sky disappear from view, and your feet realize they have nothing to stand on, and you're falling.

Your happiness is made of nothing.

Russel Kosta — to me you'll always be seven and reckless. One with the birds, and laughing into the sky. Broken bones, smile, all of that is you. Regena will forever have her hand on yours. At least, I'd like to think that way, but time and tragedy have gotten in the way.

More than anything, I wish I could go back. I wish I could redo and rethink it all, and maybe salvage some innocence, save who I could not save. If that was possible, would I trade all the future I have for just a piece of the past?

Above all, I'd like to learn to love everything. Not just the scraps of memory that appear again and again in my more pleasant dreams.

I've never liked clouds, so untimely and hateful and gray. But now I treasure them, even wish to see their cold, massive majesty. The rain, the rain. I long for it. I know that now if a hole was torn in the wall of my cell, I would reach out and grab the dust in the sky. I would wring out the rain and love every drop of it.

I think back to a day when the sky was ugly and pale, wrought with tissue-paper clouds spilling with rain. We were celebrating the beginning of May, the end of the longest winter we had seen.

"Duke Conquin looks like he's constipated," said Russel, smiling. "He has a twisty face."

"'Specially when he's mad."

"He's *always* mad, though."

"Shush, shush, he's probably out here!"

"What... hunting? Hiding in the bushes?" The group burst into laughter.

"All our parents are," I said. "Spying on us, I mean. They think we're trouble."

"We are trouble. But they'll never find us."

"Huh?"

"They never go out here anymore," said Regena. "Not even in the Green Garden. They believe every story they hear. It's too dangerous. The air's all full of ghosts. The ghosts of all the people that have ever died in the world." She waved "There's dark magic in the forests."

"You're making that up," I grumbled.

"Look at that one cloud," said Russel. "It looks like a giant mouth, swallowing the others."

We stayed out in the rain until our clothes were soaked and our stomachs hurt. Old Lady Pagele clomped out, absolutely drenched, in her best cloak, and slapped Regena across the face.

"Little fool," she hissed, clawing at her arm with long painted fingernails and leaving Russel and me in the rain. We watched them walk away. One tall figure and one small one, being pulled along like a living puppet.

We shared a glance.

It was full of things we did not understand. Violence and lovelessness. Liquor and white-colored smoke. Metallic hearts. Dark bedrooms.

It said only,
We won't become our parents.

◇

A long, damp hall, and a row of cloud-white teeth.

Through them slides a voice like bulletproof glass, straight concision.

"Make no mistake. You are a speck of dirt. Any mistake you make will reflect itself onto Kosta, and you will be, at best, expelled from the palace."

Expelled from the palace. Those words squirm mercilessly from Klosswarden's straight-line mouth, bringing all that they imply: starvation in the streets, the drudgery of poverty, the helplessness of an exiled pawn. A doubtless death sentence.

The colony boy nods, taking a gulp — off fear, of shame. Of the future. Of the dull, scrappy colors of his pawn togs.

"Y-yes." The quiver in his voice betrays him, but he straightens it right out. His obedience is in question, and that must never falter. "Kosta is our kingdom. Kosta is our master. Kosta, we must serve."

A short girl with stringy, flame-colored hair interrupts, appearing like a

ghost. "Pawnmaster Klosswarden." Klosswarden shoves the smaller child off
with just one glance, dismissing him with a wave.

"Yes..."

"Don't you think we should be allowed to go outside? Just a little? Just
sometimes?"

The man glares at her, narrowing his eyes until they're feline slits. Where
has such an absurd idea sprouted from? She wants sun.

Instead, he gives her a slow shake of the head.

"I should have known not to plant that boy in your Ward. He's a walking
wound. Bound to infect you with these ludicrous notions of freedom.
Impossible... and then there's you... always disobeying me. Always tarnishing the
name of Kosta with your impudence. You're a thief. And you're a ridiculous,
childish, love-lost little girl," he concludes. "You think that you're better than
colony filth? You think that you're fit for some special privilege? That's out of
the question, and you perfectly well know it. You're here 'till eighteen, then you
take your last shower, and you're gone."

This takes her aback, but she still speaks in a windy whisper. It takes great
courage to speak against sir Klosswarden, with his iron face and his glass
whisper. His bone-thin hands that curl into coiled fists.

"What the hell..." She shakes her head. "Where the hell has your heart
gone to?"

He turns his face to the side, ejects a whisper.

"...Excuse me, little pawn."

"Call me by name!"

"Why should I do that?"

"You're my *father*."

He lets out a humorless laugh. "That's a lie, actually."

"Th-then — "

"Do you know what you are to me?" Klosswarden spits, as if each syllable
is acid on his teeth. "You're a sickly nuisance. You're a fool that was discarded

by your whore mother and left to die in the slums. I was *kind* enough to find you at that wretched orphanage, to bring you here, for work — and even to assign you to tasks fitting of your... " — he glowers down at her — "stature. If you have the insolence to speak in that way again, you will be expelled permanently."

June gulps. "Please don't talk about my mother, sir Klosswarden."

"I'll do as I please."

"You mean to say, sir Klosswarden..." June stares at him with hopeful eyes. "You mean to say my mother is alive?"

Klosswarden raises a hand to her, and she flinches. But he doesn't strike.

"Turn your head down."

She refuses, giving him a smile instead. "Thank you."

He simply glares down at her once more as the walks away.

Remember, she tells herself, *you're nothing.*
She smiles.

CHAPTER XV:
EVERYONE IS ASLEEP

As ALWAYS, EVERYONE is asleep but the little ghost.

The stairs send aches through her legs. They are winding, enormous, seemingly neverending — shouldn't this be easier after dozens, hundreds of wandering nights? Her legs are too short, she thinks, but they refuse to grow.

This is what she loves to do, to wander. There are still parts of the palace she has yet to explore, so many parts of Belvidere to discover beyond the cramped orphanage and the walls of the palace... if she ever does leave. That's doubtful, she knows. *Your last shower, and you're gone.*

You're nothing.

Tonight she travels to the Canopies.

As she reaches the top of the stairs, she is once again astonished by the beauty of the Guest Hall, the hugeness of it. Intricate designs line the carpets, and the walls are made of sturdy bronze, decorated with gold. Velvet veils the ceiling. Dozens of towering doors extend from each end of the Hall, each labeled with a regal, lovely-sounding name: to the left, the women; the right, the men.

June trails down the left side, betting if she's caught, it's safer for a girl to find her. At the front is the room of Queen Merris, long abandoned, and now filled with roses and dust. Then the visiting nobles. Lady Inkola... Lady Odelyn... Lady Marie... Lady Charmaine... Lady Joss... on and on, and at the end, Lady Regena.

Lingering at her door for too long, she is hypnotized by the carving of *Lady Regena Pagele* in the diamond on the door. Tiny triangles, angel wings, and leaping fish have been etched into the gold. Careful not to disturb the door, quiet as a ghost, June traces the shapes with the tip of her fingers. The tiny prize for getting this far, the little luxury of observing. The plaque is so cold she nearly shivers.

She is jolted off the door by a sudden push from within. June barely conceals a gasp when she feels a warm velvet arm wrap itself around my back, drawing her inside — embracing her.

The door slams.

She stands still, pillowed by the warmth of the velvet girl. Regena Pagele. This isn't kindness, at least not alone; pure kindness doesn't shake with sobs. Regena is choking back her tears, feigning composure even with no audience but June. Shivering in her heavy nightrobe. As June cautiously edges my arms around her back, there is a long, still silence. She doesn't understand.

Suddenly Regena crumbles to the floor, taking June down with her. They sit huddled in the dark room that smells of metal and rich cloth. The room full of books she would never understand, golden cupboards and dresses worth more than her life.

Regena tightens her arms around her.

"How'd you know I was here?" June whispers.

"You're *always* here." Her voice is scratched and swollen, even more distorted in its distress than it was on the day of the fallen books. "Wandering around..."

"Wh..." What's the matter? June wants to say. Why are you so sad? But her throat won't go. She can only listen to the fragments of speech that Regena lets out.

"...tell someone." Regena's voice trembles. "I have to... to..."

"What is it?" says June, her arms still hovering slightly over her back.

"Leo," Regena says, her voice choked with pain. The name comes from her stomach, out through her throat, and into the suffocating air. The sound of it chokes her. "He... I didn't want..." She struggles to keep her voice from quivering, and June struggles to understand. "I didn't... want..."

She collapses into June's shoulders. Crying, uncontrollably. Pressing her face into her and falling apart.

"Didn't want...?" June's stomach twists, and she squeezes her tighter. She doesn't want to believe it. In fact, she barely understands it. The words are small, quiet, but they feel like screams. It's real; she know deep in her gut that it's true.

Leo. Prince Leo Lusk — the name repulses her. A name of white suits and golden goblets. She's never dared to look directly at him, she's seen him standing, never next to, always over Lady Regena, with that unvarying look of friction, of... something she can't place a name to; something that consumes; something that wreaks havoc.

That something, whatever it was, put Regena in tears. It made her collapse. June doesn't quite register the facts behind it, but she feels and knows the truth.

June strokes her hair like a sister, shocked and confused — but there is so much love in her voice. "I'm so... I'm so sorry... Reg — I mean, Regena, I'm so sorry. But... but... it's..." She struggles with words. "It's not okay, but, *you'll* be okay... because I'm here, and, and... no one will ever touch you again... I'll make sure of it."

"What can *you* do?" She shakes her head. "I'm sorry, I'm sorry, I'm sorry, I didn't mean it like..."

"It's okay."

Regena hangs onto June, clutches at her small back, and weeps. There is a long field of fertilized silence, with intervals of quiet, stifled sobs. Heavy, salt-soaked whimpers. Then nothing.

There is a soft knock on the door, and it seems to reverberate through the sorrow-filled room. Silence echoes back.

"Who is it?" June blurts.

"It's — it's me!" Russel's voice, blaring and bright, even in a whisper. Full of confusion, and wildly out of place.

Regena nods faintly, then buries her head in June's shoulder again.

"Come in," says June, supporting Regena's weight.

Russel sweeps into the room, princely and cautious. He fixes his eyes on the two girls — a duchess and a pawn, hugging like sisters — and with just an edge of concern in his voice, chirrups:

"Aww, now that's what I like to see!"

Regena pulls her black-stained face up from June's shoulder, upturning her eyebrows. She stares at Russel with stinging, jaguarish eyes, rimmed in black. Melting, leaking.

It is so goddamn frightening to him he nearly jumps, his mind tracing back once more to a lonely eight-year-old girl with mud all over her face, trying not to cry as she picked up rocks and hurled them at the ground, screaming,

"I'm not sad! I'm not sad! I'm not sad!"...

A nine-year-old girl who only wanted to read and never be bothered sat in the corner of the forest, watching him in the trees. A ten-year-old girl shared her last coconut bun. A twelve-year-old watched as the new shipment of pawns came in and said, "What a disgrace this kingdom is." A fourteen-year-old moved in permanently to the Kosta castle, due to the threat of war. And on and on, a whole bank of memories spelling themselves out in her eyes.

"That's... not." His voice is hoarse and pinched with confusion.

"June, do you mind... going?" asks Regena, stapling her composure together. June gives her shoulders one last squeeze and scurries off. She turns to Russel and looks at him for one long second, telling him a story with her eyes — he doesn't quite catch it. Then she leaves.

As June locks the door behind her, her eyes are wet and wider than ever.

Russel kneels.

"What's wrong, Reg?"

"It's nothing," Regena insists, but after a chillingly grave look from Russel, quickly comes undone. She spills out fragments of the truth.

"Leo... he... I... I didn't ~wan...t.... to, he — "

Swiftly, he knows. Russel sees something in Regena's angry, tear-blotched face that leads him to the truth.

His eyes widen, and his design is clear: "I am going to *kill* that worthless bastard son of a bitch." His voice rises through the halls. He's never been this angry, no, never in his life, his fists balling, shaking with too many emotions at once.

"I wish I hadn't told you! I shouldn't've told you!"

She has never heard him yell louder, though his voice is shaking along with his shoulders. "I'll kill him right now, I swear! This goddamn *instant*, Regena!"

"Stop it. Stop this. You're going to make it worse, you idiot!"

Russel is still grasping at the truth, clawing at it like murder. A fire is set in his evergreen eyes, a fire that threatens to chase him down the halls.

He lowers his voice to a a lethal, tremulous whisper.

"He raped you."

"Don't give it a name! Don't make it real..." She folds into herself. "You're only going to make it worse, Russel, I *told* you..."

Russel's eyes are unhinged with rage. His mouth is drawn in a straight, trembling line, no curl in his lips, no calmness in his breath, violently shaking his head. Everything about him is alarmingly humorless. "No, I can't, Regena, I'm going to find that crooked bastard, and bludgeon him so hard he'll be — "

"No! For God's sake, *stop*!"

Stricken by a pang of fear and shame, Russel tries to calm his quickened breathing. He hunches himself over, sinks his face into his palms. His eyes water, swim and shake: he imagines something sickening, and shudders violently. The face of Prince Leo, hovering over his head. Tears start trickling, and he lets them fall. His voice is softer than she's ever heard it. A hush, like the sound of wind, with his fist pressed to his face.

"I can't contain myself... around you. I d-don't know why. I'll leave you be from now on, okay? I'm sorry. I'm sorry. I'm so, so sorry. I'm sorry, I'm sorry, I'm sorry..." The wind in his voice turns to a sharp sob.

Regena squinches up her eyes, toweling the dark tears off her cheeks with the edge of her sleeve, and listens to his sobs fade and fade.

"This isn't *about* you, Russel."

Then they are both quiet as death, kneeling on the floor. Though as she knows, he can't stand silence for too long. So he sobs some more.

Russel bows his head, clutches his quivering face and stares blankly into the floor. The tears roll again. "Don't you understand, Reggie, I..."

"I *don't*. I don't understand you at all. You drive me crazy," she says. "You make me... you make me want to believe in everything again. You're so damn bright. You drive me crazy."

As he lifts his hand so slightly, he wants to embrace her, to never let her go, to wrap her in comfort, to kiss her on the eyes and tell her something that will make the room stop shaking. But he's trembling so hard he can barely sit up, and he can't lay a hand on her, cannot cannot, and Joss still sleeps in his bedroom thinking of him, and he is too scared. He is terrified. Under all that velvet and mental armor, the person in front of him is as fragile as he is. So he sits there with his hand hovering, shaking.

And he's left there, lips trembling with words he can't say.

CHAPTER XVI:
DREAMS THAT DON'T
DIE IN THE MORNING

THE NIGHTMARES ARRIVE again.

We've missed you.

They howl with frozen laughter.

This time, it all starts off suspiciously well. I'm in the forest with Russel and Regena — but we're all full-grown teenagers as we are now, and all in our sleeping clothes. I'm in my ridiculous red palace pajamas, as if I'd never left, looking up at Russel in the tallest Kosta tree.

"Reg! Ez!" Russel hollers. He's wearing light-green sleepers. "Watch this!"

Just as he lunges to jump, a speeding bullet pierces his chest.

His body plummets from the tree. All too fast. He's only a blurred ribbon in the sky, a fallen feather.

He lands in Regena's shaking arms.

He bleeds and convulses. Then the shaking stops.

"*Save him!*" she wails. "*Why couldn't you save him?*"

My expression is frozen to my face, but my hands shake even in dreams. "I... I... Regena, I couldn' — "

"You coward!" Her voice grates me. Her eyes burn and melt and spill over, as if they're not eyes at all, but swelling swamps. "You coward!"

"Regena—"

With frightening speed, her face pales and morphs. Two great dark eyes take the place of her sharp ones, unblinking and accusatory. I'm now staring at the ghostly face of June Kinsel. "You coward..." she breathes, in the sweetest voice in the world. "You coward..." and her body slumps down to the forest grass, only her unmoving back facing my direction.

The nightmare ends with her voice.

Dreams are cruel.

I wake in a violent sweat to see June's turned back, sleeping still. The rise and fall escapes me. All is frozen, all is dark and still. The nightmare has invaded my open eyes.

I extend my hand to touch her back.

"June."

She doesn't stir.

"June, wake up."

Her subtle lilt of breath goes unnoticed. I feel ribs.

"June, wake up!" My voice is sand in my throat as I lift her by the shoulderblades and shake. She feels limp. "Wake up... wake up... please wake up!"

Gone gone gone.

"*June!*"

She wakes up, but her eyes and voice are still full of sleep. Her dark lids flutter and drag, and suddenly the blur in my mind has evaporated.

"The pawn bell hasn't rung," she mumbles.

I clutch her closer and nearly crush her with my frantic, foolish fear, and suddenly my hands are struggling up her back to feel that she's still there.

"June, June..."

Breathing. Of course she is. I'm an idiot. I say nothing, because there's nothing to be said I can put to words. A tear escapes my eye. Pathetic.

Her back is warm. Her hands are warm on my chest.

"Wh—what're you *doing?*" Her arms struggle free from my hold and prop up my face. "The pawn bell hasn't rung... Go back to sleep."

"I'm sorry." The nightmare has shaken all the exhaustion out of me. My head is pounding with it. "I can't."

"Okay... that kinda hurts, y'know."

I realize I'm squeezing so hard, I can feel the bones in her back. *Relax,* I tell myself, but with little success. I can only manage to release my hold on her and calm my breathing.

It suddenly strikes me, the embarrassment of all of it. My holding onto her like she is dying, spilling my nightmares out on her. Her fingers pressing into my cold skin.

"Sorry, June. I really am sorry."

"It's okay. You're not the only one with bad dreams." She gives a smile that dies on her lips.

I let her go, and hope my dreams do the same. She was so warm. I lay on the floor, leaking from the eyes. It is terrifying to realize, that I cannot let go of her completely. That there is something about her that fills me with this terrible, beautiful feeling, like being thrown into the sun and feeling no pain. She's so warm, so warm, and I want to stay near her.

But I can't. She's just another person to lose, to fear losing.

I try to lay my head down and sleep, listen to her breathe on the opposite side of the room, choke down whatever sick, pathetic desires I have.

No.

No.

Yes. God, yes.

Her breathing seems to guard me. Her voice wards off nightmares. Her eyes see right through me, now closed in dreams. I feel sick. I feel like I could turn the wrong way and spill all of me out on the floor.

I don't deserve it.

Maybe. Maybe I should; maybe I *do*. Nothing else is good in this dark, cold place. Nothing else could save me.

◇

Sleep must have found me, because I wake in a sweat.

I am a blur. Made of nothing but sickness and hope.

The pawn hall is eerily quiet in the morning, and the sickness is gnawing at my stomach again. Everyone sits and eats quickly, shuffling over to the inker to receive their duties for the day. The occasional hacking and coughing breaks through the silence in the small room.

Bathroom sanitation. Milkwork. Crates. Upper level polish. Upper level kitchen duty. General service. The ever-rare, ever-coveted *Transportation* on Ibby's wrist.

As I stand under the Inker, the nausea strikes me. I grab at my stomach, feeling like doubling over, fainting, collapsing.

It feels as if my bones have been rearranged, and now they're all crooked and dented and bent.

"Another one with the blight," a girl says, looking at me sadly. She then shuffles off towards the engine room.

"Call Pawnmaster Klosswarden!" Noor shouts, eyes widening at my pathetic state. "Now! *Right now!*"

June scampers out in frantic shock. I catch the sight of her short legs darting away before all goes black.

◇

WARD ONE
ROOM EIGHT

Two dark, blurred circles blink at me out of her pale hovering face. My fever casts a fog over everything, sends tremors through my body at the slightest movement.

I lean to the side and let out a thin stream of vomit. Dark rags on the floor.... a whole mess of them...

"It's worse than I thought. The blight," June whispers. Tears form in her eyes, but she squeezes them back with all her might. "It's hurting you something bad."

"Whassat..." I mumble, my speech slurring with fever.

She reaches out to feel my head, then snatches her hand back. "You're... you're like a stove."

"Whyrrrn't you woooorkiiiinnng Juuuune," I drawl, half-delirious.

She sighs. "Sir Klosswarden excused me, just this once."

"Hoow'd I ged 'eeere..."

"You're not as heavy as I thought," she says, pressing a wet cloth to my face, which I realize is a torn-off piece of her sleeve. In my dazed state, the thought of her dragging me to the Ward is hilarious. I find myself laughing on the cold floor, my head still throbbing and burning.

"Feeeeeels niiice," I slur out.

"Stop talking."

"Howd'ja get the water?"

"Magic."

"Am... I gonna diiiiiee..."

I feel that strong voice in my weak stomach.

"You... will *not*... die."

Her blurry eyes are narrowed intensely. She swipes the cloth against my forehead once more, and reaches for a paper cup. Water and slowly dissolving pills.

"Drink this," she orders into the space between our faces.

Suddenly, I hear eight quick raps to the door.

"Come in!" June yelps, drawing her face back.

There stands none other than Duchess Regena Pagele, wearing a white hygiene mask, cloaked like a pawn, and carrying a white porcelain mug.

June hops up. "Lady Regena!"

Regena kneels over me. "Sip, sick boy." Her face blurs in and out of focus... eyes that could be made out of caramel... eyes I've seen before. "This coffee could wake the dead." I feel a hot mug pressing to my lips. "Also, this medicine I nicked from the infirmary," she adds with a smirk.

"M'I dreeeeeaming or...."

"No, but you passed out, it seems. Sip. Turns out you have the blight. Bad. Bad bad bad. Not contagious, though, as far as I know... *Sip.*"

I tilt my head as best as I can and sip from the cup. The taste of coffee is thick and rich and unfamiliar.

"Aam I deeeead..."

"No, but you sound like a bloody demon. You're not going to *die,*" she huffs. Then a strange smile spreads on her face. "Ezra Wickwolf."

"Thaaaaassmeeeeee."

"This poor little ragamuffin thought she had to take care of you all alone," Regena laughs, glancing at June's knotted face.

"Wheeere's Russsellll..."

"*Russel?*" She narrows her eyes. "That idiot?"

"I neeeeed to juuump... offa th'treeeeee wittthhh'mm..." All I can think of is that tree. That flying boy. With sky-colored wings sprouting from his back. "I miiiisssss hiiiim sooo muuhuhuch..."

"Won't that be nice to tell him when you're all better!"

"The blight kills people, Regena," is June's urgent whisper.

"Not him, he's strong," she insists, grabbing June by the arms.

"Nooo 'm noooooot..." I'm not strong. I'm delusional and weak and my bones feel soft and hot. I start to laugh, closing my eyes to the confusing sights that swirl before me. A pawn and a duchess in Ward One, Room Eight, nursing me like a sick baby animal. Too many colors. My vision stays dark, dark, black and dark — beautiful emptiness. The pulse of my fever aches in my temples, the nausea stirring in my stomach, mingled with June's voice:

"Yes you are."

◇

I lay on the cold ground – I know it must be cold, somewhere inside me, but it feels hot. Churning, melting.

Am I going to die at this moment? Is this my end?

The thought rolls through my stuporous head again and again, with each passing moment that I don't die.

I haven't been close to death before, but I've always felt it, ever since that day. The world closing in on me. My bones trying to break through my skin. The Regicide bullet in my own throat — they've become parts of me, unwanted visitors.

I haven't given much thought to heaven and hell until now. Is hell cold, like Russel said? Or does it burn? Is it lonely, or would the devil be there to keep you company?

I try to imagine the face of the devil, but all I can picture is a Regicide mask. The two halves, gray and white, pierce me to the ground with fear. One sharp black X in the place of an eye. Another. The cruel, curving slant of the mask is all I can see, never the face behind it.

Who does that mask belong to?

Is my father is in heaven or hell, or just buried under the earth, his heart dead forever, his eyes closed to the world?

Is heaven a bed of pearls? Would it welcome me or turn me in the opposite direction? Would the angels sing their song, and would it sound like her voice? Would I be safe from the Regicides, pawnship, and sadness? That kind of world sounds like heaven to me.

I'd like to live in that world, I think at last. But such a place can't exist.

The world is ruined for good. The land can't unsink itself so much as the sea can unswallow it.

It's not our fault. We're only trying to destroy the earth before it destroys us. Because the earth can live on without us, but we can't survive without its soil to stand on.

I know. I know. But if another end-all wave were to come now to our small shaky island, this solitary piece of earth, we'd run like overeager children to the last safe corner until there were no safe corners left. We'd run through sickness and heartbreak and death and fight until there's nothing left for the sea to swallow. That's what we're bound to do. Because we'll always believe in safe corners. And we'll always believe in "we."

 My eyes flicker shut again, sending my thoughts in a scatter.

The colors start to speak to me. A bright red. The lightest, clearest blue I can imagine, pierced by a single ray of sun.

Come, it says, in a voice that melts my worry.

Dream with me.

The sky clears. I can breathe again, feel myself against the wind.

Soon we are floating hundreds of feet in the air, the sky cornflower-blue, the sun blindingly white. The clouds roll like paint strokes.

June floats too. Her pawn uniform is gone, replaced by a sky-colored dress that catches the light of the heatless sun. I can feel our clashing heartbeats melting together, distance disappearing, rapidly synchronized, rushing like water.

We are clumsy trapeze artists. Her legs extend straight behind her, her hair floating in midair, seeming to skydive, stomach-first, towards the neverending earth below. We are parallel — perfectly side by side, fingers touching. The air rushes between us, around us, above us, inside of us and everywhere. The sun sways bulbously, and June's eyes are fixed in an infinite laugh.

The ground reels in a mist, surging up at our flying bodies until it disappears, evaporating into the whiskery rug of the Wickwolf palace. Our heartbeats clash on the floor of the palace, soaking through the fabrics of the rug, till we're not even people, but liquid, melting.

Our eyes melt together.

Then hers melt away.

Her smiling laugh turns to a tremble. A quiver strikes her chin.

Eyes like paint, spilling, spilling, spilling.

Eyes like black holes.

Holes in her head.

The paint leaks from her throat and the sockets of her eyes.

Her hair smokes like a warm bullet. A crown of fire.

I look down at my quaking hands to find they're gray and pale as death, but for the red and blue of my pumping, paintlike blood. Veins like spiderwebs, veins like tunnels. My fingers are on the trigger of a hot black gun. Paint runs out of the muzzle. The mouth of the gun vomits and everything disappears.

Her face evaporates into the unsure sky.

I'm lost in limbo.

I see scores of trumpets, dozens of wild, screeching violins, announcing my arrival. Thousands of blurred faces waving in salute to the King. And June. Wearing a dress of cobwebs and color and wind. I'm moving toward her. Forward, forward. Our lips almost touch. Are we both dead? I don't feel dead. I feel like I am walking into the surface of the sun, and I feel no pain. At first she is a firework, a spark of light, an array of bursting color. Then she is a shadow, a mere blur, fading into nothing.

My lips start to move, my voice escaping me, but disjointed and unclear. I have no doubt in my mind that I have died of blight, been picked up by the fingers of God, and been placed in that uncertain place between heaven and hell.

Of course, when I have no doubts about something, I'm always wrong.

◇

So I lay with my dead-eyed face thrown to the side, blinded by an invisible, impossible light, my eyes sucking the color from my surroundings.

There's only the blinding whiteness, and I'm sure this is the end.

But the colors spill back into my eyes. Gray walls. Gray floor. Brown hair. Flame-colored hair. All slowly inching back, slowly splattering.

When I awake all I can think of is June. The dream that became a nightmare of paint and blood, my heart that moved on its own. I look at her with eyes half-open. There is a terrible throbbing pain in my stomach, itching up my ribs, threatening to travel up my throat, to work its way into my lungs.

The same June of my dreams is staring down on me with a look of plain shock. No paint spills from her eyes. Her words are fuzzy in my head, vibrating through my ears like they're made of cotton. "What... did you say?"

"Iiii dooonnnnnnooooooooh..." I laugh, overcome with fever, still lost in dreams. "Whaaat *diiiid* I saay..."

"You said..." She bites her lip, still staring intensely at my feverish face. "It's not important."

I can still feel the trigger on my fingers.
And June's sky-soaked fingertips.

I dare to open my ironweight eyes.

I'm half-asleep and quite dazed, yet I hear the faint sound of Regena reading to June — a fantastical tale — something about oceans and stars and wanderers. She sweeps her hand across the pages. June leans in close to examine the paper, deciphering each unfamiliar word.

"You know how to read, don't you?"

"A lit'l bit — yes," says June in an uncomfortable voice. "Learnt how, but — uh — not quite... What's that word there?"

"Wanderer. It's the title of the book, too — *The Wanderer.*"

"Oh... well, y'see, we're not really allowed to read or write or anything down here, so — "

"I'll help you," says Regena. "You know what a wanderer is?"

"It's me," she says simply.

"So you're like him."

As Regena reads every bit of the tale in a clear, soft voice, June is silent as a silhouette.

CHAPTER XVII:
THE WANDERER

The Wanderer
Chapter 1: The Lighthouse Ghost

THE WANDERER COLLECTED stars and seashells that had dropped into the ocean. Although he had so many things, he couldn't help but feel sad, because he had no one to share them with. He had many clothes, but no one to admire them. He had sheets of velvet, but he always slept alone. So he wandered by the seashore, hoping to find someone to talk to.

The trouble was, the wanderer couldn't remember a single thing. His wandering had mixed up the memories in his head, and all he could remember was waking up by the shore in a strange land of sea.

In the distance, there was a storm still whispering itself away. The wanderer saw, suddenly in the moonlight, a magnificent lighthouse beaming through the stars.

Light, he thought in his exquisite loneliness. That must mean someone is in there.

Quickly, he swam towards the lighthouse. At the very least, he remembered how to swim. The building was ominous in the fading light of the sky, with great white waves clawing at its sides.

He opened the door.

What he saw sent a shiver down his spine.

There was a ghost there, with trailing red hair and eyes the color of a seastorm. Her phantom song had lured him to the lighthouse. Yet her eyes showed no ill will; they only spun with a long, slow waltz that never ended. They danced with a sadness he saw mirrored in his own.

The ghost was silent.

"What's your name?" asked the wanderer.

She couldn't remember it, and slowly shook her ghostly head.

The storm still breathed in the distance.

"You don't have a name?"

"I don't remember it, I don't remember it..."

"The wanderer isn't scared of her?" June interrupts.

"He's just an idiot," is Regena's quick reply. "Continuing — "

"Perhaps I never had a name."

"Or perhaps it was stolen from you?" asked the wanderer.

"See, he's not stupid," says June, leaning over and into the book.

"Shh. Listen."

"The lighthouse door has been locked all these years, hasn't it?" the wanderer said.

Her reply was cautious and slow; a ghostly nod of the head. "Yes."

He reached for her hand, and felt only a storm of air grasping back. A shivering presence and a steaming frost. Her hand flickered. He reached for it again, and couldn't hold on. Her fingers were mist. Her palms were moonlight.

Another question from the wanderer, who seemed to become the wonderer.

"Why are you trapped in here?"

Another floating silence from the ghost.

"I was left here."

"You can't leave this place?"

"I have nowhere else to go," she replied, lowering her faraway gaze to the floor of the lighthouse. Her eyes stared through the cracking wood, into the ocean floor.

"I'll let you go."

With that, the wanderer cracked open the escape door and the stormy wind rushed on his bare face.

The girl turned to steam and blew away. A fluttering ghost.

Everything she was disappeared. Her floating legs became wisps of smoke and whisked themselves into the storm; her stomach; her elbows and arms; her shoulders; then finally, that sweeping hair. Her lips formed a last word, perhaps goodbye, perhaps thank you, but they disappeared too.

The wanderer was alone again, but he continued his journey.

"I don't like this story," June breaks in, flipping the pages over in rejection.

"Why?"

"The ghost died again," she says, looking Regena honestly in the face and trying to articulate her floating thoughts. "She was supposed to stay. Doesn't the writer know anything? How can you become more of a ghost? How could she disappear like that? She wasn't supposed to. Now he's even more alone."

"The story can't go the way you want."

"It can if you write your own. Where ghosts stay ghosts."

The blight lessens as the days drag on, my pulse slowing, my fever cooling. The royals are certainly on a wild goose chase for Regena, who has been running back and forth between the Uppers and the pawn quarters, but they find no one. Who would guess she's been hidden in Ward One?

June shakes her head in pure confusion when Regena curls up on the floor to sleep.

"You don't want to sleep upstairs?"

Regena ignores the question. "It's hard as rocks down here, goddamnit," I hear her groan. "How do you live like this?"

"It's not that bad, really." I see two small slippered feet patter across the floor. A cold hand on my head, and an enormous sigh of relief.

"He's gotten much better," she tells Regena, who's huddled uncomfortably on the ground. Her voice breaks a little. "He's okay. Wick's okay."

"Calm down, will you?" Regena reaches to pat her on the back. "And he's Ezra."

CHAPTER XVIII:
THE BLIND WAR

"I WAS AIMING for his heart."

"Then why did it hit him in the goddamn stomach?"

Nox fumes, quietly.

"What can I say, the kid jumped like a rabbit," said Spindel. "As if he was playin' hopscotch. Playin' hopscotch with his face a bloody mess. You sure tried, though. You did good, girl. You got *one*."

She fixes her eyes on his. "Is this a game to you?"

This quiets him a bit. He still smirks – the misfired bullet is the most hysterical thing in the world to him.

"Isn't it, though. You capture the king, and you win. So you'll have to try a bit harder, girl." He turns and pats her on the back, and in one quick motion, she has her gun to his large forehead. One bullet clicked into the chamber.

"Woah, woah – I'm sorry, Nox. Sorry as hell. No need to polish me off."

She holds her gun steady for a moment more, and breathes, slow and mocking, into his face. Back in the scabbard.

She smiles like a victorious child.

"I don't care enough to kill you."

Two large white beds against a white wall, clear tubes streaming from all corners. Dark blue liquid, pale yellow liquid, bandages stained with blood. Green eyes closed in sleep. Blue eyes open, seeing nothing.

The medic takes his hand to two hollow eyes, and closes them forever.

He wheels around on flat white shoes and looks at Regena, who appears like a painted statue, frozen and hovering over Russel's sleeping body.

"Prince Kosta will live. He is still recuperating, but he's fit to be returned to his room for some rest, as long as he is given proper supervision and medicine."

"I'll carry him, then."

"Excuse me, Lady Regena – that's pawn's work."

"I don't care. Let me do it."

"It's not right... you don't know how to properly—"

"No, actually, I do know, sir."

Regena pays no attention to the medic's sputtering protests. She takes the limp, heavy body in her arms and starts up the stairs. Russel is completely silent and perfectly still – in a full, drowning sleep, deeply medicated. She carries him along with his medicine, packed in tubes. Each step is agony, and she silently hopes that he'll stay unconscious, that he'll sleep in peace. That no more blood will spill, no tears from his eyes.

The hall is dimly lit. His room is the first on the mens' side, the most extravagant – gold lining his door, his plaque carved with more care, a never-dying light seeping out from inside, into the gloom of the night. The door doesn't make a sound.

An unfamiliar room, but one that is obviously his. The whole room reflects fluorescent green and yellow light, filled with leafy artificial flowers, flowers that never wither. Thin golden pillars rise from the floor, lined with thick, painted vines. The four-poster bed stands at the other side, the canopy falling in translucent golden waves. Regena carefully places him on the end of the bed, pulls a loose blanket over him, so he might be carelessly sleeping. She brushes a lock of curly hair away from his eyes.

You idiot.

You didn't do me any favors.

She hears a stifled gasp from outside.

Lady Joss – her pale hair illuminated, her eyes startled, her white hand coiled around the half-opened door. She stands in a sheer, ribbonned excuse for a nightgown, legs trembling.

"Go," says Regena, but it comes out as a pinched, choking sound. Her voice breaks, and Joss stands still for a moment.

"*Leave!*"

Joss is frozen to the spot. Then, with a shuddering breath, she runs back to her own dark room.

Tonight, the stars hang themselves like nightmares from the sleepy, stringy moon. They sink into the unseen sky. Everything is at peace in the gutters, in the Great Hall, in the guest rooms, in the royal bedrooms. Dark and quiet. Silently bleeding, silently sleeping into the morning.

In the morning, the kingdom wakes up dead.

The streets are silent. The newspapers don't arrive.

Between the walls of the palace, the prince sits in the light of his room, completely alone. A score of golden pillars are raised around him. Russel heads to the bathroom, his feet failing him. He falls, only once, struggles to raise himself from the cushioned floor. He opens the extravagant cupboard, with its beautiful assortments. Gels. Sleeping pills. Mascara that Joss used to keep. He takes a handful of gelcaps as usual, and swallows them whole.

His stomach throbs. One bullet. Five pills.

Alive.

Snow. There was a cushiony blanket of snow over the Green Garden... an unnaturally red puddle. A long stream of blood, only growing larger... A low moan from the ground – "Is this the end...?" Another shot, from further away... a piercing pain. A piercing, distant pain... warmth. Warmth. Her voice. The sharp taste of the infirmary. Clear liquid... his bed again. The folds of her purple dress against his beside. Her hand. Her hand.

Alive.

If I had jumped a little lower...

A thought he would never finish.

◇

The low-hanging chandelier threatens to shake, the discarded goblets toppled over and leaking dark wine.

The playing cards from earlier in the day still sit on the Dining Hall table, but the game is gone. King Lusk seethes, his hands pressed into the porcelain, his face staring blankly, blazingly down.

"The Regicides have killed him. They have *killed* my *son*."

His huge fists grind against the porcelain table. His massive shoulders curl.

"A plot — a plot by *Kosta!*"

The words rebound off the walls. Gasps echo all around.

Rage escalates, more and more and more.

"*KOSTA!*"

Another day added to the mourning toll.   Another prince by the Regicides. Black-printed headlines, screaming PRINCE LUSK DEAD. WAR BETWEEN ALLIES. The sick murmuring of the radio.

Outside the wall of the castle, on the streets made of lesser stones, the chaos only continues. Peasants drudge down the streets. A wrinkled old man mutters: "Seems unfit to wage war on a kingdom without a king."

Several whip around and raise their eyebrows.

Fear bites down into the features of every man and woman, confusion crossing the faces of children. There is no crying, no screaming, just a thick, silent chaos like a blanket, smothering all sound.

The Kingdom without a King is in similar disarray. In the Kosta palace, there are hushed whispers, muffled exclamations. All of war.

"War."

War ~war ~war ~war. It's the only word on anyone's lips. It overwhelms the great yellow hall, turning its portraits into mockery, its pillars into farce. The windows are bolted closed, but an imaginary wind sweeps over everything.

"A declaration?" Joss whispers, her unpainted eyes filling with fear. Her hair is tousled, her nightgown is wind-whipped, and without her velvet gloves and tight-laced corset, she looks strangely like a sad little girl.

"Yes," replies Klosswarden.

"L-lusk and Kosta? Klosswarden!" She grips at his robe. "Tell me!"

Klosswarden detaches her hand from his side. "Yes, madame, yes," he mutters, his voice lost to the wind. Then he rushes off in silent frenzy, the swish of his cape like a fleeing bird.

Joss lets her hand fall. Her face is still as she reaches into the lining of her nightdress for a gelcap.

She gulps and drowns in the sweet medicated indifference. She is welcomed to a white-cloud world, with nothing but sleep.

Leo is dead, and war is alive once again.

In every kingdom, every quarter, academy, university, nursery, pub, shack, bar, brothel in Belvidere, his name is an echo. An echo and nothing more.

His last words were heard by no one. But maybe, as usual, he didn't say anything at all.

I still remember when he'd sit in the corner of the room at summer galas, hulking and ridiculous. Even when he was surrounded by duchesses, there was an emptiness in his eyes, a blankness to his smile. At the core of it, he was a sad, lonely man who filled his vacant heart with liquor, who couldn't look beyond himself. I hate him, I *hate* him, but I can't help but feel the slightest bit sorry for him.

Black dresses again.

The duchesses unleash a wild chatter upon the walls as they make their last leave from the palace. It's as if the war to them is another spectacular event, another lovely carriage ride. I notice, panic filling my head, that Russel is absent from the scene. The gossip continues without him.

"Put a trigger to Russel, Leo did."

"Let it go on him, too."

"Beat him senseless, I hear. He's bruised up badly... he was in the infirmary for days."

"And he's still *alive?*"

"One of them had to be."

There are so many questions.

How did Russel end up in a duel with Leo Lusk? What did Russel do to deserve it — or rather, why did Leo think Russel deserved it?

But you can't ask a corpse about his motives. He wouldn't even tell them alive, anyway.

In actual, unvarnished truth — who killed Leo? Behind the painted faces and alarmed scraps of gossip, is there anything left to believe?

"Russel did *not* kill him," I tell June, trembling in the dark of Ward One,

Room Eight. With the declaration of war and the darkening skies, it has become more and more like a prison cell for the both of us. "He would never kill anyone. He would never even *hurt* anyone..."

"I know." She shakes the cold out of her head. "I know."

"He would never hurt anyone, June... I mean it..."

"I know."

"It's the Regicides, rearing their ugly goddamn head again." The words are insufficient and useless. No one will listen to me, and I'll change nothing.

"I know."

"That's all you're gonna say, huh?"

June shakes her head, then stands herself up. "Yes! That's all I *can* say! That's all I have the *right* to say!" She balls her hands into fists and pounds on the wall, stomps her feet into the cold ground, skitters around the room in a frantic fit. Her nails dig into the stone with pure anger. Everything is in her eyes: I know that look. She wants these walls to collapse; we both do. Her breath is heavy, her energy quickly draining. "You can't make people into saints! He did his share of bruising... Russel was bound to – just like *anyone* else... Leo – he... Russel had *reason* to... if–" She heaves breath into the wall.

"Hey, don't tire yourself out—"

"Oh, *shut up!*" I'm shocked – not by her words, but her voice. She uses a tone of disgust usually reserved for talking about cleaning up Leo Lusk's vomit.

"Please, you need to sleep—"

"What do you care?!" Her feet are still stomping relentlessly on the ground, her fists tightened against the wall. Her voice breaks. "You know, I'm getting tired of it! You drive me mad... always, like you're drowning, you're drowning and I can't for the life of me *save* you!"

"You've already—"

"I can't do a thing about it, I really can't, so don't lean on me!"

"It's just, I–"

Her teeth clash. Her anger makes her eyes huge. "You *what*, huh? Feel sorry for me? For yourself? For *all* of us?"

"I like you."

She freezes. Everything goes quiet, too quiet, as if all the sound has been sucked from the stones. Her voice is a ghost against the wall. "You sure?"

"Yeah." It's a watered-down word. Like.

June starts to laugh, a nervous collection of breaths, then turns to me. "Don't make fun of me. What d'you mean?"

"I don't really have the words for it."

She stares at me for what seems like a long expanse of time. Four seconds, maybe. "Uh... m... th-that's... if that's all you'll say." She sighs. "Tell me everything'll be fine, after all."

"It will, it will. Everything will be fine."

"You're a terrible liar, you know that? You can see it in your *eyes*. They're the most honest eyes I've ever seen. And those are not eyes that say everything will be okay. They're just *not*."

Without thinking, I take hold of her by the curve of the elbow and pull her in. I touch her back, her shoulders, her neck, gathering her to me. This time, she immediately buries herself into my shirt. "I'm not lying."

She's right. I was drowning. I was weighed down by a thousand bricks, and drowning along with them. But I've gotten a grip of the shore. The water's still washing in, but it's not such a bad feeling when I'm not alone.

"I just don't know what to do. I don't," she whispers, every ounce of anger gone from her voice. "Everything's wrong, and I'm so tired."

"Then sleep."

"You're shaking again," she says, grabbing my wrists, soft and fierce. "Stop it."

"Mm."

"We'll get through this rotten mess," she says, reading my face and apparently finding no story printed there. "You're right. You are."

"Mhm."

In that moment, I know I have misjudged her. She is not a little ghost or imp or pawn, or any of the tired thoughts I'd attached to her. In her wide eyes is malice and indignation – an impossible dream – and in her small arms a hidden strength.

I don't mind if she twists my bones with it. I don't mind if she hurts me.

June flicks the lantern off, though I hadn't noticed it was on in the first place. The dark is all around us, a beautiful, numbing blindness.

Everything is black. There's nothing, everything to fear. I'm free from harm, where no one can see me. Suddenly I feel so warm and safe, I barely want to sleep. Then I remember who I am.

The scene is red and white in my mind, stains in the snow. All I can know I have collected from scraps of gossip from the nobility. The soft, familiar murmuring of the radio.

I didn't see the blood, only the bruises on his face.

The whispers of the Kosta duchesses tell me: "*She* was the one to see him." I don't have to think twice about who *she* is.

"Miss Regena..."

Regena saw him in the back corner of the palace, near the frozen-over Green Garden, crouching, clutching his face with one hand and his stomach with the other. Shuddering. She ran up to him, I suppose, and... she must have been so scared.

She saw him with a red-smeared jaw, some fresh blue bruises, blood streaming from his nostrils and mouth. A bullet still lodged in his torso.

"What the hell happened?"

"Nothing..."

"*Nothing?* Blood is seeping out of you!"

He turned his face aside and spat blood at the ground. "Okay — don't look at me like that, Reg — I got in a... a duel... with Leo... ungh."

"Idiot! You idiot!" She grabbed Russel and embraced him tightly, trying to soothe him, but she kept saying "idiot" and digging her fingers into his back. Blood pooled on the floor.

"S'okay. I wanted him to hit me. I wanted him to wreck my beautiful face." He smiled like a dying lunatic, sending a trickle of blood down her shirt.

"Russel," she said, and tightened her grip on him. "Infirmary." She sobbed quietly into the bruise on his neck.

"You're hurting me."

A trail of blood snaked its way down his chin, and onto his throat, and suddenly, so suddenly, he collapsed — toppled like a playing card into Regena.

She hauled him into the castle with frantic tenderness, anger filling her throat. The back door was heavy, Russel was heavy, and blood was still spilling from his half-conscious mouth.

"I have to leave, Regena," he coughed out, vomiting blood and words. His voice was broken into pieces, pouring onto the floor.

"No, you don't."

"Yes, I do, I have to leave..." He slumped his head against her shoulder and his eyes went sad and blank.

A helpless little boy. They were seven and eight again. Him diving from trees, her scoffingly watching, wishing. He looked at her, and this time she did not slap away his closeness.

She hoisted him up by the arms, and the words came spilling out, desperate and true. "Not without me. Please, not without me."

Not without me.

He touched her face with a blood-smeared hand and watched the soft, injured expression that rested there.

The tourniquets, the heavy dosage, the clear blue liquids. The palace medics could never heal him like those three words.

He replied with three more, quick and soft and gurgled with blood:

"I love you."

Truth shone from each word. A glorious declaration. A foolish spasm of the heart. But they got caught in his throat, drowned by the blood in his teeth and the pain in his stomach, and he fell to a heavy, aching silence.

CHAPTER XIX:
THE SUN THIEF

I WAKE TO an empty room, no cloak bundled on the floor. Only a note, torn off from a scrap of a book.

Russel is ok.

That youd wanna no.

come to the hall after the day is over

whare you'd expect me to be.

trust me,

if you want.

June.

◇

Pawnmaster Klosswarden enters the hall, a deadly expression on his white, skeletal face. His mouth is an unwavering line, and his hands are set neatly behind his back.

"I've been sent to alert you of orders from Duke Calixte Conquin." A tombstone of a stare. "The war against Lusk requires a large militia. He has declared a pawn purge. All pawns of any age will be sent into the troops, male or female. You will be delivered to the underground of Victoria, Kosta tomorrow night. Goodbye and good day."

Good day, says the man sending us to slaughter.

The pawns are frozen.

They meet their certain death with compliance, and head to the inker once more. There is only silence now, from Ibby, from Noor, from everyone.

June is absent from the table this morning.

Suddenly, Noor breaks out crying, though trying to stifle it.

"H-hey, get up," Ibby whispers, picking him up by the arms.

I head down the hall, feeling an all-too familiar tremble in my legs, contemplating how to escape. It has to be tonight. It's selfish, but I never want to hear another gun fire in my life, and I certainly don't want to watch anyone else die...

And there is Klosswarden, looking like a reaper, his eyes hollow under the shadows of the pawn quarter. The human manifestation of my panic. It's everything I can do not to attack him.

"Can't you do anything about this?" I whisper, and hear my small, useless echo through the hall.

"Listen..." Klosswarden says, expressionless as ever. "Listen to me. You have no duty to save these people. None. It is a delusion. You are just a child, and I'll treat you no differently. Your birth does not make you a hero." His voice starts to boil. "Nothing will – nothing! There are no villains and no heroes. There is only one, and it breathes through our lungs. It is an ancient disease..."

"Oh, don't give me your dross," I spit. My voice is dangerously loud in this musty old dungeon, but he's making me physically sick at this point. "There are villains! And you are one of them!"

He gives a low, creaking laugh.

"Let me remind you who orchestrated your rescue."

"So can't you... save me again? And – and *please*, if you can't help me, make sure that the rest –"

"I can't move *mountains*, boy." Klosswarden shies from my glare. "I can only do what my duty dictates. But remember..." Can't he finish a damn thought? He reaches out to touch my shoulder, but I flinch away.

"Your duty dictates nothing," I say. "The King is dead."

He smiles again. "There are millions of bodies buried under the oceans and no one mourns for them. You spend four fine years of your life mourning one soul to make up for it."

"I wasn't mourning one soul," I say. "I was mourning a kindgom."

My kingdom of four people. My mother, Emelin, my tutor, and the man in the streets. No. His children. His family. His family in the gutters. He smoked into a sky made of ash. He shook his bald head at me, as if I could grow a thousand times my size, hang over the island, and break the fall of bombs.

You're despicable.

Klosswarden stares into my eyes like a threat, like a promise. "Remember, boy. Remember who the hell you *are*. You're not entirely helpless."

With this, he walks into the nothingness to which he belongs.

They corridor is too long, and his legs ache. The wings on his feet won't fly.

Where is Leo? Dead. Not laughing in the corridor any longer. Not stuffing himself with food and liquor. *Ashes. Gone. Buried. Shouldn't I be happier?* No. His mouth jerks to one side. *I am going to kill that worthless bastard son of a bitch.* He was so damn proud of himself. *Shouldn't I be satisifed, now?*

No. It's wrong to be happy. It's wrong to feel anything.

A pale head of vanilla-blonde hair, looped into three buns. A tightly-knotted corset. Eyes that blame and accuse and refuse to laugh along with him. It's the last he will see of her.

"Where do you think you're going?" Joss forces a smile, gripping Russel by the sleeve, barely glancing at his exhausted face. She just stares at the arrangement of flowers that he knocked down when stumbling in.

"Anywhere." He takes her hand and weakly detaches it from his shaking arm. "Nowhere? Everywhere? I'm sorry."

"You're not making sense." Her face is terrified. She just now notices the heavy bandages across his stomach, the gauze and the dressings on his cheeks. "What happened to you? Truly?"

"You must've heard by now. Leo taught me a lesson," Russel mutters, "as he called it. Don't think I learned anything, though, except that I'm a damned fool." He makes his way towards the door, dragging himself along.

She catches him by the arm.

"Don't do that. Don't *leave*, Russel."

"I'm sorry." He places a bruised hand on her cheekbone, and she gives a delicate, disgusted flinch. "This is the end."

"Please," she whispers.

"I really do care for you, you know." He tries to smile, and runs a hand over her face again. "Even if—"

"Please," she blurts, training her eyes at the floor. "don't finish that sentence."

Please don't let me haunt your dreams when I die, he thinks deliriously. In truth, though, hers are not dreams composed of sinking boats and salt-choked hopes. Hers are dreams where nobody dies.

Don't look to me with that battered, broken face. Don't show me your demise.

The poor, miserable creature, once strong and fast, now wrapped in bandages and weakened by bullets. She won't allow him to tarnish her precious life with blood and sadness; she will sweep him under the velvet rug – she will brush him off like dirt.

Even if...

Even if I never did get around to loving you.

◇

Near the showers, there is a sudden rush of pawns, all walking quietly off for what could be their final four hours of sleep. June stands among the crowd, completely still, with a lantern in hand. Right where she said she'd be.

There is the clacking of a dozen doors. Suddenly, the pawn corridors are empty as death, all except for June and me in our hooded cloaks.

"I'm setting off," she declares. "I'm leaving."

Something tugs at my heart. "No."

"This war... all the wars — another one, another one, it's never going to end, is it?" The quiver in her voice tells me she doesn't want to believe it, but must. "I refuse to go fight. I'm leaving. I can't take this place. Goddamnit, I can't, I can't take this. I don't care if it makes me a criminal, I gotta— "

"How can you leave them like that?"

"Leave who?"

"Ibby and Noor and... all of the others..." It's rather awful, I realize, that I can't name a single pawn other than those two. They don't dare open their mouths. They are the same to me as they are to the royals and aristocrats — nameless faces, virtually invisible, existing only to serve. Nonetheless, they matter. "How can you leave them?"

"Quite easily, Wick, I have no friend here but you."

"So you'll leave me behind, too?"

"I..." June lowers her face to the ground, sending the white flickering of the lantern into her eyes.

"You can't...." I feel the desperation edging its way into my voice. "...Break me in half, June, I—"

Before I know it, the light's gone from view and she's on her tiptoes with her chin tipped up. Her hand tugs on the neck of my robe, and her mouth just hits me on the lower lip, but it's gone before I can lean in.

"Sorry," she mutters. But I can't respond. I can't even move. It takes me a moment before I realize she just kissed me.

"I–"

"Please..." she raises her head. "Please come with me."

My hands are bleeding again.

I imagine the sky is dim by now. I imagine the sickness growing in every pawn's heart. I don't need to imagine Noor, shuddering on the ground, stooped in the exact spot where I first found June.

"Noor."

He looks up, unabashedly wiping his face. "Wick."

I look around, but there's no one. Nothing but silence.

"Go to the Pipes. Down in the oubliette – trust me. There's no monsters down there or anything. *Trust me.* Dig a hole in the wall, and run. Run to the safest place you can find. Tell the others."

His face is startled, but he nods.

"Meet me there."

The only light to be found is the kerosone lantern shaking slightly in June's small hand. In her other hand she holds a coarsely-threaded sack of palace loot and leftover goods from One-Eight.

"How do you do it?"

"Do what?"

"Your thieving."

"Don't you know I'm a little ghost?" She smiles vaguely.

No one else. Not Noor, not Ibby. No slippered feet in the dirt, no more dull-glowing kersone lanterns.

From the darkness comes a third voice.

"It's too damn cold down here."

I watch as the light from June's lantern spills onto a familiar face. Tiger eyes. A small sneer. All wrapped up in a purple scarf.

"*Regena?*"

She smiles. "Obviously."

"You— how did you even know—"

A new figure sprints up to the group, his coppery curls leaping, his teeth chattering, and I have to blink twice before registering it – it's him. Russel. In all his glory. Well, most of it. He clutches his stomach, wincing with dull pain. It seems that he doesn't ignore the ache in his gut; he just forgets it's even there at all.

Still, his face seems set aflame with something — joy? I don't know. An idea, a thought is forming; it swells in his eyes.

When he catches sight of my face, he throws his arms around me — a real labor in his current state. His stomach is still vibrating, writhing with the impact of Leo's bullet. But he nearly knocks me to the floor.

"Ezra!" he says, wincing a bit. "Ezra, it's you!"

"Hey – it's great to see you, too."

"It's you, oh my god, it really is! You're here again!" At this point he's started to shake and cry like a child. He smells like my most beautiful memory. He smells like pine needles and shampoo and the salt of the Kosta shore.

"Take it easy." Some extremely hypocritical advice coming from me, who has mastered the art of anxiety.

"How can he do *that?*" It's Regena's voice this time, hushed, unsmiling. She stares at me, evaluating and questioning, tossing aside childhood joy. "He just got shot and beaten, and we'll probably all get caught and *killed* before the night is done."

Eternally optimistic Regena.

"No we won't," says Russel, his eyes bruised and brighter than ever in the dark. "Come on, this can't be all bad."

"Yes it can."

"Nothing's ever *all* bad."

June inhales deeply, sucking in the stale air. "Should I leave a note for Klosswarden?"

"Don't," I tell her. "We've got to leave nothing behind. Nothing at all."

We don't, too. The scars stay with us.

"We'll go through the Pipes, right?" Russel asks, plunging a metal spade through the wall and digging it around. He cringes with each jab, the exertion shooting pain through his day-old duel wounds.

I watch him spasm. "Are you sure you should dig, Russ?"

"I'm fine."

June twists her face in confusion. "The Pipes?"

"The underground network that winds through Kosta. Tunnels," Regena explains, aiding Russel's effort with her own shovel, gouging deep into the filthy Oubliette wall. "They're in *Anatomy of Kosta, Volume II*. And they were built about fifty years ago."

"They're how I came here," I say. "Klosswarden helped me."

June's face is once again contorted in wonder. "Sir Klosswarden... *helped* you?"

"Once. It won't happen again." I laugh as quietly as possible. "The man's a piece of work."

I find Russel staring at us with a strange, awestruck smile. Then he carries on with his digging.

"I'll take over, Russ." I swipe the rusty spade from him and take his spot in the dirt. "If you keep on like that, you'll cave in."

"Why can't I dig?" June asks, throwing her fist into the wall.

"Cause I'm made of muscle, clearly."

"You are *not!* Let me dig!"

"At least you've grown about thirty more feet," Regena smirks, tossing dirt at my face.

I smile back, watching the mound on the ground grow by the minute. June starts tearing at it with her bare hands.

I hit iron. The clang of the knife sends a tiny echo through the Oubliette.

"Now," I announce.

One by one, we load ourselves into the Pipes. The view is surreal from the grimy Oubliette: a sleek silver tube winding through the ground, with no foreseeable ending. The ceiling is about twenty feet tall, the width around ten. It's like we're walking around in Kosta's giant bloodstream — a mechanical beast with iron veins.

I try not to think about anything but the Pipes.

But escaping, but running.

I'm running away once again.

We've walked for hours, and over time, the Pipes have gradually decreased in size. The further away from the palace, the less space. I have to crouch and hunch down as I walk through, and everyone is clumped quite closely together.

"Don't you think it's getting smaller in here?"

"Maybe we're getting *bigger*, Ez."

"Russ, you're an idiot."

Our footsteps clang. Every breath shakes through metal and mist.

The thick metal ceiling of the Pipes is interrupted by a thin spray of water. "Look at that," Russel murmurs, mesmerized by the flow. "It's got a break

— "

Suddenly, a jet of water bursts from the break in the Pipe ceiling, echoing loudly throughout the silver tubes. The spray grows and grows, throughout, outward, everywhere, piercing our ears with its liquidy wheeze — soon it has escalated into a hissing flood of sour water.

"*Run!*" June shouts, grabbing my and Regena's hands, and shoving a stupefied Russel forward. Her terror mingles with the sound of the flood. Her legs start to move, jolting herself forward, and she shrieks again: "It's about to *explode, goddamnit!*"

We run as far and fast as our legs will carry us, through hissing metal and heavy breaths.

Thank God, thank God, is the collective, rushing gasp, as we claw our way out through a thin chute in the ceiling.

"We made it out," Russel cries, his eyes positioned toward the sky.

I expect sun, but I'm greeted with a cloud-infested horizon. June's eyes sigh and swallow the sky, sun or no sun. Then the weather makes a sharp, wet curve, and the thick clouds give way to a frosty winter rain.

"Shit," says Regena — a very aristocratic remark. She yanks her hood on tighter, but it just keeps sliding down.

"It's nice," June says, letting the rain streak down her face. She twirls in small circles, her feet catching on the robe. "It's kind of beautiful. It makes me feel lonely, but... in a good way."

Regena snarls, "If you call one more thing *beautiful*, I think I might strangle you."

"Be nice," Russel coos obnoxiously. He tugs her hood back up and kisses the top of her head.

"Get offa me."

Regena's irritation is lukewarm and half-hearted. As he kisses her hood, there is a tiny flare in her eyes. She lets his mouth rest there for a moment, maybe because he's so terribly tired and beaten up. But the look on Russel's face is almost euphoric. The rain pours down on him, and he silently revels in the ghost of her rain-soaked head on his lips.

"And... for God's sake, be quiet."

We've been walking through the open air for hours, and June is almost in tears. "It's beautiful." She touches her cheek and points to the pale winter sun. "I'm sorry, but it is. It's peeking out behind there. Look."

She dances in a slice of sunlight.

"Been a while since I've seen it, too." Russel smiles.

"It's the sun," mutters Regena, scowling.

The sloping hills spread out before us, in all their twig-cluttered glory. The sky is a calm grayish blue, with the sun squinting nervously behind the dovelike clouds. Finally, the sun. Even the thorns look soft in the mist. The scurry of animals, the quiet bird songs, everything seems to melt and mix together, and there's no word more fitting for this place than serene.

"It's strange this place will be a battlefield by morning," I whisper, and it seems to send an echo through the trees, the boot-tromped edges of the valley.

It's strange, it's strange, it's strange this place will be a battlefield by morning.

"*This* place won't," Regena says, looking out at the expanse of unravaged land. "Under it, maybe. This one's mostly an underground war. But it won't stay that way for long, will it? They'll bring the pipe rats out and take it to the ground. and the sky, and the galaxy, while they're at it. It's just never enough until they burn the whole world to the ground, and for nothing."

"*They?*" June asks.

"They," she says, staring into the sun as it sinks behind a cloud. "Everyone."

$$\Diamond$$

The day is dying, and my legs ache. The group lies huddled in another cold, clumped-together piece of forest. The trees sway around us, blowing cool wind on our faces.

There's a hush now, in the darkness of the forest.

"To Uppica, right?" June whispers.

"To Uppica," Russel agrees. His stomach rumbles loudly, and he turns himself over to sleep on the damp ground.

"Soon enough. In the morning, we'll set off."

June leans back into the ground, staring intently at the sky. "I wish the morning would never come."

"Why?"

"I don't like the morning. I just like the stars."

"Yeah. They're really shining bright tonight." Shining isn't the right word. They seem to be pulsing, dimming, but I don't want to ruin any delusions she has about the stars. Let her enjoy them for the first time in a long time. "God, there are so many..."

"Did you know the stars are all dead?"

"Not... not all of them," I whisper, with an edge of defense. "You know, my father used to tell me the dead turn into stars. You think so?"

"Your father..." she says. "I guess so."

Another moment passes, and the stars pulse again. I watch her hand hover as she points aimlessly into the sky.

"Is that him there?"

Just empty silence.

"I'm going to get more wood, okay? For tomorrow."

"Mhm."

I lay there tracing her silhouette against the sky.

"Goodnight."

Goodnight. Much better than goodbye. It echoes in my head just the same, staples itself to the wild grass, glued to the starlight, radiating through my veins, mushrooming through my skull. Goodnight, goodnight.

"Night."

"The stars outside your window," he said, "are made of ancient souls."

"How old?"

"Older than your can imagine. Older than the old world."

I was eight, and warm, and vulnerable. My father's voice was the ultimate authority in my world. Why, it carried a kingdom!

To me, the stars were mystical. They seemed just pinpricks on a blanket of blackness. They say when the world ended, the sky was white – for nothingness is not black. I looked out at the sky and thought of what the black blanket must be made of. *No,* I thought deliriously. *The stars are not souls. The darkness of the sky is made of souls, and they grow more tired and more dark with each day. Stars are made when you throw rocks at the sky.*

I drowsily wondered how many rocks it took to make a star.

Uppica is a fabricated dream, made out of sneered words and hushed conversations.

I've been acting like a leader in this uncertain escapade, but I know nothing of Uppica but its symbol of the cobalt arrowhead, its crest of the fish. In all truth, I rarely met with King Victor, Prince Clayr, Queen Ayana, or the trio of princesses before they were murdered, God rest their souls. They were shadows in the hallway; they were quiet and unextravagant. They were never the same as us. The Uppicans are ineffectual, poor, I've heard, with deficient weaponry and supplies — second to Wickwolf as the most commonly mocked kingdom. Second, but a very close second.

They did not seem poor, though. Princess Fey was always in rich blue, with silver in her hair.

Uppica is untouchable in its vulnerability. *War* is a word that never leaves its lips. The land of humble fishermen and clean water, of five dead royals, killed in their own castle. They'd never survive in a war against the unburnt kingdoms: Kosta is a giant, grassy giant; Lusk, a man made out of gold.

But what is Uppica?

No one gets involved with them, the backward Uppicans; I've even overheard Uppica being called the fool kingdom, the primitive wasteland, the ninth colony. I suppose that's better than being the ghost kingdom, with no good human soul walking our grounds – the long-dead Wickwolves. We haunt them with our still-burning soil, our broken buildings, our toppled castle. The dead corner of the island, eternally spouting smoke, our queen an icon of misery, our king an accidental martyr.

Uppica remains silent. Even the surviving royals haven't made a sound. The kingdom seems to have detached itself into its own separate island. A rumor.

It won't speak.

Russel nudges me with a stick. "I'll tell you another story, but you won't like this one."

"Yeah?" I inch closer to his spot on the ground, but the smile's lost on his face.

"You want to know, don't you?"

"Wanna know *what?*"

"What... went on, when he – died."

His father? No. I know how that happened...

Oh.

"Won't tell a soul."

He sighs and traces lines in the ground. A crude, hulking figure. A boy with wings on his feet. Spiky flowers surrounding them.

"I said something like, 'You wanna *die*?' Something stupid like that. I didn't know what the hell I was *doing*. But I was trying to look really strong. He said, 'What the hell's this about?' like he had no clue. And I said, 'You *know* what it's about', and he still didn't get it for awhile. God, I acted like I knew what I was doing, and he acted like he didn't. He just snorted and said, 'Oh?' and, something else, I don't even want to talk about it – then he said 'Don't worry, I was *gentle*.' Of all the vile things to —— I... I said I don't care *how* goddamn *gentle* you were with her, you sick bastard, and God, then he said, '*In that case*—'"

He grits his teeth and drops the stick.

"I threw the first punch, like an idiot. You can't let someone say those kind of – anyway. I kept hitting him and hoping it would work or help me or something, but it just made me feel more like shit. It didn't really help that he was hitting back and he was about twice my size and I was so angry I could barely fight him. I could barely even—"

His voice breaks. We sit in silence for awhile.

Put a trigger to Russel, Leo did.

I don't say anything. Not a single word.

Let it go on him, too.

"I don't know where the shots came from. From nowhere. It wasn't his gun. It wasn't mine. I don't know. I didn't really know what was going on, you know – he sorta punched my lights out, and everything looked wrong, but I didn't stick a finger to that trigger, Ezra. You've gotta trust me. I didn't shoot him. I full well *wish* I'd murdered him, if we're telling the truth. I'd bring him back to *life* and murder him. Without blinking an eye."

Silence.

"Russel."

He's all curled into himself now, and it's just about the most pathetic sight I've ever seen. He stomps out the drawing in the ground, dragging his feet until it's only dirt. Miraculously, tragically – he says nothing.

"Russel," as if saying it twice will help anything.

He throws his arms around me like we're seven years old. "I don't mean it," he says. "Not really."

If he had told me he had killed him, I don't know what I would have done.

"It's a terrible thing to take someone's life... it wouldn't have been as easy as you think... Even if they are despicable, even if you believe so strongly that they deserve it... you can talk all you want... but with his eyes and his face right in front of you, and you looking right at him... if he looked scared, could you still pull the trigger?"

He says nothing.

And I wish he wouldn't.

◇

Some things are too painful for conversation, even for thought. But especially for dreams.

Then that line — that ever-precious line — it starts to blur, and the false and the true get so tangled together, sorting them out becomes near impossible. The trouble is, I can't do much distinguishing even while I'm awake.

Tonight all four of us shake with cold and nightmares.

I reach for my father and mother, both lost to me now. But they look at me with heavy-lidded eyes, fogged over, misted with age and death. Their lips are cracking. Their hair is filled with snow. Buried. They're both buried, sleeping quiet in the ground, hundreds of feet into the frozen, unforgiving earth. Calling to me. But the Regicides shovel mound after mound of dirt onto their bodies. Laugh at me with masked mouths. Then one of them slings off that wicked, two-sided mask, but their face is lost to me.

My mother's misery, my father's grave, my terror and trembling and pain...

And when the nightmare gets too unbearable, I violently wake up. Drenched in my parents' blood, it's seeping into my skin, seeping. It takes me a few minutes before I realize it's just my own sweat.

My mother is alive, I think, hope, pray to myself. *Alive.* With just the force of my thoughts, I can pretend I'm right.

The truth?

She hasn't been alive for years, I know; simply surviving, breathing and letting her heart beat slow and sure. But that sprawled-out woman, miserable and paralyzed in her luxurious agony, is by no means alive.

The heartbeats, the sleepy breaths next to me remind me I'm not alone.

Not alone, what a wonderful thing to be. Alive, and not alone.

Everyone else is lost to their own nightmares now, and I feel my face furrow along with theirs; their pain projects itself onto me and into me, and their individual aches reach my own chest.

June's hands are curled around her folded legs.

Regena fights in her sleep. She writhes on the solid ground. In my heart, I want her ghosts to leave her alone.

A good five feet away, Russel clutches the hole in his stomach, weeping for his mother, God rest her soul, to come back from the dead. For a certain girl that lies two feet away, fighting in her own nightmares. And another, in a distant castle, whose dreams are full of him. It's bizarre — simply, sickeningly, staggeringly bizarre, to see his cheerful face so warped. His shoulders so bent, crushed down by the weight of his world. His victorious kingdom, his utopia of sun and spirit, weighs so heavily down. The War, the duel, the Regicides, and her.

His cries are the loudest of them all; his sleeping self doesn't even try and stifle them. In my heart, I want him to be calm. I want his misery to be finished once and for all. But true misery is never finished.

For a fleeting second, I think of how easy it would be to abandon them all — to abandon everything, and take care of myself and myself only. I'd take care of me, and give care to nothing. I'd fend for myself and it would all be simple and detached. I could make it. I wouldn't have to carry their hearts along with mine, which is heavy enough on its own. Sometimes I can feel their lives weighing me down. The agonized glare of old Lady Pagele, golden-hard. The shadows of the palace. Silk and liquor and screaming for help. The gorgeous feeling of two broken legs. The thick smell of forest leaves. The darkness of solitude and the cold slap of a faraway hand.

I don't need your sorrows. I don't.

It's easiest to love nothing and no one.

As much as I try, I can't. I don't want to.

CHAPTER XX:
CORINTH

THE FOREST AWAKENS us with a pearly light, sliding its fingers through the tall Kosta trees. The frosty grass of the forest takes on a morning dew, and I shiver in my pawn robe.

I feel a warm arm around my back, the brush of old bandages. "Morning!"

"Hey, Russel."

"Shut *up*, Russel." Regena's voice.

The trees let us go.

◇

"What is this place?"

Russel's face sinks at the collection of dilapidated houses and shacks that makes up the Kosta slums. To say the least, they're in bad repair. There are no guards, no gates. Nothing to protect. The streets are dirty; the air is filled with smoke. Not the smoke of decimated castles – tobacco, exhaust, and factory wase.

A great shock, a building disgust, a mounting confusion in his evergreen eyes. And then they flutter to the red-and-yellow neon bulbs, flashing dimly in the sunlit streets.

June sinks into her shoulders.

"Over there," he actually whispers — a disconcerting tone of voice for him — "Looks like civilization." In the streets, I see a whitewashed sign has been toppled over, reading, in bulbous paintstrokes, *CORINTH*.

Corinth, Kosta.

"We have to go through Corinth to Uppica," I instruct the group, my mind jittering with information pulled from childhood libraries and my father's ink-stained map. "It's right on the border."

There is a darkness to the Wickwolf slums — a narrowness to the streets, and the inescapable smog. But Corinth is different. There is too much light, too much to look at — dull colors and artificial brightness.

The markets along the streets are the most colorful, miserable collection of kiosks I've ever seen, with a different worn-down face and different bits and pieces at each stand. Ragged people mingle in with polished ones, shoved aside by shopping bags — and behind them the selection of goods. Beaten ocean apples, scraps of cloth, old wires, expired custard in glass bottles, halfhearted sandwiches, petroleum, lighter fluid, cigarettes. Bottled dyes, picked up with delicate fingers. Young hands swatting for fruit. Half-mona candy in plastic wrap, bags of seagrapes, packets of white powder, spare metal parts, bottles of ale and whiskey and rum in every vile color you can name. An abandoned shack of a shop with rubble on its windows and a red X on its door. Sweet perfume leaking from a store called Indigo. Then a butcher shop to the right, reeking with blood and fish and formaldehyde.

It's unignorable. The red and yellow lights scream at us us, blaring from across the street.

My eyes widen and blink again to check if all of this is real. On the edge of all the bedraggled shops and markets is a bona fide brothel. Women pour in and out and about, and intoxicated men follow.

Women is not the right word for most of them. They're girls. Most are so terribly young.

In the middle of it all is a scruffy middle-aged man in thousand-pocketed brown pants. He stands pale and tall and proud, smoking relentlessly. His head is surrounded by a warped halo of pure smog.

We walk through in a disorderly line, aiming for the edge of Kosta, and the man's eyes meet our group.

"You," he drawls, pointing at Regena. He approaches her with a lazy, arrogant amble and sour breath. She flicks her eyes away, not daring to look at him. "You here for work?"

"*Work?*"

I recognize her distressed expression. It matches my own after a long nightmare. She has caught the details of his face and doesn't dare look back.

Suddenly, he grips her arm with his free hand and she's frozen to the spot.

Russel curls his knuckles, tensing himself, and prepares to charge. His eyes are scrunched and cheerless. "Don't," I hiss, restraining him by the arms. "You know you're in no state to do anything." I walk over to the smoking, centerpiece man with a flickering anger set in my eyes. He has Leo's eyes, all roaming, shallow paleness – full of pride he damn well doesn't deserve.

I lunge forward and punch him square in the jaw, knocking the smoke out of his mouth. His cigarette hits the dirt floor. It smolders weakly.

I can feel his face on my fist; the stares are widening on me.

"Dammit, kid," he mumbles.

He throws his own fist at my face. It's harder and more callous than my own, and delivered with more force, but less anger. The impact makes my head throb, and blood stream from my nose.

I hear the quick patter of feet. Closer.

June's voice.

"Don't you dare hit him." A shout-sized whisper of a voice. She doesn't lay a finger on him, but her words grab him by the neck and throttle. "You horrible, *horrible* man."

I wipe the blood from my nose and watch his flat eyes go wide.

Let me go.

— her pale collarbones in the red dress and her chopped-off waves of

brown hair and the knocking of her knees and the anger on her lips and the
sadness of her large eyes that he never cared to acknowledge and —

You horrible, horrible...

That one burning sentence finished at last.

He nears her.

"You," he utters, scrutinizing her face. "I know you, little girl." The man
points a shaking, golden-ringed finger at her, and his eyes take on a faraway look.
"I *know* you, little girl..."

"You don't," she objects, injecting disgust into every word, her eyes
flicking around, anywhere but his face. "I've never been around *here* before."

The man lowers his foot to stamp out the still-burning cigarette.

"Of course," he mutters to himself, staring absently to the smoked-over
sky. "Of course she wouldn't be this young."

June's eyes waver.

"...What?"

"That kid. And her," the man wheezes. His voice is like smoke and gravel.
"You look like her. You look just like her, dear God..." His eyes are on her face.
The dark saucer eyes, the small bowstring mouth — the paleness of her face.
The smallness of her, the nervousness of her expression.

The tired, quiet anger, written on her, carved into her.

It ties a string inside of him.

A smoke-scented murmur.

"Jette, was it... Jette Chajkia..."

"Jette?" The name is unfamiliar in her mouth.

His words are slow and convinced. "You carry her shadow – like a copy,
like... oh, Jesus Christ. you've gotta be her kid. That girl... your mother..." He
laughs. He laughs like heaven has sent him a miracle, and there's something in
those shallow eyes that makes my hate for him disintegrate a bit.

A flicker in her eyes. "M — my mother? Are you mad?"

The man grinds his foot to the ground, extinguishing the last of the cigarette stub. He places another between his yellowed teeth, and lights it without a thought. "She left here a long time back, quit being a peddle for good. Went somewhere far off. Skipped town, crossed the border, didn't she... with that damned university kid..."

"So you're saying... she's in Uppica?" June stares into his stubbled face with goggling eyes.

"That stupid, stupid girl," the man scoffs, hurling smoke at her. "She could be goddamn anywhere. Now, you don't belong here, babyface. Run off, will you?"

She decides not to retort, though she could kill him with words if she wanted to. This man has given her *something*, somehow — a vague clue. It is something, be it true or not.

"Thanks, old man," she says, tossing him some pity and making a visible effort not to spit in his face.

Someone she never even knew is tugging at her again, working her from the inside out. She runs off with anger in her eyes and her mother's whereabouts stirring in her mind.

What can we do but follow?

"There's bound to be a decent place around here," she mumbles, catching her breath and softening her pace. We walk among the edge of the slums, keeping our distance from the red and yellow lights. The miserable-looking people. "To rest from all this."

"I could use some food," says Russel, grinning. "That was a good load of entertainment, though, wasn't it?" He slings his arms around me and June. "This cute bastard unleashing it on that brothel guy? I mean, damn, I didn't know you had it in you!"

"Oh, shut up, will you?" I say, brushing his arm off of her.

"Grouchy as always, I see."

June laughs. "You really didn't have to make a holy show of yourself, though."

I kick away rocks and pebbles that scatter the path. The roads are narrow, but the sky lasts forever.

Regena's steps falter. "That wooden building looks promising."

At first I take this as something of a joke: the little temple has gone to rack and ruin. Then I see the subtle glint of stained-glass windows, the pillars of crosses, the tiny congregation within, and it seems a degree less desolate.

"Who in God's name puts a chapel smack next to a brothel?" she snorts. "Oh, well, let's go. *They* probably won't want to take the likes of us."

"You sure we're allowed in here?"

"Have we ever cared where we're *allowed* before?"

The floorboards rasp beneath our feet; I've never seen a place more decrepit and alive at once. The hymn rings through the walls, sung by only a dozen or so people, some half-hearted and mumbled, some ringing clear and strong. There are red-dressed women mixed into the crowd, pressing their palms together and staring at the peeling paintings on the walls. There are gamblers and drunks and saints and schoolgirls and sinners. Bags stuffed with tin cans and empty beer bottles. At the front of the procession is an altar decked with bouquets, wrapped in day-old newspaper. No one takes notice of us but one little girl in black.

"Mama," she whispers, tugging on her ragged sleeve. She points to Russel. "I's the *prince,* right b'hind you! Lookit!"

"Shhh, shh." She turns her head to the altar again and talks in a hush. "Let's not talk nonsense and fairytales. It is a sad, sad day today, my darling, and we must be quiet."

"Why?" She tugs on her sleeve once more. "Why?"

"Father Lot has died just yesterday," she whispers.

"F-father?" the girl whimpers. She breaks into tears. "Why'd you gotta tell me that, Mama?" Her praying hands reach her face. "I thought he was just sick."

"He was, indeed, and that is why," the woman murmurs. "Shh, don't cry, doll, he's in Heaven now. It's better for him than this place. He's singing now. With the angels."

"The angels can't have him," the little girl says, burying her face in her hands, indistinguishable from a prayer.

We redirect ourselves from the scene and sit in the back pews, lit by the sinking of the sun. Here, we soak up the music that drifts across the old wood, the small collection of ill-matched, harmonious people, much like ourselves. I can barely tell what god they're worshipping, but it doesn't matter to me. Their voices are rough and beautiful.

June sings, and she sounds like the sun behind the clouds.

Father Lot's name rises from each corner, each crack in the chapel, an enigma, a blur in the distant sun that will never be seen again.

At the end of the service, a red-dressed girl leaves her last bouquet of flowers for the Father. Makeup is smeared across her face. She glances up at us for a moment, surveying our faces with a wide, peculiar stare.

"What're you looking at?" She aims it in the form of an insult, but there's no venom to it. Her eyes are watery. "What're you..." She bows at the altar, wiping at her nose. More makeup is rubbed off. "H-have you no respect for him?"

"We didn't know him, miss," Regena says.

"He is... he was a saint, you see. You'd see if you had known him. It's a shame." Her voice quivers. "It's a damn shame. And I never got to say goodbye..."

I lay a careful hand on her shoulder. "It's okay."

She shudders and looks up in surprise. "Did you just put me in a trance, sir?" Her voice is loud and friendly now, like she wasn't just crying.

I laugh. "No. You'll be okay, alright?"

"Thank you, kind stranger?" Black liquid is dripping over her cheeks now, but she's smiling. "I'll see you around town, I hope?"

"Ah, no, I—" I scratch the back of my head. "I'm not from around here. I come and go. More of a traveler, to tell you the tr—" I feel a sharp tug on the side of my shirt, unnerving dark blue eyes staring up at me. "I'd best be going, then."

She looks vaguely disappointed. Then she smirks. "I'll show you yet, charming lad! I'll make something of myself beyond this town! Don't be so repelled by me at first glance."

"I'm sure you will, honest. You can become a queen if you like." Another tug from June. "I've really got to go."

On our way from the chapel, the sky has darkened; the sun is nowhere to be found. A faint glimmer of stars can be seen again.

Russel seems childishly amused, trying not to choke himself with laughter. "Charming lad... charming lad!"

"Please close your mouth for a split second or remove all sounds from your vocal cords," I say, pulling him into a headlock.

"You have the strangest way of expressing your love for me."

"Oh, and with your little flirtation, you upset June." Regena pats her on the head.

"Nope," she mutters.

"I did no such thing! There was no *fl*—"

"*You can become a queeeeen, if you like.*" June imitates me in a deep, oafish voice. "*I come and goooo.*" Her tone changes to a high-pitched purr. "*I'll see you around town, I hope?*"

"Are you done?"

"Yes, charming lad. Oh..." she pulls a sheet of newspaper from the pack, called *THE RAG.* "I kinda took this back there."

Regena swipes it from her.

"THE ROYAL RUNAWAYS – Several sources confirm sightings of four traveling youths – two of whom are suspected to be the missing princes of Melchor and Ordim. This correlates with the disappearances of Prince Russel Kosta, Prince Ezra Wickwolf, Duchess Regena Pagele, and Duchess Joss Conquin, all of whom have fled their homes. (Read more about the royal crisis on page 4, section 3.) Whether these disappearances relate to the recent death of Prince Leo Lusk has yet to be known. Young Lady Pagele's mother, Lady Alexia, is very distressed about these disappearances. She reports, '*My daughter was engaged to Prince Lusk, so of course she has run off in grief. She was always somewhat impuslive and made unwise decisions, but we do hope she gets home safely.*' — What a load of absolute piss — 'Her father, Duke Constantine, declines to comment."

"No offense, but your mother's terrible," says Russel.

"Obviously. – Oh, and here's a load of garbage on page 4... 'Every royal who has fled their respective castles has suffered a terrible loss by the Regicides, except Lady Joss Conquin, who is thought to have fled the kingdom with Prince Kosta; Kostan citizens have reported sightings of a curly-haired boy and a very short girl traveling together—'"

"Citizens have also reported fairies in the forest and monsters in shallow water," I say.

June shrugs. She attaches herself to Russel and says, in a very high-pitched voice, "Guess I'm Lady Joss now."

"Pray to God you're not," I mumble.

"–'Prince Wickwolf, who was believed to have committed suicide some seven months ago, was reportedly seen clawing his way out of the earth. (Oh, that's rich.) Onlooker, a citizen of Kosta, describes the sighting as 'incredibly odd... the boy was covered in dirt and running quite fast, as if being chased.' Another source assumes the prince to be already dead, but not by suicide, but murder. She suspects the Regicides have added another victim to their toll. Keep reading The Rag to find out more about–' Ugh, I despise newspapers."

She folds it in half and hands it back to June. "You can have it."

We pause to sit in the sunset, salmon-red, golden orange, and deep purple – the kind of sunset I've always loved.

From the edge of Kosta, the dregs and the dirt, the other side is visible. The sturdy apartment buildings, schools, and factories climb over the hideous atmosphere of the slums. The ground is tensing its muscles for the flow of soldiers and fire. The sky is a warning, the buildings a line of victims.

They lay in waiting for the raids that will surely come.

CHAPTER XXI:
UPPICA

THE MORNING IS achingly, violently bright, the stars sapped from the sky. The leaves shows the smallest signs of spring, and birds cry in the distance.

We gather in the woodlands at the very edge of Uppica, a tight-packed circle of grubby refugees, and June empties out the burlap sack she swiped from the palace. A heap of memories pour out.

The Wanderer, left unfinished. A strange, raggedy stuffed animal with button eyes – the same one she kept in Ward One. The brown shirt I wore when I arrived at Kosta, now frayed and limp. Russel's rusty spade. A sizeable bag of nuts, rolls, tiny cakes, and apple slices, so we don't starve before we jump into the unknown. A single half-inked pen. My red Wickwolf pendant. A bronze compass. My father's map – on it, the name *Loupe Wickwolf,* in his graceful, swooping letters. A dangerous name.

"Beautiful," she says, eyeing the pendant. "Is that yours, Ezra?"

The name sounds foreign in her voice. "No, it's yours," I say, handing her a roll.

"I didn't mean the *roll,* Ezra—"

"Don't say that name," hisses Regena, pawing along for some cakes in the grass. Her eyes are smudged with the residue of black paint, her hair falling from its artificial curl. "Who knows who's watching."

"You're right."

"We need false names," Russel concludes, already devouring half the stash.

"I'll keep Wick."

"I'm Sophie Engeldower," says Regena. We all hand her curious looks, but she just shrugs. "First thing that came to mind."

"Okay, Sophie Engeldower," Russel says, attempting to laugh in his pathetic condition. His ribs visibly ache, sending him into a small convulsion that he disregards. He smiles as if he's only coughed. "I'll be Charles. Charles Curley."

"Where are you coming up with these?" I say, bewildered. "Okay, I'm, er, Wick... Brown."

"How unimaginative," says Regena.

June joins in. "Can I be June Kinsel?"

I hear her in my memory: *I don't like nicknames.*

The sound of a small, collective laugh is strange to me. To allow ourselves to be happy or give a simple, single smile – sometimes that's the best way to cope with everything. It's certainly better than anything else.

"No, seriously, you need a false name," Regena tells her.

"Jette," she decides. "Jette Chajkia."

There's a strange familiarity to all of this. I'm a runaway once more, striking fire with forest branches. I heap the firewood into the flames and hear that same old electric crackle speaking back to me. I feel young and ancient at once, but most of all, I feel that I belong. There's something about a fire that makes you feel you're where you are supposed to be.

"Oh, wow," says Regena, her eyes flickering gold. "I haven't seen a real fire in ages. Everything's fake in the– "

"Shh!" Russel warns. "Let's not mention that kind of thing, okay?"

"Fine." She forms a fist to jokingly sock him in the arm, but uncoils her fingers. There are still fresh bruises on his cheeks and a subtle sadness in his eyes.

"No talk of the past, then," says June, "so what's there to talk about? The future's too unsure... and the present is just — us, sitting around this fire."

"That's all we need," I say.

"Marvelous." Russel's spirit hasn't died. Neither has his ridiculous storytelling. He plants a stick in the dirt and draws the image of a very muscular, curly-haired man. "Presently, Charles Curley is a fantastically strong woodsman traversing through the forests and chasing the heart of Sophie Engeldower..." His smile is a turned page. His stick traces along in the dirt, creating the smiling face of Regena.

The real Regena scowls. "*Charles,* Reggie, not me."

"He has settled into a clearing in the woods and made a fire for himself. But what is that? In the distance? Could it be? A long, skinny lad comes out from the trees, lost and — "

"Are you talking about me?" I observe the dotted stick figure in the fire-flicked dirt.

" — yes — lost and afraid, like a baby."

"Wow. A masterpiece."

"Thank you. — Now, this lankyish babyish lad sits next to Charles Curley and pleads for help, all cow-eyed. He says, 'Charles, a massive fleet of rabid rabbits is attacking my home! They're going to tear it down, brick by brick, with their little teeth! You've gotta help me, Charles! I love you, Charles! You're my hero!' So Charles just says, 'Rabbits are no match for me. I am their ruler.'"

"You've outdone yourself, Charles."

At this point June is snickering at the sharp teeth Russel has drawn on the dozen or so rabbits.

"And then," Regena chimes in, taking her own stick from the ground, "Sophie Engeldower watches Charles get eaten alive by rabbits."

June laughs along.

"The end." That old smirk.

Russel's face looks yellow in the fire, and he draws his bandanged foot across the dirt.

The sparks of the fire are lessening as we talk on for hours about nothing. Our quiet voices hover in the darkness, and our faces grow dark.

"I'll go get more firewood," I say.

June suddenly shoots up in her seat on the log. "And you think you have the authority to do that?"

"Uh, sure? Even a lowly peasant such as I..."

"I can do it! We can't gamble on you or Russel–"

"–*Charles*–"

"*Charles* – wandering around the forest at night! Can we be done with this game? There's no one around!"

"Okay, then come with me!"

"Fine!"

"This is the most useless argument I've ever heard," Regena mutters.

The fire dies out slow and lovely, and we plant ourselves in the middle of the forest, huddled in a clump.

"Happen to have any blankets in that pack?" Russel asks.

"Nope," says June. "Sorry."

He pats her on the head, then gives her a hug. "Well, goodnight, then."

There is the subtle fluttering of birds' wings, the churn of a distant river, the coo of crickets. The sky blackens as if it's burning, stars searing like little fires. Regena falls asleep quickly, and Russel sets himself down two feet away, in a kind of delusional attempt to safeguard her. Soon he drifts off too. It's only me and the little ghost.

In the night, June's face is like the moon, her voice like the whisper in the trees. It shocks me even now.

"You told me not to disappear."

"Huh?" I sit up. I can barely hear her.

"Oh, I mean..." A simple murmur, and a reddened face. She struggles. She covers her mouth with her hand, to staunch the flow of words. They spill out anyway. Once they come, they don't stop.

"You just said... don't disappear, that time. When you had the blight, I mean. I thought you were going to die... but, you didn't, and — you were worried about *me*. *Me*, even though you were half-dead." Slowly, she removes the hand from her mouth. Her sentences still stumble. "Your fever was dangerous... and your eyes were half-closed... somewhere in the middle of it, you grabbed my hand. Your hand was a fire. It burned me. And you — well, some part of you, I guess — said, 'Please don't disappear.'"

June looks down at her feet, which are twiddling uncontrollably. "It made me happy." Then she stares me straight in the eyes.

"I won't disappear."

I trust the colors in her eyes and the sound of her words. I trust her wavering voice and her small, hidden smile. That ever-rare smile. When it comes, it's worth every frown in her arsenal. Her voice could kill, but it brought me to life, more alive than I ever hoped to be.

It's not the time or place, but I lean over and press my mouth to hers.

I stay, and I feel her respond. I feel her startled eyes and the confusion on her face, so close that I can taste the words on her lips. I feel even now, as her face is pressed to mine, that she'll fizzle off into the sky. Evaporate and be lost to me forever. But she's not a dream, and even when I draw back, she doesn't disappear.

"Me, either. I won't disappear."

Her eyes widen. Then close. She extends a hand to touch my face, and I grip it just to feel its small warmth. It's so different. We're not trapped in a stone cage. No castle walls. No cold concrete. We're not hidden in darkness with a single pulsing lantern. There are scores of stars dotting the sky. There are good dreams flickering in my head. So I pull her closer, and do things I've never dared to do, and hope Russel and Regena are fast asleep. Stroke her moonlit hair. Press my mouth to her ear. Trail my fingers down the deep scar on her neck and listen to her breath pick up. She kisses my shoulder, my throat, my mouth, and something shakes in the trees. No words. No sound. A shock settles over us, and our embrace turns to an embarrassed huddle.

Those familiar dark eyes blink as we both draw away. We look at eachother's hungry eyes and startled, swollen lips, and decide it's best to go to sleep.

The sun is not quite up when we wake, but Regena squints at the sky. She jostles Russel awake, and he cracks a huge smile.

"Did I die? Am I in heaven?"

She slaps him lightly across the face. "Quite the opposite. Uppica."

We only have to walk a couple of yards before Uppica is in our eyes, its buildings and hills and sky, all blue and white through the blackness of the trees.

The awe grows, tangible around us.

Their first foolish act was planting the Kingdom City just over the border. Their second was having no substantial guard, so riffraff like us can trespass easily.

The steel-blue palace is clearly visible in the light of day. This palace, though, is foreign to me — it's not so much a castle as a skyscraping collection of blocks and steely rectangles. It's out of a different kind of world.

I'm infiltrating another kingdom, but this time I'm not alone.

June, with quiet strength and a voice that could kill you. Russel, with bravery in his eyes and wings on his back. Regena, made of metal and a heart of gold. Me, with my nightmares and wobbling courage, and friends.

Friends.

Remember. You're not entirely helpless. Saved by the devil himself. Those words, once muttered in the coldest of voices, from the sharpest of mouths, now sends something warm stirring in my chest.

Come what may, I'm not alone.

CHAPTER XXII:
RUNAWAYS

The first word out of my mouth when I wake:

"God."

A plea, a question. A whispered scream.

A cold sweat, a trembling body, again.

My fears don't die at night; they all manifest themselves in my nightmares, and grow with each passing day that I feed them. The loud ticking of clocks filling every corner. Walls and roomfuls and castles full of clocks. Worms crawling all over my body, blue paint leaking from the guns I assembled at the palace. Noor in the proud, green outfit of a soldier, still the size of a child, running into the fire of guns. Digging his way through the underground veins of Kosta and finding his way to a haven of bullets. Russel's murder, with no sharp edges and no sense – all red, red everywhere, in his eyes and legs and hair, his mouth gaping – and a group of Regicides stealing away from the crime scene, their masks taunting me.

A black-cloaked man sings as he digs my grave.

My night terrors always seem to begin with the loudness of clocks, and end with that Regicide mask. They are usually broken apart by the face of Russel, or Regena, or June. His concerned smile, maybe — or the rough shake of her hands — or the wind of her voice in my ears. A voice I could get lost in. A land without invisible monsters and living ghosts.

Please don't leave me, please, you set me free.

◇

Somewhere in the distance, bullets clash and bodies fall. It's all because of me, isn't it? My fault, my fault, always. I was born a despicable person. A person who was never worth the throne he sat on, the hair in his head, the name he was born to. Please, let me become someone who is worth all of this.

Am I allowed to hope for anything more than this? I've been handed everything. From birth, I was showered with wealth, prosperity, nobility, love. All undeserved.

There are people better than me in the slums of Uppica, in the dregs of Kosta and Lusk and Wickwolf, I can tell you that. There are people more deserving. There are pawns who smile and sing. There are little slum boys who believe in themselves.

Please, not Ibby and Noor. Please, God, don't let them die. It's all I ask. Please, don't let the kingdoms destroy each other.

The nightmare clings for a second and releases me from its claws, but the shallow burn in my chest won't let go. All I can remember is a tower of flames in my dreams. Burning into nothing. I've heard it said so often that love is like a fire, but it can't be true. No – love doesn't feel like this; nothing could hurt more than this tugging feeling of change. I'm tethered to a pole and the fire is coming at me, licking at my legs and turning me into smoke – there's nothing I can do.

If this is love, then love is a monster. A dragon.

My velvet bed is so far away. And I want it to be. I want to sleep on rags. I want to feel the burn of hunger, and I want to live like I deserve to. I want to feel the air around me, and become the land. Like a little death.

There's a war inside of me and inside of my land.

On our way to civilization, we come across a blue forest coated in dust, sparkling with dew. Toppled logs, bristled leaves, crawling vines like the ones so common to Kosta. Then one strange pile of blackened sticks, obviously the remants of a campfire. A discarded glove lies in the grass, a rip running through its fingers.

"There are others?"

"Well, did you expect we'd be alone?" Regena shrugs. "We should be more careful, then."

"Oh," says June, and the group comes to a stop.

In the underbrush, there's a collection of woven baskets stuffed with nondescript blue and white clothing and dirty rags, lying abandoned in the middle of a dead grass patch.

I inspect the heaps of clothing and our own shapeless pawn robes. The robes match; the Uppican clothes match. "We might as well look like Uppicans, huh?"

"A heist," says Russel, pawing through garments.

"A poor excuse for a heist," Regena whispers. "A laundry-basket heist."

"Shhh," I warn them.

"There's no one around to care."

His innocent smile is met by a dark hiss of a voice. "Maybe the people we're shamelessly robbing?"

"Oh, relax."

June picks up some small blue pants and a floppy white shirt that's at least four sizes too big. "Quick." Together, we dive into the forest and make a rapid change of clothes.

"These pants are too short," I mumble.

"Your legs are too long," Regena says, glaring at me. "Just wear your damn boots."

A knife lies in the middle of a clearing, gleaming innocently. It's rough and rusted, and beneath the grime, a beautiful shade of suncast silver.

Cautiously, I reach down for it, as if it will sit up and attack me. It stings my fingers, but I don't drop it. It might be of use.

"Hand it over," June whispers, though backing away a bit.

After a confused change of hands, she holds the knife in her palm. Her fingers rest with determined delicacy, a near-invisible tremble. The dagger is foreign in her hand. She seems to have no idea what to make of it.

She reaches behind her head with the knife and my heart stops for a second. With a slow swipe, she drags the knife across, and a foot of wispy hair flutters to the dirt. June leans down to catch, feeling the absence of it, and I watch the feathers of cut-off hair that drag on her cheeks.

June says nothing, but keeps her eyes down for half a minute. When she looks up, she gives a small smile and waves goodbye to the ground.

"For God's sake, June, the back of your neck." Regena digs a scarf from our sack of loot and wraps it around June three times. "Why did you do that?"

She shrugs. "I dunno. To look more like a boy, I guess."

"You really don't, though!"

"You two are going to have to look more..." I place a hand on Russel and Regena. "More... grubby."

They work at tearing their clothes into convincing shabbiness and swiping mud on their faces.

"Alright, you look terrible enough."

"Impossible," Russel says with a toss of the head. "I'm gorgeous."

"You're drunk," I laugh.

He spins his arms in the sky and jumps up and down like a child. He leaps through the forest, shaking the grass. "Yes, I am. I'm drunk on fresh air, and flowers, and the big beautiful sky and−" He begins to hack, jolted forward by a spasm in his stomach. Regena holds him by the arm, fright in her face. He keeps talking through his cough, and his knees curl helplessly forward. "And the smell of the sea, and..." A single tear tracks down his cheek through the swiped-on mud and day-old bruises, and he splutters up a bit of blood. "Christ, they didn't fix me up that much."

"Stop." It's all I can manage to say. The twenty-odd broken bones he's accumulated throughout childhood don't compare to this. He's really hurt this time, and he refuses to acknowledge it.

"Be careful, for God's sake."

I hear Regena whisper to him, "If you die, I'll kill you."

Where the forest ends, there's a sign plastered with only an enormous Uppican arrowhead, no trace of lettering. Straight ahead are the glass chambers that lead to the city.

Around us is a long, straight tunnel of thick glass. It has a cold blue tint to it, like a high-heat fire. Its ceiling shoots straight through the air into darkness and smog, its corners rigid. I feel as if I'm being swallowed by metal. Suffocated, caged. My breath fails me.

Overheard, there are blinking, jerking metal eyes, shooting out from the ceiling from cold shiny vines.

Glass. All around me, surrounding and enclosing me —

I'm in the chariot —

The bullet is coming —

"Wick, are you okay?"

I didn't realize it: I'm shaking hard. "Y-yeah, sorry, R— " I correct myself — "um, Charles-"

The bullet is closer —

"Watch out!" I hear myself scream, but the voice is detached from my body. It sounds thick and desperate; I watch myself like a stranger. I don't belong to me as I leap in front of Russel and extend my arms straight out, like a shield.

The look that crosses his face is lost to me. I stand in panic and false bravery. I can't quiet the voice in my head that screams, always, *danger*.

"Be calm, I've got it," he mumbles, not looking very calm himself, and starts to reach into his pocket out of habit. No pocket, no pills. "Oh — well — nevermind."

"This is good for you," Regena tells him, clutching his shoulder. His face relaxes. "You can't keep taking those damned pills. You're going to kill yourself."

"Quite right, Reg, I can't keep taking those damned pills, because I don't *have* any."

"Good. You're better off."

I don't know if Regena is right. His face is pale white and his eyes seem both crazed and drained, pink-ridged. The sound of his chattering teeth fills the glass chas, and doesn't stop until we have reached their end. The echoing dies, and my heartbeat slows.

We head for the city square — another large block of Uppican glass, but this time filled with citizens. A pure mob of white and blue. Everyone in the crowd wear tattered, stiff clothes of identical fit and color — an Uppican uniform, covering them from throat to toe.

"Let's head to the crowd," I say.

CHAPTER XXIII:
THE STORY
WITHOUT AN ENDING

"C'MON. C'MON, NOW, babyface."

The green soldiers had stopped by again, hollering of another battle won against Wickwolf, another grand peddle festival. Spring was coming, slow and sure, but snow still speckled the ground, and the Pedlar still held onto her like a doll.

She looked out, at the whole rented world. People borrowed time and promises, broke each other and broke themselves. They bought love with their last coin. She watched the dark shadows of legs against the lights, day and night. Nothing ever changed. The same circulation of men, only with different faces. The same girl, over and over again, in a different form. Nowhere to go. Nothing to lose. She was no different.

She clung to the ground in her tent, and his golden-ringed hands tightened around her waist.

"C'mon."

"I don't need any money. I *really* don't! Don't make me go back there. Leave me alone, you promised, you *prom*ised!"

With some hesitation, he let her fall to the ground. "Fine."

Then Jette saw his brown boots tromp their way out of her tent. She batted away the smoke that lingered, and her mind wandered back to the orphanage. Those dark, haunting eyes. Whose child was she now? Whose was she before?

She lay on the dirt floor, looking at the wreckage of her life, smelling spring in the air for the first time.

It was the last time she would see those wooden pillars, those lamplit ceilings, those red-dressed girls, legs crossed and shivering. If her journey was successful. If not...

She didn't want to give it a single thought.

"Where are you going, bunny rabbit?"

Jette turned around to face Lila, whose dark face was covered in powder. Her black hair shone with the beaming red and yellow lights. She stared at Jette's white robe with questioning eyes.

"Nowhere, really." She meant it. Anywhere was nowhere. Anywhere was a blank-face street, all indefinite color and all curiosity. Hope was not essential, only change.

"Bye, Lila."

"Wait, wait — " Lila grabbed her by the arm. "You're really leaving?"

No answer. Just her frightened face, turned to the side.

"Jette?"

"Yes," she whispered, finally.

She could control one thing only. Herself. She could make her feet walk out the door, she could run without saying goodbye, she could fight and claw the world away.

The sky was black and graying with stars. Each one handed her a cold, white stare. They burned her — but this was a soft burn, unlike the blaze of the peddle lights. The stars held no judgements, no malevolence, only whispers of what was to come. Her legs were brisk in the grasping air, but her head was veiled in white.

He saw her.

The Pedlar caught hold of her arm. A rough, graceless grip, the force of it knocking the hood off her head. "Where do you think you're going, little girl?"

"I'm not your little girl," she fired back immediately, baring teeth and jerking from his hold. "And I'm not your peddle."

"Yeah, you're not mine." His eyes focused on hers, looking strangely bruised, like he'd been up for days and nights on end. "But you're *theirs*." The Pedlar's thick arm gestured out to the peddles' grounds, the midnight bustling, the bright commotion. She could see the shadows of girls, soldiers, late-night drunks, constantly moving in the darkness.

Jette shook her head. "I'm my own. You're the one who belongs to them." She resisted the urge to spit up at him. It would only reach his vested chest.

He tried to clutch her shoulder, but she only wrestled more.

His voice softened a little, from sandpaper to the texture of gravel and smoke. "You're just a kid, you know that?"

"I'm not a kid, Pedlar. Not to you. Not to *you*. I'm not a person... I'm a piece of furniture to you. Nothing belongs to me, and I'm supposed to belong to everyone. They use me. They mess me up. They pay their last filthy coin to lay their filthy selves on me. I never wanted this."

He considered her for a moment.

"You're more than a piece of furniture."

"Don't," she whispered. "Don't. Let go of me."

His hand fell, and Jette was gone.

One last time, she told herself, breathing deeply. The chapel stood nervously, like a poor-postured child. Its wooden walls sank with the weight of the night. She remembered the nights she had spent sleeping in the chapel pews, heavy with grief and love. *He must be in there.*

When she entered, he was there again, indeed, sitting still under the yellowed picture of the mother and the son, with their tiny, painted smiles.

"Good evening, visitor."

His words sparked tears in her eyes. They grew and grew until they spilled out as she bounded toward him and threw her arms around his white-cloak shoulders. "I'll miss you, Father Lot."

"And you." His face was serene, his eyes full of calm and peace; of sleep and love. Never questioning, always answering. "You're always welcome back here, Jette. I'll stay. I'll always be with you."

Even the strange exhaustion in Father Lot's eyes was golden. She allowed herself to look at him one last time. She couldn't place a name to him. He was a sleepy glow, a dying sun – and she was a quick-shooting moonbeam.

She slept in the church again, that night.

She dreamed of the vast poisoned sea, lands long buried, warm jackets and Christmas snow. Then the true dreams — dead days, sleepless nights, rough hands. The bad dreams made her cry out in her sleep, but they sang no songs, gave no quick-buried hope. Flowers wilted so easily. Good dreams did not comfort her.

He did come, after all.

The snow shrouded him, a thin shadow.

She realized, then, how absurd it all was, how much she was asking of him. A silly, filthy girl, looking to flee the kingdom. But she saw it in his watery eyes: he had some strange sense of duty to her – as if he hadn't bought her fairly. As if he knew for certain the child was his.

"It's a long road. Let's go."

CHAPTER XXIV:
THE FACELESS VOICE

SCHROLEN'S EDGE.

The sign sits perched on its high ledge, its letters thick and dark blue, surrounded by lights that blink in the dark of the night. It stares down at us, at the crowd of thick-bodied Uppicans leaving us no room to get in, their blend of voices overwhelming our words.

"I think it's a pub," says Russel.

"Great deduction," says Regena. "Outstanding."

We wrestle through burly men carrying sacks of loot, worn-looking travelers, snide-faced teenagers – some hooting, some absolutely silent. They push through the wooden doorway. Near the doorway, someone has scrawled

Regena swipes the sack of loot away from me. "Hey, Russel – can we–"

"YES."

She glares. "You didn't let me finish, you idiot – can we get some food?"

"How much money's in there?" I ask.

Regena shrugs. "Don't need money," she says, leading us to a wooden table. "Sit down."

With that, she marches up to the bartender, a dark-haired girl with silver bracelets and a thick fur scarf – and I don't know how she does it, but within a minute, she's back at the table carrying a plate piled with ham sandwiches, brown rice, and water.

Russel looks like he might cry. "Truly, your beauty and intelligence transcends all—"

"Oh, shut it. And you two. Stop playing footsie under the table."

We sit, eating and no one saying a word. A figure approaches with soft stomps – I flinch, but it's a harmless-looking, tiny man with a pathetic beard. He holds a mug of golden liquid.

"Liquid fire! Cures all your problems, one swig."

Regena rapidly shakes her head. "That's fine, sir."

"Suit yourselves, then. You kids going to the rally today?"

"Where is it?" says Regena, looking endlessly bored.

"The city square, o'course."

"A rally for what?" asks June.

"Uppica, my girl!" He laughs, and his voice grows hushed. "The likes of you... must be from far off. Don't worry, there's lots like you 'round here. You'll be fine as long as you take cover."

He leaves, and takes the thick smell of the golden liquid with him.

The people around us join in on his excitement for the rally. Mostly burly men in ragged white, and their reluctant wives, scowling at the piled tables. Thin, tired wandering men, dozing in the corners, doubtlessly escaping from something.

"How'd you get the food?" June whispers.

"Told her I'm set to work here starting next week. Shh."

"Come on," says Regena. "I haven't seen any of Uppica at all."

"It doesn't own any colonies, though," says Russel. "It doesn't own anything. All of its royalty is dead. It has no army, no ships – there's no use. It can't help us."

"For God's sake, do you believe that?"

Down the road, kids kick a battered rubber ball around. A girl leans down to pick a copper coin out of the gutter. Black water runs down the streets, puddling around bare feet.

"Let me see your father's map," Regena whispers, and I hand it over with a reluctant toss.

We round the cobblestone corner, deeper into a city of glass.

Even from a distance, his voice travels. It only grows louder and louder as we near the crowd and the pedestal.

From our position at the bottom end of the crowd, we blend nicely with the masses. All I can see of the man is his perfectly-pressed blue pants, his polished shoes. He stands in front of a vast sheet of blue curtains that hang from pure glass. There is a silence in the organized mob of Uppicans, then broken by the clear, booming sound of his words. His voice has the richness and vastness of an ocean, yet no clear origin, no mouth to pin it to. He pronounces each syllable with gravity usually reserved for royalty.

"All rise for the Salute of Uppica."

The crowd is silent, but the voice thunders on, growing into a chant, all rising and falling and rumbling. Calculated, without passion. But loud as the rumbling of a thousand seas, a million buzzing flies.

"We are purity.
We are solitude.
We are unity.
We are justice.
We are peace.
We are order.

We are wholeness."

The crowd repeats, in a voice like a thousand worker bees, "We are purity, we are solitude, we are unity, we are justice, we are peace, we are order, we are wholeness..."

The words start to blend. They lose their meaning and their sense, all nothing more than shades of white. I feel my mouth moving along with the crowd. I am just a piece of a colossal machine. *Purity. Solitude. Unity. Justice. Peace. Order. Wholeness....*

They mean nothing, when you get right down to it.

But to this crowd, they mean *everything*. They mean Uppica. They watch with enchanted eyes.

Suddenly, the blue curtains draw back as if by the pull of thousands. The blue man steps closer to the edge of the pedestal, and the curtains are gone. Behind them is a long, vertical glass box.

In it is a girl.

Her straight black hair shines with a blue glint from under the glass. Her face is so flat and plain as to be featureless, a small nose and mouth, and two tiny, dust-blue eyes staring out, unblinking and entranced — no eyebrows and pinpoints for pupils. She wears a long dress and a crown of cobalt blue. And says nothing.

Princess Fey.

It's her – it has to be her. In the glimpses I saw of her in my chilhood, I saw those watery eyes, that sheet of black hair, rounding corners in hallways. Never really seeing eye to eye, never knowing there would be a time when I would shake in my shoes to see her face.

The last surviving princess.

The blue man speaks in her place, and attaches a new name to her nearly unblinking eyes.

"Hail the Jewel of Uppica!"
"Hail the Jewel of Uppica!"

"Hail Uppica!"

"HAIL UPPICA!" This time the crowd is in a triumphant, tranquilized hysteria — a swarm of locusts, swaying methodically. The curtain is drawn, and the Jewel of Uppica, their secret survivor, is hidden again.

The voice dismisses them and they scatter.

CHAPTER XXV:
THE BROKEN MIRROR

GLORIA SAW EYES that were not hers, and hair that shone with an unfamiliar glow. Her reflection never matched what she imagined, but this time it showed the vision of a dark-cloth goddess. Not the confused human girl she knew herself to be.

The reflection had hair of pure black, long and straight and curling softly at the edges, eyes like gemstones. She wore deep, regal Wickwolf red. The girl in front of the mirror trembled.

Her mother clutched her by the shoulders. "You're going to love him," she yelped, more of an order than an optimistic prediction. Gloria nodded and feigned a smile.

"Yes, he's very — handsome," she told her, putting her black-bead pendant in place. At the very least, she didn't have to lie about that.

"Yes. And you are beautiful, Gloria. The loveliest pair in Belvidere."

Her future husband had the deep, clear skin and the curling black hair of the Wickwolves. Eyes the color of bitter chocolate and a pouting bottom lip. At their first encounter, he was an enigma. Their second, a stranger. Their sixth, still yet a stranger. The young King Loupe Wickwolf was cold and distant, and never looked her in the eye, always held her at a distance. This was constantly blamed on shyness, and she accepted the excuse. His shyness would evaporate soon enough.

After a month, she learned this was not shyness alone. He came at her with his lips and hands but never with his heart.

Their wedding ceremony ended in fireworks that boomed so bright and large and far across the kingdom, she was sure even the peasants of Uppica could see them. They created shapes of horns and crests and stars and flowers, all in Wickwolf red. She hoped somewhere, anywhere, the fireworks made someone happy. Because they did nothing for her but reinforce the drained color of his eyes as they flicked away from hers. Nervousness did not look like this, she was sure; what she saw in his eyes was apathy.

"Why are you crying?" he asked her, the vital notes of concern absent in his voice. There was an edge of intoxication to him after the spirit-filled ceremonies and royal galas.

"I'm just so... happy," she lied, and buried herself in his unresponsive chest. His heartbeat was steady and sure, but too faint.

One long day, Gloria decided to wander out of the palace. Loupe had left her alone in her bedroom to go off in a chariot and deal with Lusk. A brusque dismissal with an unemotional kiss.

"Goodbye, Gloria."

"Goodbye, Loupe." She looked at him with startled eyes. This time he actually spoke her name.

And thus began her wandering. The freezing rain had died off, so Gloria could leave the castle without getting pelted. She wore a brown cloak, and the red-dressed knights did not haggle her. Strangely, they paid no attention to her.

But she wandered too far. The luxury diminished and the architecture dropped and shrank. She was lost in the country she ruled over. A buzzing heat drifted about, and in it milled a hundred beggars.

"Miss?"

A rake-thin young girl with straw-colored hair and no shoes stared at her with wide eyes. As she looked back, she noticed one was brown, the other green. A peasant mutation, perhaps — but she couldn't help thinking it looked fascinating. The girl's clothes were dingy and torn, but her face was like palace porcelain, and innocent as a child's.

"'Scuse me, miss, are you an angel?"

The girl's voice sounded soft and smooth, not at all how she had imagined a commoner to sound, and her words rang sincere.

She couldn't help thinking she was the one who echoed an angel.

"Oh, um, thank you," she said. "No, I'm just a lost human."

"Well — you're beautiful," said the girl with the mismatched eyes, without embarrassment or inhibition.

Oh, a streetwalker calls me beautiful, she thought, *but never him.*

"Thank you — ah — what is your name?"

"It's Olive. Nice t'meet you, miss."

"You, as well."

"Might I see you 'round?" She smiled like a child, and reminded her that she was one as well.

A married child, who held a kingdom halfheartedly in her fingertips.

(A sad bride. A catatonic grace. A single scream through the city.)

Gloria hesitated. "Perhaps you will." She hated to lie, so everything she said, everything she did, she did halfway. Maybe. Perhaps. We'll see. She couldn't look at her eyes anymore. Her ragged clothes. The dismal streets that surrounded her.

It was a mistake. All of it.

Loupe remained a stranger to her.

His absence settled and lingered on. As the months of their wedlock dragged, his love failed to grow; if anything, it shrank or never existed in the first place. She wanted him to love her, but much more than that, she wanted to love him. She wanted to feel something, anything at all, for the man she slept next to, and would sleep next to every day for the rest of her life.

They settled in their twenty-foot velvet bed as stars swelled in the black-ink sky. "I love you," she tried, in the softest whisper she could manage, reaching for his distant face.

The silence didn't last. She wished it would. Instead he said, "Yes," and leaned in to kiss her. She grabbed hold of his face and his eyes opened again, startled.

She had to say it. The words rose in her throat. They sprang from her lips before she could stop them.

"Do you love me, Loupe?"

He just nodded and leaned toward her once more, but Gloria drew away. *No, no — I need words.*

Tiny lines grew in her face. Her eyes paled and her hair darkened. She longed to break down the walls of the palace and travel to the outskirts again, where he would be waiting with two colors in his eyes and raw, beautiful words in his mouth.

It was all a dream, just as she liked it. If it stayed inside her head, it could never change. It would always be beautiful. She loved the world she built inside of herself. In it, there was no trouble, and so many words.

The royal conferences and treaties and galas and corsets and ribbon coats began to suffocate her. The weather froze, the trees sank, and she grew tired of her life.

She strayed at last. The cloak was warm.

"Have you seen a girl called Olive?"

I don't know, I don't know, they told her. Who?
Her heart struggled with it. Maybe she was just a dream, after all.
It had grown so cold since the last time.

As she walked home, the wind sang her a nocturne.

Words came at last.

Loupe arrived home, dark-eyed with exhaustion, his hair in slight, curling disarray. His lips shook with snow. "Gloria, Gloria."

She approached him quietly, still in shock at the sound of her name, this time spoken twice.

"Yes?"

"My Gloria..." A third time. He neared her. "Don't you know I love you?"

Her eyes were pried open with surprise, with the the urgency of his voice. She could only manage to say "What?"

"I love you," he whispered again, his bottom lip trembling. "I'll say it as many times as you want. Please listen to me."

"I'm listening."

"But you don't love me..." There was a strange brokenness to his voice, and also a surrender. She had never seen him so physically cold, but with such warmth in his voice.

"I — " She paused. "I don't *know* you, Loupe. We don't know each other. We never even knew each other at all..." The words echoed around the velvet room. "I just want to know you."

"I'm a bad man, Gloria," Loupe whispered, shaking his head of snow. The white of the snowflakes stood out in the black of his hair. "That is all you really must know about me."

He looked back at a bewildered face.

"I haven't been faithful to you, Gloria." A lonely tear rolled from a long, dark eyelash. "I have disgraced you. And for that I'm sorry. I'm a bad man. What's done can never be undone. But..."

"I know that," she said under her breath. "I know. You're wrong. It can be fixed, Loupe. It never happened. It's alright." She spoke of his affair like an unfortunate accident, a tug of fate, that had simply jostled and wronged him. She ignored his wrongdoing and replaced it with the notion of a broken man.

The broken man stared back at her and embraced her along with the lie, and they became two broken people, cracks in a palace mirror, glued back together to form a splintered reflection.

At last.

After years of the kingdom's impatient waiting, Gloria and Loupe finally had one child, a boy. Ezra Loupe Aymeric Nikolas Kira Wickwolf, a long string of names that meant little to her and even less to the babbling boy. The baby's eyes were deep brown, but a softer, yellower color than his father's. As he grew, dark hair sprouted in his head and freckles appeared on his cheeks. His eyelashes matched those of his father, dark and curling and long. He learned to read with ease and tore down the Wickwolf library in search of story after story. As the days passed, Gloria treasured his footsteps, his sleepy eyes scanning pages; she grew to love him. As he chased around Belvidere with his two strange friends, she grew to love him even more. From the picture window she saw a boy with a future; a fate of golden happiness, one untouched by the wars of her childhood. But it could have been just another dream.

Inside the Kosta castle, before the war, I ran up to her with urgency. My eyes pleaded and sang.

"Mother, I like them a lot."

"Yes, yes, I can tell."

"But they say – mother, come closer."

"Yes?"

"They whisper. They say Regena's below us."

"Who does?"

"All the grown-ups. They don't like it when we're all in the forest together. They think we're doing dangerous things, and causing trouble, and being a disgrace."

"It doesn't matter, Ezra," Gloria said. "I'll tell you a secret. Being born to a king doesn't change if you're good or bad."

My wide eyes lit. "Of course I know that."

She stared sadly into her glass of icewater. Her eyelashes stooped. I knew this expression. Of longing, of regret, the kind of expression a child would never want to see on his mother's face.

"What is it?"

Her response would puzzle me for years.

"You don't speak like a child anymore."

◇

That fateful day came.

The city was too cold, frostier than usual. The Wickwolf royal family paraded down the road by the pull of white horses and angel-carved golden wheels. Gloria Wickwolf watched the waltz of the white mist in the sky. Her son sat between her and the King, fidgeting in his seat and staring out, with a childish awe that echoed that of the crowd's.

Through the silence and the dancing air, it broke in. The glass, the mirror, all of it shattered in one irretrievable second.

From an invisible gun came the strike of a Regicide bullet.

The horses neighed and screeched and sped in the street, their hooves knocking and their mouths gaping. Their eyes were on fire with fear. Everything was loud, the howls of the crowd, and that eternal scream that cut through the mist and rang through the kingdom and remained in the city forever.

The world screamed along with them, and fell to pieces.

Gloria cradled the body of the King in her cold, shaking hands. At first she did not believe it. It was a particularly bad nightmare, that's all. That's all. In a matter of seconds, the truth began to eat at her eyes. They were first. They shook. They sank to the still-bleeding man that had always slept beside her. Then came her mouth — it expanded as if swallowing the contents of a soul. But not yet her voice. It struggled through her throat, it failed her. It had broken itself to pieces with its grappling to come free.

Finally, the scream sliced her throat.

Don't die. Please! Not when I had just begun to love you... Her thoughts screamed along with siren of her voice, but no one and nothing listened.

Words let her down her this time. Her body moved on its own, huddling down to protect the only person she had left to love. Thick black hair on faint eyes. Her world was in fragments, but her son was still alive.

"Ezra," she whispered to me, the scream drained from her voice. Hoarse and jolted. My unconscious, trauma-struck body failed to listen, a slight twitch of the shoulder. "You are safe."

Deliriously, her son thought of the songs she used to sing.

Swing low,

sweet chariot...

She collapsed into her last grain of hope, and another gunshot sounded. The second bullet missed and shot straight through the heavens.

CHAPTER XXVI:
THE GIRL WHO
BECAME THE NIGHT

She used to hide at night, when her mother's rage was the most potent. Or when she sometimes brought home drunken men, trailing unwanted into *her* home.

Calling her mother vile names.

This man was particularly filthy. He wore a big coat and a greedy smile. Her mother trailed after him, repeating his words.

"We can just go to my place instead–"

"Your place."

"I've got a big parlor–"

"A *parlor.*"

The girl who was not yet Nox hid in her room. She threw makeshift darts at the wall, wished herself deaf. She tore out pieces of parchment, to write the same line again and again.

This is the last of it. The last of it. The last of it.

It has to end. It has to end. It has to end. It has to end.

Who was the man with the big coat? Was he a hidden king? Was he a man of powder or a magician? Did he cast a spell over her mother, as the ink-man had? And what of her weak, turbulent heart – would he break her, too? Would he leave her to her rags and rages, swatting uselessly at the sky?

Or would he wrap them up in his big coat and take them to his big white parlor, out of their crumbling wooden reality?

Would he bring them out of this?

No. He only filled the house with smoke and sound.

"Maya."

No answer.

"Maya, you keep quiet."

Silence and white smoke.

She wanted to say,

LEAVE US ALONE

She wanted to say,

DON'T COME NEAR ME

but she didn't have the words.

So she took him while he was sleeping, and drowned him in the river.

"Locke."

She sits hunched, breathing like a slumbering viper, clutching her Regicide mask in her raw-chewed fingernails. Her boots dig into the dirt. The trees clamp around her. Their trunks are handgrips, their branches triggers, and everything is hers.

"Where is he?"

"The target is in Uppica," Locke tells her with absolute certainty. "He has trespassed on foreign ground again and aims to conceal himself. He travels in a group."

"A *group*, Locke?"

"Yes, with — unidentified fugitives — although evidence leads me to believe that Prince Kosta and Duchess Pagele have escaped with him. They're absent from the castle – ah, but so is the little Duchess Conquin."

"That fool," she spits into the distance. "Coward. Run all you want, you'll get caught like the rat you are. I'll make you bleed."

Her eyes are clocks, ticking away the nights and days; time bombs, swinging into their own detonation. The most passive eyes you can imagine, but with a secret, feelingless fire.

Her skin, her bones are bulletproof glass, decaying fast.

The leaves of the trees shake their heads in disapproval, and the sun backs away in fear. The grass surrounding her dies, the moisture in the air avoids her. The sun grows cold around her. Nature cowers to her grin.

Her counterfeit smile spreads, and abandons all pretense of happiness.

She shouts to a sky as cold as her own soul. "*Catch me!*" She raises her pitch, more and more and more. "*CATCH ME, YOU COWARD!*" Emotionless tears stream in rapid lines down her face, the sun biting into her eyes. "*CATCH ME!*"

That is Nox.

CHAPTER XXVII:
A WARM WELCOME

Russel stares at the empty stage in disbelief, watches the crowd scatter back to their alleys and homes.

"What was that?"

"Fey," I whisper back. He tilts his head at me, not yet understanding. I keep my voice low. "Princess Fey."

Through the Uppican crowd of white and blue, a figure makes its way toward us. It is kind-looking, with soft edges — a plump woman of about fifty or so.

The woman's eyes are tired and her hair is in curly disarray. She raises a concerned hand to her cheek as her eyes scan over our tight, jumbled group. Her voice is like honey, but with the distinct tint of age.

"Oh, you four look like you've been through something awful."

"I suppose we have," Russel tells her, always the first to speak up. His eyes are heavy-lidded, and dimmer than usual. It worries me.

"You have somewhere to stay?"

"Afraid not, ma'am."

"Oh, dear." The hand is raised to her face again. "Come with me, then."

The town square's lines end and make way to a straight line of white-shouldered, unarmed soldiers. The old woman passes through, but I feel the sharp slap of a hand on my shoulderblade. "Excuse me," says a man with a long scar running across his throat. "Where have I seen you before?"

I can only stare at him in confusion. "I– I've been in the papers before. For community work, and–"

"Oh," he sighs, on a clear note of disappointment.

Uppica has lost its voice after the big, triumphant rally. They've ran out of nonsense to spout, I suppose – but everything is quiet, muted of all loud noise, as if I'm walking in a dream.

Before I know it, the noise picks up again. Beggars swing their hopeless fists until I hear the plunk of silver coins in a cup. Little kids dance in the streets, dirt on their bare feet, flipping ragged ropes in the air and singing.

The mean old man all down the way
Said missy, don't you go
But I said don't you talk to strangers
Mama told me so!
The strange old lady down the street
Tells stories I don't know
But I said don't you look my way
Or out my sight you'll go!
The radio that mama hid
Said there's somethin' a-brew
But I said don't you make up tales
Or I'll unwire you!
And Mama said don't make up tales
Or I'll break you in two.

Soon the moon lurks overhead, in a starless sky, the streets cast with dancing shadows. Scraggly ropes lay on the ground, all the songs done for the day.

The woman leads us through the steely streets and crowded alleys to a long row of tenements. They are much better than the hopeless Corinth slums, it seems, but still bedraggled. The writing on the sign is unprofessional and quick, reading LOSTHOME, marked by graffiti and childish scribbles.

The noise of commotion immediately greets us, the bustling of many men, women, and children. Hungry voices and eager feet.

"Mommy, look! Lookit!"

"Shhh, dear."

I can't help wondering whose hands assembled the imported Kosta clock on the wall. Its ticking is all I hear. It drowns out the warm voice of the woman and the voices of my friends. My eyes keep flickering back to that goddamned clock with its unbending hands going too fast, too slow. That's my problem with clocks: I can't ignore them. They make me nervous. They frighten me, actually. I can't help the pull of my eyes along the ever-moving hands, yet I want to demolish them all.

Stop. Stop ticking.

Time shouldn't have a sound.

I try to tune out the clock. New sounds break in. The creaking of the wooden floor beneath the weight of too many people, the wind shaking the feeble foundation. A comforting kind of wooden creak against the ticking clock. Overpacked lines shuffling on. The clacking of spoons, the rush of people to the meal line, scattered voices, low and high and rough and clear.

I silently thank God there are windows here – they let the moonlight in, let the near-noiseless streets distract me from the ticking of the clock.

The woman examines us with bright, tired green eyes. She hands us cold chamomile tea in frayed paper cups.

"I'm Allanora, by the way."

"J– Jette, and this is Wick... Charles... and Sophie."

"Ah, I see."

"Thank you," June tells her, "for helping us." She squeezes my shoulder to remind me I'm among the living.

"Y-yeah, thank you," I blurt. "Is there anything we can do to help?"

"Take care of yourself, boy." She smiles. It's a smile made of sympathy and concern, a smile stitched out of generosity and knotted with pity.

She knows it. She knows I'm a godforsaken raving lunatic.

CHAPTER XXVIII:
THE LOSTHOME

THEY DANCE IN my mind, those bedtime stories of long ago – of lands called Europe and Africa, kingdoms that once existed, kings that met their end long before the ruin, long before the Regicides.

The grass grew. The gardens bloomed. Everything looked like books, and words sounded sweeter. People spoke in rich tongues.

When I was old enough to understand, my father sat at the end of the bed and told me how that world had ended.

"For years, the oceans swallowed the land and spared us, only us. What the sea didn't eat, the fires did. But the drowned world lives on in our hearts. We carry it with us, and we resurrect it."

We resurrect nothing.

We only recycle.

We sit in a circle in a crumbling corner of the losthome. Hushed voices, lowered faces, dawn light slipping in from the window cracks.

"She's alive, Russel, she was there in the flesh."

"They could've... I dunno, cloned her." He laughs. "It's all kind of a blur.

The whole rally was loud and confusing, you know. Hate to say it, but you might be wrong?"

"No, this was... that was her," I say. "That's why they call her the Jewel – she's their hidden treasure. How could they have kept that from all the kingdoms, that the... the Regicides didn't do the job?"

"They're cut off," says Regena. "We don't even associate with them. If they were burnt to the ground, we'd only know if we smelled the smoke." She flicks her head towards me. "Sorry."

"Uh, it's okay..."

"Alright, I'll take your ridiculous theory into consideration, I guess," she sighs.

"I don't think it's ridiculous." June traces lines through dust on the ground. "I'd like to think there's still a princess in the world."

As the weeks pass on and give way to new days, everyone changes around me. Regena's hair loses its curl and gloss, her eyes revealing themselves, black paint fading. Russel pales, his curly locks darkening and uncoiling themselves from their ringlets. He looks younger, but older at the same time — new. We shrink and grow. Each day we hide ourselves in the losthome, eating sparingly and busying ourselves with memories and conversations. Our words repeat themselves as we avoid the future.

Russel has abandoned hollow happiness and fills himself with what little hope he has. He keeps planting flowers in the dank soil by the entrance. "Wick, Wick," he'll say. "The clouds look like rain today, so those flowers of mine will grow."

Regena is made of ink and anger. "No, they'll get stomped upon by some drunk."

And June – she plants flowers in the cracks in the wood, in a corner of the hall. No one will dare stomp on them.

A corner of the corridor has been given to us where four rumpled cots lay. Our palace bag's been stuffed in a gap in the wall, where white paint is stripping off and the concrete crumbles. The floor sag beneath us as we sleep. I lay between Russel and June, trying desperately to be calm.

But each night, my dreams hunt after me. Each night, a new ingredient of nightmare mixes itself into the old ones, creating a brew. Each night, I wish I could wipe the diamond burn off of June's pale neck as she tosses to the side in her sleep. And each day I wake up to the sight of her in the losthome cot next to mine, those little pale blue flowers sprouting out of nothing. This day is no different.

This particular morning, I wake in the afterglow of a dream. I wake to find her arms coiled around my shoulders, her legs knotting into my own. Her head is pressed to my chest. I would attribute this to nightmares, but there's a deep calmness to her closed eyes that suggests something else. No shaking, no disturbed stirring. Tiny freckles on her nose.

"Bad dream?"

Her eyes flicker open, her face waking up, and she stays for a second, dazed. Then she jolts back, as if by an electric shock. An incoherent exclamation of embarrassment and feathers of hair flying into her eyes. "Oh — ah, I didn't mean to— "

"Be quiet," Regena groans from a neighboring cot. "What *is* it with you two? Good God."

"Good morning, sunshine!" I can hear Russel's buttery voice from one foot away, directed at the pillow-headed girl. "Sleep well?"

"Terrible, actually," I say. He responds with a warm, sleep-filled laugh.

I realize that June's hands are still holding onto me.

"Oh! I knew it!" He smiles a ridiculous smile. "I knew it, I knew it!"

June turns to face him. "Huh?"

"Oh, nothing!"

Though not as heavy as he was before, the floorboards still creak under him as he makes his way to the breakfast line.

The clusters of people that surround us come and go, but we remain. As I look at each group of newcomers, I see a new story in their tired eyes and dragging feet. I quickly attach names to faces. Bene, the tiny boy who always chews his fingernails, and keeps bugs in a jar. Questa, who always sings in the meal line without any music. Ilo, the old man who claims he's been here since the dawn of human existence. The deep lines in his face agree.

The nights grow warmer and the sky gives way to rain.

On the nights where I know I can't leave, I wish I was a cloud. I'd be born as free-flowing water, travel across the earth, and be sucked up into the sky. I'd collect every droplet of water and empty myself into the atmosphere. I would live forever, and I would always have a story to tell.

Right now, we're living like ghosts, just floating by the cracks in our lives and trespassing upon a world that does not belong to us, and never will.

We hide from the world in our tight-packed corner of Uppica, where paint peels and eyes close and candles quiver. Kit bags shuffle in and out, and Allanora gives us a sad, questioning smile with each new morning we decide to wait. Cowards, all of us, but I'm the worst of the lot. Her old eyes know it.

A morning arrives that seems longer and emptier than the others. The sky outside the losthome window is pure white. A blank canvas. It needs color, it needs scratches in its surface, it needs ink. I want to dig my fingernails into it and drag them down.

I just can't shake the feeling that something needs to be done. We have to move, we have to change. It takes a while before I can put my thoughts into words.

"We've got to pull ourselves out of this place sooner or later," I whisper to the group.

Allanora hands us a parcel of her very best cookies before she waves goodbye. Her smile, this time, is more forlorn than ever. I wonder fleetingly if she can read minds. When she looks at us, does she see our stories and know our thoughts? Our pasts? I don't want to believe it. But there is something knowing in the sad curl of her lips.

Before leaving, June approaches her one last time.

"Excuse me," she whispers. "D'you happen to know anyone by the name of Jette Chajkia?"

The woman's face is puzzled; the wrinkles in her brow grow deeper. "Chajkia? No," she utters. "Though I do know of a Jette Gretling. A pretty young woman, though, isn't she? Lives somewhere in the Kingdom City, I b'lieve — "

"I'm sorry, I... was mistaken." June touches the woman on the arm — softly, apologetically. "Thanks, Allanora."

Why is it always the woods?

Why do I always run?

The forest welcomes us back like old friends. It embraces us in its barren arms. After it all, we've run out of mundane things to talk about, theories to concoct – and the painful words are scratching at the surface. I can feel it, like a scent hanging in the air. It's a matter of time before they break through.

And break through they do.

But only once the night has come and everyone is asleep once more, only then do the words make their entrance. The darkness is interrupted by the tiny glow of the wheezing campfire. Russel and June are rolled over in the dead grass, but neither Regena or I can seem to settle down and sleep.

I still can't believe the person sitting next to me is real.

When I first met her, she was an chubby, short-tempered eight-year-old duchess with her face permanently planted in *The Princess Dragon* and her hand always unenthusiastically attached to Russel's. She evolved into someone I could never know, someone above me, and by some twist of fate, became who she is now. The girl sitting next to me, with matted hair, sleepy skin, and a hood over her forehead.

The silence is heavy, but outweighed by her salt-soaked voice.

"That goddamned castle is gone."

Regena's face is a flickering fire, her words spilling over into a storm. Thick locks of brown hair shield her eyes, her whisper.

"The first word I said to him was 'no'. Just that... 'no'. The last were 'stay the hell away from me.' My mother, too. 'Stay the hell away from me.'"

I tremble along with her, despite the strange warmth of the night. "Y... you know, you don't have to talk about it if you don't want to."

"I need to," she tells me with broken certainty.

We curl into ourselves, and sit in silence for a moment.

"I can't get that castle off of me." Her voice joins her hands in the constant, rhythmic tremble that mirrors mine. "I could stand under the shower for all my life and it would never work. I could try, I'd never be clean, I'd never be right again and... it might just be that it's my fault that they all detest me..."

"No." I feel my voice breaking, but I struggle to keep it strong. Her eyes are an orange flame, struggling to keep burning on. "No, Regena, you... no one could detest you."

"I can trust you, can't I?" she asks, the fire in her voice deteriorating by the second. "Ezra?"

"Of course you can."

She embraces me like the child is, like the friend she has always been, so snug it almost hurts. But she won't allow herself to cry again. Not ever. Not over the distant past of castles and confinement.

"You know everything will be okay, right? That everything bad will end sooner or later?"

I wish I could claim these words, but they seem to be coming from somebody else, unreal on my lips.

She lowers her head to a nod.

"Please believe me."

The ghost of the fire floats beside and watches over our camp. The song of rain sings us to sleep.

◇

A trail of tangled black hair and dirty boots drag along. The thin mouth curls, and the siren eyes watch the distant city.

The buildings are blue blocks against the sky, as if sculpted by a child. Smoke streams from factories.

Despite the change of the weather, Uppica grows cold around her. Its steely buildings and glass chambers and blue silk curtains and grimy pathways. Warmth runs from her, and so does her target.

"Uppica at last," says Spindel, but she pays him no attention.

Her mouth opens slightly, baring teeth.

Her eyes are the color of a polluted sky.

"The game is mine, Prince Wickwolf. You lose."

◇

Without moving or even breathing too loudly, I open my eyes. The dying sparks of fire fizzle out beside me, but a new light washes over the forest. The sunlight burns for a moment, but then the colors come. I wake to the sight of home.

They sit on a fallen tree.

Russel holds Regena's hand in his, with a strange and sunny cautiousness. The other hand he uses to make swirls of black ink on her fingers and knuckles, working his way up to her wrist. He looks like a child, though his face is worn and pale. His eyes have the focus of an expert craftsman, but Regena looks like she could drift off to sleep at any moment. The forest seems to have brightened him; his drooping curls are illuminated by the white forest sun, his expression wide awake. For the first time in a long time, he sits up straight on the log.

I drift in and out of sleep, and they stay at their spots in the sun.

"You know," I hear her say, "when you're not talking, you kind of look like an angel."

I don't catch the look on his face, but I'm sure it's a startled smile. "You got a fever or something, Reg?" His pale hand is pressed to her forehead now, as he lets out the music of nervous laughter.

There is a long stretch of quiet that I'm not sure I should be intruding upon. I can't help it. I glance back to see Regena slant into him and — no, no, it's just my imagination.

A question comes from her mouth, and its name is Joss. The small conversation falls to a hush.

"She's gone now."

"You can't just make someone *gone*."

"It was just because of my father. You know that, don't you? Arranged. He was the one who set it up." He picks up her hand again and absently draws swirls and stars and curling vines, like the ones that congregated the castle walls. He's concentrating more on the patterns he draws on her skin than anything else.

She speaks. "He was right, though, wasn't he..."

A pause in the whispering. The ink moves again.

"No."

Regena plucks the marker out of his hand just as he's finishing another vine. Their quiet discourse shifts to ink. She takes his large, pale, sunlit palm. She writes, in quick letters,

I'M SORRY

When he raises his gaze from the black ink, she's in tears.

"For what?" He puts a palm to her cheek. "For what, Reg?"

She takes the pen to her untouched cheek.

EVERYTHING'S RUINED

Russel reclaims the pen. He licks his thumb and rubs it across the black ink on her face.

EVERYTHING'S RUINED

His fingers and ink work along the curve of her cheek. Tears sprout in his eyes and his regal posture falls again. In the place of those two heavy words, he draws flowers. A dozen black-line magnolias are blooming from her cheek.

Russel takes her hand again, just lightly by the fingertips, and finds an uninked spot on her wrist. The ink spills harder this time, the pen failing to catch it.

I meant it

Regena stares at the ink on her wrist and the water in his fast-blinking eyes. Her mouth twists, trying to form a response. She bites her lip so hard it bleeds. Russel looks away. He's terrified of her answer, which will undoubtedly be an exhausted dismissal. A child-like slap to the face. If he's lucky, she'll spit on his arm. I love you was a ridiculous thing to say. Now, with no blood spilling from his mouth, he must realize it.

"S-sorry. If you..."

Her lips interrupt him, just softly.

This moment doesn't belong to me. I try to look away, but I can't hide the smile that settles. I steal a glance. She's drawn away. I expect his face to be a shooting star, a monument to the years of hopeless pining, but no – he's crying.

The tears make tracks down the grime on his face, and his mouth is a trembling, stupefied parody of a smile.

"I'm sorry," he repeats.

CHAPTER XXIX:
SCREAMING SKY

THE CURIOSITY IS unbearable. I need to investigate, I need to move. Sleep is too chaotic, and I feel like a fool – slowing my terrified breathing, desperately clinging to comfort when I wake, crying into her familiar shoulder. Like a child. The ground is too silent now, and silence is the worst pain in the world.

My only weapon is a gleaming, sunlit knife that still smells of hair.

Somewhere between midnight and dawn, I wander out of the forest. I leave behind the dozing forms of Regena, Russel, and June, with guilt in my gut. *I won't be long.* Then my legs move on their own. My restless legs, like the turning hands of clocks. They can't seem to stop once they start.

I feel the words form on my mouth. *Princess Fey. Is Princess Fey alive?* I practice them under my breath, and they taste like hope. The leaves of the trees are dancing for me. The sky is a warm river. Uppica is a good place to be.

The first discovery comes quick, as I look on the farming house that lies just over the border of the woods. It is revealed to me in the form of a shackle-kneed young man in black rags. His face is distraught. His arms are accepting.

Not only kings keep pawns here.

"You useless pawn, get the hell in here!"

I hear it in a quick bark from within. They, too, are branded - I remember the swollen scar on June's neck, more visible now then ever. But unlike hers, they are not diamonds; they are not arrowheads. They are numbers. And they are burned straight across their foreheads.

I dare to approach the farmhouse, crossing the short, innocent fence.

The pawn, branded Sixty-One, speaks to me in an indistinguishable foreign language, rich and thick and beautiful, with words I've never heard or imagined.

"Hello?"

"Ah... ah... help!" He switches languages. "Please!"

"You speak the King's tongue?" I ask.

"Yes − not good − help. Help? You help me?"

"Yes," I say, misjudging. His face is so miserable, so desperate, I can't help it. "Yes, I can help you." I realize now that this boy looks vaguely like me. Dark skin. Freckled. Black hair, his falling over his shoulders. Tall in stature, but with the unmistakable hunch of a pawn. But his eyes are green, the color of a river.

"The knife... the knife..." I remove it from my pocket. His eyes looks frightened; he thinks I'll hurt him. *Why is that always the assumption?* I begin to think, but quickly correct myself. The boy's like June, in a way. He's like all the pawns − who flinch at the sight of a sharp edge, an extended arm, a smile. When you are beaten on your whole life, you expect every hand to hurt you.

I cut a fringe for the boy, and it covers his brand adequately. With his pawn number covered, I realize I don't know his name.

"Your name," I whisper. "What is your name?"

"Sixty-One," he whimpers, echoing the burn on his head. "That all."

"What the hell are you doing?" A rocky, malicious voice. Its owner reveals himself, a man of tall stature and momentous girth, in the usual Uppican colors. A whip, as well. He cracks it immediately at number Sixty-One. "*Get back!*"

The whip lashes again, this time carving the boy's face. Without thought. I hear his wail carry across the land. Once more. I hear broken words on broken ground. This time, the word is lit on fire. "Please!"

"And you! Geddoff my *goddamn* property!"

I stop the venom of the whip with my shoulder. It catches a strip of muscle and bone - and burns like absolute hell. The sting is unbearable. It cooks my skin, it reaches inside me. A strangled groan escapes my throat before I can explain myself. But judging from the look in this man's eyes, explaining won't do it.

"I did not kill the cows!" Sixty-One insists, cowering from the whip. "I did not kill the cows, my master. It was girl — *girl!* She kill it. Skin it! She take cow to eat! Hair, long, black. Skin of white. Mask. She wear mask, my master. Two X."

A mask.

Two X.

I swallow a scream.

The word sends me running, reeling, bolting from the hideous farm. I hear the man's heavy voice call after me, another crack of the whip, but he matters little to me. What can he do? He can only whip me. A pathetic old pawnmaster on the side of the island. He's no great threat. Not when they are near.

They are near.

The Regicides are coming for me, their masks and guns and shrieking silence. Running is the only choice I have. Running, running again. I can't keep living in a forest, sleeping, dreaming –

Any other time, the trees might have felt like a rescue, a heroic embrace. But now they feel like scratchy fingers and nails, gripping at my back. *Why did I do it? I left him behind. He trusted me –*

His eyes like rivers, sad and neverending–

Their leaves flog me. Twigs lash at the jagged gash of the whip on my shoulder. I realize, with my heart dragging along in my body, I am so damaged.

They're still here.

They still lie sleeping, all of them. Russel taking flight, maybe freefalling in his sleep. Regena curled into a ball. June turned to the side. They lie in a cluster, unaware — I picture a Regicide net snatching them like fish. It seems even my imagination is out to get me.

I jostle them all at once, ignoring the pounding in my head.

"You snuck out?!" Regena grips my bleeding shoulder until it stings, thrashing against me with gritted teeth. "You absolute, godforsaken idiot, have you got a deathwish?"

Yes, I think fleetingly.

"Run!" I cry. "Back to the city! We have to run!"

CHAPTER XXX:
MOTHER

THE KINGDOM CITY is alive again, with the calculated music of chanting. White and blue, blue and white. At first, the ground is stony and dead on my slippered feet, but the continuous stomping brings it to life. It seems that the whole of the city has been congregated in this one square, watching the blue curtains and the man without a face.

Uppica! Uppica! Uppica! The chant is endless. Their faces are focused on his familiar blue pants and polished shoes, and the voice with no origin. They are loud and bright. Stirring. Roaring. All with vacant eyes.

I wait to see her again with my own eyes. Princess Fey, the Jewel of Uppica, the girl whose eyes are made of glass.

"The sun is shining still," June hums to herself, scanning the crowd. Her voice grows louder above the Uppican chant. In her hands she holds the stuffed animal from the Ward.

She slips through the cracks in the crowd like water, like air. As she continues to sing, the confused looks multiply on the entranced faces around her. They stare at her – some with awe, some with contempt. She has disrupted their daily ceremony.

> *"Out by your windowsill...*
> *The angels sing their song,*
> *Quiet, low, and long.*
> *I love you still today,*
> *Don't ever go away.*
> *My courage reappears*
> *Whenever you are near.*
> *Your face is like the sun.*
> *The day has just begun.*
> *I'll always be with you,*
> *The song I sing*
> *is true..."*

She sings the last few notes in the strongest, clearest notes she can muster, and in the most vulnerable of voices. She mixes with the wind. She searches the crowd for a woman of about forty-five, with kind wrinkles in her face. *Please be here.*

The woman who approaches her is no more than thirty-one.

The milky brown hair has faded and darkened with time. Her coffee eyes have a natural look of sadness, but slightly aged — and now pried open with astonishment. Her expression is a question.

She holds the hand of a fluffy-haired man, and a tiny, teetering child with dirt on her face.

The sun is shining still...

The dark side of the moon.

Out by your windowsill.

A baby born in snow.

A girl born from hope. From longing.

A girl made from a springtime song.

She dares to say it.

"J... june?"

The name barely makes it to her ears in the Uppican buzz.

Her face lights up, flickers, makes sense of the tiny family in front of her.

She says the word hesitantly at first, unaccustomed to the sound of it.

"Mama?"

"It's you." Jette takes a step forward and clutches her daughter by the pale, frightened face. "It's... it's you, isn't it?" She tosses her arms around the girl.

June's confused sputters are interrupted by the man to her side. "This... is..." He raises a palm to his mouth. "Oh, Christ in heaven, Jette, you were right."

"Hail the Jewel of Uppica!"

"*Hail the Jewel of Uppica!*"

The glass eyes blink, just once. I watch her small face, her unmoving mouth. Then suddenly, I swear for just a second, her eyes latch onto me. The line of her mouth wavers.

Almost imperceptibly, it happens.

She draws her fingers in a straight X.

I feel my fear swell inside me. She's alive, but she's not safe beyond the shallow walls of their little charade, the thin glass they've encased her in. She knows she isn't.

Somebody. Anybody. I rush through the crowd, crying out, trying to find the words these people will listen to, words that will make them understand. But nobody will listen to me.

Someone. Anyone — this middle-aged woman in front of me.

"They're here!" I tell her. "The Regicides. They've come back!"

"Excuse me, boy?" She eyes me like I'm speaking in different tongues. Every word is a question. "You'll have to repeat yourself?"

"Haven't you heard of the Regicides?" I ask, feeling the despair in my voice, willing myself not to step in and rattle her by the shoulders. "Haven't you heard of the War?"

"I haven't the foggiest clue what you're going on about," the woman mumbles, dismissing me and rejoining the crowd. Her eyes are wide with concern, like I'm a raving drunk. Seems likely: I haven't had proper sleep in weeks — if you'd like to be meticulous, years —, my hair is ruffled up into chaos, my eyes are probably beyond bloodshot, my cheeks have hollowed out considerably. I'm a madman to her.

"Please!" I scream, my voice just a drop of water in a foreign ocean. "Please listen to me!"

No one can hear me. No one wants to. I'm an undesirable.

I wrestle through the crowd, climbing for the steely blue stage, jumping with all my might. I feel a leathery glove at my ankle and frantically kick free.

"You've been lied to!" I shout, and watch the crowd grow silent. "The Regicides are here! In *Uppica*!"

Without warning, a large surveillance guard plucks me from the stage. He is voiceless, his cold breath seeping out from his slot of a mouth. He offers no explanation, no words at all.

Suddenly, I see my friends ripping through the crowd, pumping their hands in the air to catch my attention, calling for me, drowning in the churning ocean of Uppica.

"Wick! WICK!"

But their calls are useless.

I feel a sharp blow to the neck and everything goes cold.

CHAPTER XXXI:
THE KNIGHT'S PRISONER

THE AIR IS DANK and murky, but the noise leaking out from the pub gladly smothers their conversation, guarding their hushed, gruff voices. Several layers of dirt cake the walls behind them, Some wear Uppican blue, some brown leather; all blend in perfectly with the battle-worn travelers. In pink rags and a white sunbonnet, Nox stands tall, perfectly still in her suppressed rage.

She wraps a white, long-fingered hand around Locke's neck. "Where the hell is he?"

"There's news in the square — some lunatic boy shouting about — can you please let go—"

Nox laughs, high and loud, and looses her grip on his throat. "Locke, *where the hell is he?*"

"If you'd care to know, Lady Nox, Prince Kosta was sighted among the crowd – poorly disguised, obviously– aside from that, Fey's not quite *done with,* would you say–"

"You know perfectly well," she breathes, "that's not who I'm after."

"If you'll allow me to say it, your grace, our mission isn't fixed upon Prince Wickwolf."

"*Our* mission!" she sneers. "It was always *mine*, always!"

Locke's eyes are wide, bright, almost childlike in their shock. He stands still for what seems like a long expanse of time, staring at the trembling face before him – the pale, glittering eyes, the thin-lipped mouth, black hair falling from the bonnet in riverlike twists.

"I have to say, I thought you to be better than this. This personal vendetta against the boy, because you share a father." His voice shakes. "Pathetic."

Nox is frozen to the spot, nostrils flaring, eyes dangerously wide. No one dares to speak.

"How dare you..." It would be less frightening if she'd raise her voice, if she'd raise a hand and slap him across the face. Instead, she whispers so low only Locke can hear. "How dare you speak of that man."

He bows his head now, shaking. "Lady Nox, I apolog—"

She clamps a hand over his mouth, so he can smell the metal of her gun. "It'd do you well to keep your mouth shut."

This cell he has thrown me in is even smaller than Ward One, Room Eight. It's a solitary cell — I suppose my crime was awful enough to separate me from any and all human contact. It smells overwhelmingly of rust and dried blood, despite its polished blue walls, as if there are many unseen layers to this place. Acid. Rust. Cleaning fluid. Soap. Lye. They've scrubbed these walls so ridiculously hard. I'll break them down, I'll break this whole rotten place, I'll whittle it down to its rotten bones. I pound my fists on the walls, and call "No! No!" but the man does not linger. The last metal clomp of his boot. I'm another criminal.

Everything I have done until now has led up to this. I have fled. I have toiled. I have dreamed. I have ran and ran and ran. But I'll never, never escape. They will always catch me and drag me back to one prison or another, alone.

I will myself to relax, feel my muscles melt. *Draw your mind away. Catch your breath and throw it back.* It was bound to end this way. Things were never going to end well for me. *Focus on nothing but what surrounds you.* The smell that drifts in reminds me of the bomb shelter – scrubbed endlessly, but never clean, reeking of concrete. I hear the tired moans of a dozen other men, waiting for their verdicts.

Suddenly I hear a voice that sounds like rescue in my ears.

"Does *this* mean anything to you?"

Russel speaks to the surveillance guard, holding the Wickwolf pendant in his hand. From the temporary-hold cell, I see his desperate face. I see June, Regena, and a couple of older strangers with their hands clasped tight. A little kid, too. I don't know what to make of it.

"Ah..." The bulky guard grabs at the tiny, gleaming red wolf. "Ah, where did you find this — "

Russel points a distraught finger in the direction of my prison cell. I can just discern the shape of his mouth, his voice colored with desperation. His lips twitch into a smile. "My good man, you've just thrown Prince Wickwolf in jail."

At first, the guard's lips form the beginnings of a laugh. What a ridiculous excuse for a breakout.

"That kid — he... he..." Then his face widens, brightens with epiphany. "By God, he's alive!"

His enormous feet stomp to my cell, and he jams a key into the rusted slot. Its twist is music. "Come out, now," he hollers. I obey. "I'll take you to Lusk."

"Lusk?" I croak. The word is heavy.

"Yes," he tells me. He reaches down, and I flinch out of reflex – but from his pocket he pulls a circular badge. On it is printed the curving shape of the island, and it reads 'Belvidere Knights'. His voice now lowers to a hush. "It's my duty to keep you alive."

The knight grips my wrist and pulls me back to the small group in the prison front. "I believe this belongs to you," he says, slipping the pendant into my shaking hand. The Wickwolf crimson has faded to a resigned shade of red.

"Thank you."

The man now looks me straight on. His eyes are dark and narrow, unmoving but kind. He paws along in his pocket, and finds a slick white key, labeled *Knightpilot*.

"Prince Wickwolf, have you ever before been in an airplane?"

CHAPTER XXXII:
THE UNDERGROUND INN

AN AIRPLANE.

"I haven't, sir. I don't — I don't know what that is."

I know full well what an airplane is. Years ago, my father's troops sent out our supply; Kosta sent back their sturdier ones, with better bombs to drop. From thousands of feet in the sky, they wreaked havoc on our kingdom. At that point, the military men had taken control of it all. They didn't bother with my mother; she was always asleep. I only remember bits and pieces of the truth; all else has drowned in my memory. The head of our Army rose his head from its cloud of cigar smoke and spoke to his lieutenant in a voice he made no effort to conceal.

"The boy's traumatized," he spat, like my trauma was a character flaw that could be easily fixed. "Best to let him alone."

Yes, I'm sure it was much more comforting to be locked in my room alone with my thoughts than to have a hand to hold. Did me a lot of good.

The lines in the knight's face move as he speaks. His voice is oddly proud, almost enthusiastic. "An aircraft. It flies through the sky, and it can take you anywhere. This one carries up to thirty passengers. It's the first one we've reconstructed in Uppica."

"Reconstructed?"

"Yes, from a crash, long ago. Airplanes were not as sturdy at the start. They often collapsed. But this" — he pipes a laugh — "this is a miracle if I ever saw one."

"A miracle," I repeat. A miracle that will take me back to Wickwolf, a miracle that could save or destroy me. "But sir... the Regicides will find me. I'm not safe in the castle."

"We're not going to your castle."

He takes us out in the open air, behind the prison. The sight of it is not comforting – a slapped-together contraption or metal and plastic, complete with shabby seating. *It's something. It's something.* As he loads us in, there's a strange jolt in my heart.

"Captain Annike at your service," the man laughs. "Didn't properly introduce myself."

The airplane shakes in the sky. The seats are strapped in precariously, and the floor feels rickety on my feet. Sturdy, my eye. I can feel the lurch and pitch of it, a constant irregular sway – this is a step above death trap. But that doesn't quell the infinite gratitude I have for the knight.

June echoes my thanks. "How can we repay you, sir?"

"Keep safe." He pats her on the head. They always seem to do that. "I'm sick of it, you know. I've had enough of this war. Everywhere it's fire and people running for safety. I've had enough of watching bodies fall." His face grows solemn. A definite soldier. I see it in the lines of his face, his rigid stance, the slight hesitation in his laugh.

"Where are the Regicides?" I struggle even to ask.

"Oh, they're now situated in Uppica. Miles below our feet, I dare say."

"They'll shoot at us." I imagine dozens of men with blank-mask faces, lead X's over their eyes, aiming their firearms up at our creaking contraption of an air carrier. I can't hide my shudder.

The knight speaks to me from the pilot's seat. "We're flying too high for their bullets to reach, my boy."

I can only hope he's right.

The ride is long and lurching, with June's head nestled in my shoulder, jolting occasionally. Russel and Regena sit opposite to us, with their hands set courteously in their laps. Real royals.

A single question from Russel, who's eyeing a basket of breadtwists: "Can we have some food?" Regena elbows him in the shoulder. "Aye!"

"Er, yes, and who may you be?"

"Prince of Kosta," Russel drawls, a childish smile widening on his face. He takes two breadtwists, handing one to Regena.

"*Another* one?" He laughs again, keeping his eyes focused on the sky. I'm quite enjoying his complete lack of formality. "My God."

I hadn't yet paid any attention to the man and woman sitting behind us, not to mention their kid. I turn my head back to them, careful not to disturb June.

"Hello," I whisper, which seems to startle them. Oh, that's right — I'm a prince, after all, talking to foreign civilians. "Excuse me... who might you be?"

"I'm Cole, and this is Jette," the fluffy-haired man informs me, placing a hand on the shoulder of who I assume is his wife. "We're the parents of this little girl." He pats his tiny daughter on the head. His hand travels to June's sleeping head. "And this one."

"Ah!" My reaction is immediate, and my face feels strangely hot. I'm all too aware of her cheek on my neck. "Nice to meet you." Jette and Cole smile back at me, and it's all just like a dream. Who are these people? What have I done to get where I am now?

"It'll be another few hours," Annike hollers from the front of the plane.

The Wanderer still sits in the palace pack.

"That old book again?" Regena smiles. I see Russel has drifted into sleep on her shoulder.

"Look," I say, gesturing to June. "We match."

She just glares. "She's probably not *drooling*, though."

The Wanderer
Chapter 2: The Paralian Village

The wanderer meandered on, ignoring the heaviness of his feet and the faint dragging of his memories. He was looking for a place called home, but he had wandered so long he could not remember it. It was somewhere, without a doubt. Somewhere in his memory, a grand piano sang across the halls. The waves washed against a glass castle, and a little boy looked out. He had forgotten now who that little boy was.

The wanderer's chest felt strangely empty since he'd last taken this path. Before, he had a hand to old. Since then, he'd replaced his heartbeats with an ocean metronome. And he'd learned that if you hollow out your heart, you'll only create an echo larger than you can contain.

The sky looked dismal to him now. He'd read plenty of books that talked about the sky, and being children of the stars, but at that moment the wanderer felt like a disowned son. He firmly believed that the stars were crossed against him.

There seemed to be no place to go for a man with a hollow heart. A man who looked out upon the sea and saw emptiness. Where were the fallen stars and broken bits of seashell? Nowhere to be found. The pirates and rogues and storybook mermaids, all absent from the scene.

A voice called out to him, but he couldn't see a single soul.

He thought of all the people he had left behind. He felt their pain in his bones, and wondered for a second if they did too.

When you hurt someone, you hurt yourself. It isn't any different.

At the time of our arrival, it is already night.

The plane whirs to a halt in the clearing of an unfamiliar forest. As it goes down, nausea rises in my stomach, but my struggle against it is successful. All I allow myself to think of is the destination. Not my past. Not what caused me to run to this godforsaken forest. Not the blurry uncertainty of my future.

In the spot where I discarded my palace knife so long ago, an underground inn has been built. I can see the path it makes into the ground, but not what lies inside of it.

I clutch the coarse shirt of the Knightpilot as he begins to walk forward. "My mother," I whisper, "is she back in the castle?"

"No, Ezra." He looks directly at me. "She's in the underground inn."

It takes me a minute to register.

She's here.

My first steps into the ground are cautious, measuring. It's a lie, isn't it? It's another trap with Wickwolf bait.

No. No. It can't be. The rest follow me, including the Knightpilot.

Inside the candlelit inn, there is a long bed of fabric and feathers, and two tired bodies seated on it. Emelin, staring in disbelief. The queen — my mother. She rests there, but it isn't that same old comatose sprawl. My mother lies across the bed, diagonally, propped up against the dirt wall. My nightmares disintegrate. Queen Gloria Wickwolf is alive. *Alive.*

"Mother." I nudge her shoulder in disbelief. "Mother, wake up."

This time, her eyes open. I had forgotten their color — it's a soft, muted brown, and there are sleepy crinkles around the edges. I can't help but think of the torment I must have caused her, the sleepless nights she must have spent in an empty palace bed, watching the empty world outside her window, thinking of the two who have left her. Oh, what did she do to deserve it? Her skin looks paler than before, but with a rich candle glow. She wears the dark red nightgown I last saw her in – it seems like a century ago. Tears collect in my eyes, but I hold them back, *for God's sake, don't let the sight of a nightgown make me cry.*

"Ezra," she whispers, clasping me to her. Her hair smells of regret in a velvet bed, of long empty sleeping years, of the glass in the broken chariot and the second bullet that shot into the sky, the roll of my father's skull. "You are safe."

I try to believe her words.

You'll look for me one day in your frenzy of fury. You'll aim a gun at an invisible man, a prince who no longer exists. You'll look for me, but you won't find me, because I know how to disappear from you.

I know.

As my mother lies down to sleep, I fear she will stop living again. She'll turn herself off and escape. We're the same, in that way. But June walks on softly over to her. Without fear, she begins to stroke her hair with a shivering hand. She starts talking to her about the wanderer and the lighthouse ghost. She tells her about Kinsel Orphanage and the wind blowing in the windows and Klosswarden. She tells her about Ward One, Room Eight, and what my dreams looked like to her, like a man fighting an invisible monster. How she doesn't like to be alone anymore. About the Pipes. About the losthome. About how everything will be okay. The war can only last so long.

"If the world burns to the ground," she says, "I'll still be here. But the world's already burned to the ground, a long time back, you know."

By the time she is finished, the whole of the inn is in tears. The duchess

and the prince. Her mother and her father. The Knightpilot. Next to her, the
queen has drifted into quiet, cloudless sleep, and candlelight fills the
underground room.

We are drowned in the purest and most vivid shade of yellow that the
dim room can manage. I know this light is only a reflection of the battlefields
and bullets. The gunshots and bombs thrown into innocent taverns. It flickers
like the mob fires in the Kosta streets. Lusk headquarters, raided and ruined.
Children I once knew are tunnel rats. And still the candle glows, like there's
nothing in the world but this hole in the ground and the people in it. The light
sends shadows to our worn-down faces. It illuminates the cracks in the dirt-
caked walls, oblivious to the world and its war.

But it's beautiful all the same.

There are so many of us that our breaths mix together.

June's mother is a woman of, I'd guess, a little above thirty years, with
thick curly hair that glows in the candlelight. Her husband, Cole, has June's
wispy hair and dark eyes, but nothing of her voice. He holds his littlest daughter,
whose eyes are closed in shallow sleep. He speaks to her in a reverent whisper:
"Eshne, Eshne."

The sight of me startles him.

"It's an honor to meet you," he tells me, nervously shaking my hand.
"Really. I remember the day you were born... I was sixteen... and Kosta and
Wickwolf were still on good terms, you know..."

I can feel my cheeks redden. "Oh, thanks – uh – where'd you grow up,
exactly, sir?"

"Corinth, in Kosta."

"I was just there a week ago. God... it was – no offense, sir, but it was
pretty awful. The side we were on, anyway. The minute I got there, this old

brothel-keeper just grabbed my friend and I got in kind of a scrap with him—
kind of punched him—"

June's mother pivots in her seat. "The Pedlar."

"Excuse me?"

"Oh, good holy lord, you punched that man in the face? June must have
left that out of her story."

"He wasn't too happy about it. Strong old man, he punched me back."

Jette looks suddenly misty-eyed, angry. A Junish look. "The smoking
hasn't killed him yet?"

With a wave of embarrassment, I realize that *this* is the Jette Chajkia the
Pedlar was referring to: the one who fled Kosta, who quit being a peddle, who at
some point left June in a shabby old orphanage.

"No, ma'am."

I wake to the sound of moving earth, dozens of people digging their way
through the ground. Sunken-faced, with familiar dirt-caked cheeks, brown eyes
begging for help. Wrestling through in faulty armor. Two Kostan soldiers.

"Where the hell are we, Noor?!"

"Jesus *Christ*, stop running!"

The dirt-caked soldiers slow to a halt, bayonets in their gloved hands.

"It's a goddamn *campsite!*" shouts the girl. Ibby.

At this point, my arms have crossed in front of my face in self-defense,
but no bayonets are lifted to me. A few have woken around me, sleepy and
startled.

I feel a solid, sickly warmth smothering me, filthy gloves pressed to my
back.

"Noor?"

"*Ezra*," he says breathlessly. That dangerous name. His eyes look at me in an entirely new way – an urgent, frightened way. "Lady Josselin... Duke Conquin... Both dead. The Kosta castle – burnt straight down to the ground. The Regicides..." He pulls away with a crazed look in his eyes. They've changed, lost their shine. He's seen many things, things someone so young should never see, things that have nibbled at his heart and shaken him beyond repair.

His breath hitches.

"They're coming for you."

CHAPTER XXXIII:
YOUR GHOST
WILL FOLLOW ME

I SIT IN the sick afterglow of a beautiful dream. The underground room is suddenly full of ghosts, ghosts that claw at the skin of everyone and everything I have left to love. They crawl through honey-colored hair and wounded shoulders, try to burrow through my chest again. I can't let them win.

I see the outline of long black hair against a roaring fire. Shoulders shaking with laughter, smiling and celebrating the ultimate bonfire. Violent yellow flames consuming the palace – first the oubliette, the fire eating away at long-forgotten bones. Then the pawn quarters, deserted. The fire would climb up each step, taking its sweet time. By then, the royals would have evacuated – all but two, pale and idle. With the pawns gone, their stomachs would ache and their eyes would be bleary. The flowers would wilt. The pillars would burn. The bright-cheeked children would watch the pretty orange flames and the crumbling blackness. They wouldn't understand the screams – their eyes would be hypnotized by the dance of gold and red and orange. They would see the real sun for the very first time, outshined by the spreading fire, and reach for it. A jeweled hand would pull them away. Block their view. Their silk skirts turned to ash. Smoke would get in their eyes, and their legs would falter as they ran to safety.

A vast flash of gold. Then a black hole, consuming everything.

I have to be strong this time.

"Excuse me?" Annike says, sitting up authoritatively in his seat on the floor. "Who are you?"

"I don't know," Noor mumbles, vacant as can be. Then his eyes refill with fire, his face contorting like a madman. "*Run*. Run while you can!"

"We'll fly to the colonies, Prince Wickwolf," Annike says. "There is no war there. No kings. It's the wisest choice, please believe me. We must ensure your safety – for the purposes of your kingdoms. Both Prince Kosta and you. You must be kept *alive*. The Regicides won't make it to the colonies."

"It's me alone." I allow my voice to fill the underground inn. "Alone, this time. So many have died already, Knight. So I... have to kill them. The Regicides. Every last one."

"Prince Wickwolf, You think that's the answer? More fire? More killing to requite the killing?"

"It has to be, sir," I whisper. "It must be."

He looks at me with genuine pity, eyes that have seen a hundred bodies fall, legs blown off and bombs cascade from an ancient sky.

"But it isn't. It never will be."

When Russel awakes, Annike softly tells him the news.

The hectic glow of sad green eyes.

The palace, he doesn't care. It is a distant dream. All useless towers and bastions, filled with empty things to fill the emptiness. No. He thinks of pale blue eyes and a head against his pillow.

"No, no no no *no*..."

He clutches his stomach and sobs.

◇

Her horde surrounds her by the poisoned river, all dark forms, tall and armed and never, never trusted.

In her restless lull of sleep, Nox dreams of the fire again. Yellow and licking at the godforsaken sky. The golden pillars to ash. The swell of fire in their eyes. Beautiful.

She lies on her side, half in dreams. Black hair coils into itself, making its own dark river on the ground. She sings sickly-sweet tunes in her lightest hint of sleep, drags her fingernails across the dirt, keeps her pale eyes open as if to suck out the light of day.

She longs for fire again.

Fire for fortune.

Where had she heard those words before?

"What is done in darkness ends in light," she repeats, keeping her hand fixed on her loaded gun. "What is done in darkness ends in light. What's done can never be undone."

She takes Locke's sleeping form in her bandaged arms, and he does not wake. His body is heavy and strong, too strong, his hands too quick, his mind a damning shame to hers.

"Freedom is always incomplete, unless it is stolen."

His hands are stirring now, his eyes opening slightly.

"Unless it is stolen..."

She longs for fire, but water will suffice.

She fixes his feet with heavy stones. Quiet fingers. The lowest of breaths, as if she is dead after all, singing from the grave. She hauls him to the river and lowers him in, bandaged hands in bandaged hands.

His eyes flicker open for a second. Childlike and strange. Pried open in fear, sucking in the last of their sight.

A black river, opening for him.

"Oh, it pains me to do this, my Locke." She lets her teeth show.

He screams for a split second before she lets both of his hands go. He's pulled under.

The last thing he sees is her smile.

She watches his sleeping mouth fill with black water, waits until his lungs are full, waits until his arms stop their hideous jerking. *The charade is done.* She lets out the sweetest of sighs, and sinks a bullet into the sky, savors the sound of his split-second scream.

Her lips twist into a slight, scared smile.

You won't make a fool of me.

"I am a king's daughter," she whispers, only to herself. "I am a king's daughter."

◇

Here the streets are paved with dirt and sludge, the single factory spouting fat gray ribbons into the sky. A newspaper lies, discarded and speckled with dirt, in the snow. All snow-smeared black type, gnarled letters –

Joss won't dare look at it, or the fire it describes.

The wind in the streets gnaws at her face, the hood is rough against her hair, and her stomach growls for food, but nothing matters anymore. She's lost all interest in pretty things, but she's not yet accustomed to the ugliness of the streets. She's traded her dresses for thick rags and jeweled flowers for grime. Everything she's ever known, burnt to the ground. No longer a Duke's daughter. No longer a prince's bride. No longer anyone that matters. The freedom spreads through her like fresh oxygen, the afterglow of escape – but tainted with a thousand new sorrows.

A sudden barrage of shouts comes from the side of the street.

"You useless bastard!" A gruff, murderous voice, stomping feet.

All silence from the other end, until a fist strikes a stomach –

a sharp blow from an invisible object –

the silhouette of a dying man, splattered blood on the sidewalk.

A crowd gathers, and someone points and and laughs, giving a cruel kick to the victim on the stones. She sees his face now. The face on the stones. Greasy hair, red blood splaying out in all directions. Mangled and dark.

The riots in the street, the outrage, men and women spilling their hatred to the streets. It doesn't match up – this isn't life. This isn't day-long parties and galas, fresh bread rolls and pomegranates, dresses from an invisible hand. This isn't life. This isn't *life*. Joss flees with bare feet, and tries to make sense of it all. She finds none.

Joss clenches her hands around her ears as if to block out the horrible sounds in the streets, the dreadful newspaper sentences echoing through her head. *The plot to kill Prince Kosta.... devised by none other than the Duke, who is suspected to have ties to the infamous Regicides....*

She nearly chokes on the pain of it. The banquet is done. The beautiful summer wedding is abandoned.

So she kneels by the paving stones and cries, violently, silently. For everything that could have been, and everything that never was, and everything that never will be.

Annike approaches me. "Is it time?"

"It's past time. It's far too late."

He shakes his head and takes a jangle of keys from his pocket. "I don't quite know where you want to *go*, boy."

"He wants to go to the colonies," June whispers, only to me.

The air outside the inn is warm, sickeningly, heartlessly warm, but sapped of all wetness. The trees have sprouted new, warped leaves, twisted and yellow, and the clouds sag with invisible weight. Our group is large and varied to an almost comical degree. Princes and soldiers, civilians, refugee pawns, a dangling daughter. Nothing is how it was at the beginning, wherever that was.

The face behind the mask, and me. We're both cowards. We're both so damn good at hiding.

June throws her arms around me, burrowing her face into my chest. "The colonies." She grips both of my hands, and the warmth in her fingers strikes some sense into me. Her eyes shine with a familiar starlight. "Ezra. Please."

"You're not ready," Regena says, placing her own hand on my shoulder. "Not yet. I know you want to be brave, but you can be brave without being stupid."

I look from one face to another. Their eyes hold on to me. I have everything to lose, and everywhere to explore. The fabled moons beyond our Jupiter, the starling-filled forests where the wolf never dared to venture. She's right. I'm not ready, not ready at all, to look into the black X-mark eyes or see the face behind them. Perhaps I never was all along. Still, I know within my heart: the day will come.

Just not now.

"Yes," I decide. "Yes. The colonies."

Russel leaps forward, enclosing us all in a giant embrace, and the light in the sky flares again. More people join the group, my mother's arms strong again, the deep scars obvious on Annike's shoulder, the child clinging to my legs. We are traitors. We are free. We are all we have chosen to be. The war that does not belong to us thunders madly on, and the sun beats down on our beautiful selfishness.

The sun doesn't last for long.

A dark, rickety boat waits for us in the river. Annike takes the front, and as we gather in, I realize it's much sturdier than it looks. My cowardice is eating away at me, but, I assure myself, it's better than death. Better than death... *and less deserved,* says that snickering, hateful part of my mind that so badly wants to drive me into my own destruction.

Finally, I let myself sleep. No dreams come.

When I awake, the darkness seem to have taken over the day. As the sky dims and the boat lurches across the water, Captain Annike's hands are steady on the wheel, listening to muffled commands through his headset.

"We'll go to Kallichore," he says. "Right now, it's the safest place to be. Hold on... I'm getting s...."

He goes quiet. Too quiet.

"*What?*" he says, incredulous, to the person on the other end of the microphone. "Oh, well, that's ridiculous— it can't be *proven*—"

"Are we safe?" says Russel. "Is everything okay?"

"Yes... of course," he says, keeping his eyes on the water. "We're almost to Kallichore. The Regicides are still in Uppica, as reported. Everything's fine. It will be fine, Prince Kosta."

"What is it, then?" asks June.

"It's just... I've just received some very disturbing information. No doubt, it's just a ridiculous rumor."

He pauses, and I can hear him swallow.

"The leader of the Regicides — she calls herself Nox — the very girl who murdered King Wickwolf... claims to be his illegitimate daughter."

That hideous voice, those cold eyes taunting me in my dreams, that gunshot from the crowd, from that girl. A sick laugh climbs up my throat, a tremor through my legs.

I know the boat is not shaking. Only me.

My mother. I look to her, and I want to shield her – *no*, I want her to defend herself.

Her eyebrows furl. Her face says nothing I can read. No self-protection. No declarations, no denials.

"It's a *lie*." My throat is hoarse, strained, as if bled dry.

Annike's deep, worried voice breaks through. "Please be calm, Prince

Wickwolf. It's a rumor. Slander. Propaganda, I daresay. After all, she is..."

"Completely insane," I finish for him. "Wrong."

One thought washes over me, almost serene: *Aren't we all?*

I watch the ground grow closer as the plane lands, look into a sky dotted with more stars than I've seen in my life. Regena drags a sleeping Russel out of his seat. Noor and Ibby amble out, both clearly exhausted and stumbling. We climb out in aching, empty silence, everyone but June and my mother keeping a good distance away from me.

Kallichore smells like soil and damp air and ocean salt, the faint lights of a town glinting weakly in the distance. I wonder vaguely if anyone will recognize me here, if the news about the kingdoms reaches the ears of the colonies – if I can be a person, or a piece of news, a mockery...

My mother's face, sixteen years old, on the front of every paper. Sad-eyed and scared. Her cold love. A bedroom made of silence, velvet sheets, secrets. A kingdom that encased her. Books that never told her quite enough. Then the scream that sliced the kingdom in half. Everything she treasured, burnt; everyone she loved, ripped away.

All but me.

I wrap my arms around her.

"I'm sorry."

"There's no reason to be." She whispers it now: "Ezra."

"Mother, this slander – I'm sorry. I am..."

My mother lays a hand on my shoulder. "Forgive your father."

I wait for an explanation. Nothing. It hangs in the air; it slices the space between us. *Forgive your father.*

"He strayed from you," I mumble, too shocked, too angry to raise my voice. "He strayed from you and brought about his own–"

I can't bring myself to finish the sentece. It's the hurt in my mother's eyes, the tiny sparkling tears, the secrets she carries that she'd never dare tell me. I loved my father. I trusted him. Some part of me still does, but it's nowhere near the pit of my stomach, where there is only empty anger.

Her tears stand in her eyes, waiting.

Exhale.

"Hey!" Russel shouts. "Are we all here?"

Everyone pitches in some form of answer: some quiet yelps, some inaudible grunts.

"We'll keep safe," says Annike, "if we keep undercover, and we stay together."

"Damn straight," says Russel, too loudly.

The rest of the group is on the ground, rubbing slabs of wood together to make a large campfire. As they pile stick after stick, the orange flames grow into a bonfire worthy of Wickwolf.

"Flames for fortune," my mother says, and I think I see a tear sliding down her cheek.

Regena smirks and turns to me. "Everything'll be okay, you know? After all."

I find myself nodding, almost smiling as I watch my friends' faces shining yellow over the flames. I breathe my anger out, watch my breath dissolve into the dark air.

She has my blood. She has my father. But as the fire roars, I know she will never have me.

The laughter. The feeling of escape. Memories of tree-cluttered forests, barren lakes. The fragile magic of the dreams that pile in my head.

Some things cannot be stolen.

◇

TO BE CONTINUED

BELVIDERE
archipelago

FOUR KINDGOMS:
Kosta, Lusk, Uppica, Wickwolf

EIGHT COLONIES:
KOSTA TERRIOTY: Kallichore, Orion, Rioghnach, Usha (Usha
ceded after Wickwolf defeat)
LUSK TERRITORY: Alcyone, Heidrun
WICKWOLF TERRITORY: Shanta, Ondine
UPPICA TERRITORY: none

Square miles: 4,287
Main island population: 178,970
Total colonies population: 397,823

LUSK
Shield: Lion
Symbol: teardrop
Capital: Kassa
Demonym: Lusks
King: Leocor
Queen: Callista
Currency: gold

WICKWOLF
Shield: Wolf
Symbol: horn
Capital: Melchor
Demonym: Wickwolves
King: Loupe (deceased)
Queen: Gloria
Currency: silver

KOSTA
Shield: Eagle
Symbol: diamond
Capital: Ordim
Demonym: Kostans
King: Karan (deceased)
Queen: Merris (deceased)
Currency: coinage (copper monas)

UPPICA
Shield: Fish
Symbol: arrowhead
Capital: Kingdom City
Demonym: Uppicans
King: Victor
Queen: Ayana (deceased)
Currency: paper money

41984055R00158

Made in the USA
Lexington, KY
04 June 2015